The Deal Mak

I find it hard to answer your letter because I agree with almost everything you say.

> – **Milton Friedman** [Nobel laureate (Economics) and advisor to US Presidents. Friedman also adjudged Rakesh Wadhwa as the best writer on free markets in the International Policy Network's Bastiat Prize for Journalism.]

A skillful combination of doctrines of Good Governance and Economic Freedom ... a racy, compelling and page turning drama of passion, intrigue and love; a potent script for a promising Bollywood flick.

> – **Sanjay Khan** (Bollywood Actor, Producer and Director)

The Deal Maker

Rakesh Wadhwa
With
Leon Louw

Rupa & Co

Published 2010 by
Rupa Publications India Pvt. Ltd.
7/16, Ansari Road, Daryaganj,
New Delhi 110 002

Sales Centres:

Allahabad Bengaluru Chandigarh Chennai
Hyderabad Jaipur Kathmandu
Kolkata Mumbai

Typeset by
Mindways Design
1410 Chiranjiv Tower
43 Nehru Place
New Delhi 110 019

Printed in India by
Nutech Photolithographers
B-240, Okhla Industrial Area, Phase-I,
New Delhi 110 020, India

Part One

Part One

Jaipur, 15 October 2023

The Rambagh Palace Hotel of Jaipur stood in all its glory. Water from the fountains gently splashed lending a magical charm to the evening. Peacocks posed gracefully and enamoured the surroundings displaying their brightly hued plumes.

The Prime Minister of India, escorted by a phalanx of guards, climbed its sparkling white marble stairs leading to the city side of the hotel to join a meeting with his closest allies. The leader of the welcoming group walked ahead and greeted his honoured guest with a smile.

His smile froze within seconds as he saw a crimson dot appear on the Prime Minister's chest. It was followed by a sharp crack and the Prime Minister's steps faltered. The laser beam moved swiftly to his temple. Another shot rang out and he collapsed to the ground.

The nation heard the shattering news: one shot in the heart and another in the head had caused the Prime Minister's immediate death.

Within seconds the security team cordoned off the area and sealed all exits from the premises.

Sophisticated forensic equipment calculated the trajectory of the bullets as having been fired from a room on the first floor. Details were radioed to the search team.

Entering the room, guns drawn, the guards found a high calibre rifle lying on a table by the window but the assassin had vanished into thin air. How he got into the room and disappeared puzzled experts for many years.

Shock waves rippled across every corner of the world.

One

A village near Delhi, 1989

Seven-year-old Inder Bhati sat playing on the parched mud bed outside his father's shop when five masked men approached.

The shop was little more than a few square metres, painted a lively turquoise colour with a Thumbs Up sign above the door.

Four of the men entered the shop. Inder froze as the fifth, lit a cigarette and walked towards him. He towered over Inder, casting a long shadow over the boy. Then he crouched and took a lengthy drag, slowly exhaling in the little boy's face. He smiled. Inder jumped to his feet to flee but the man flung him over his shoulder and carried him into the shop.

The men were hurling tins and bottles, packets of rice, chips, and an assortment of goods across the floor. One of the men carried a silver baton that was twice as tall as Inder. He walked towards the tiny twelve-inch television mounted on the wall and swung, sending it flying across the room into a glass cabinet, shattering it.

'Put my son down!' demanded Janak Bhati.

The man carrying Inder released his hold making Inder fall on the hardened clay floor. Janak rushed to his son's aid but was restrained by three men. Two held him as one of them slammed the baton into his stomach repeatedly. Janak gasped for air between blows.

Inder darted towards the nearest man and bit his arm as hard as he could. The man grabbed him by the neck and flung him against the brick wall. He watched, helplessly, his father shrieking on being beaten mercilessly. Finally, the thug's club ricocheted off his dad's head, knocking him senseless to the floor.

Inder stared in horror at the blood trickling from a wound on his father's head. Its dark stream ran down over Janak's closed eye, across the high bridge of his nose and dripped soundlessly onto the floor.

Terrified, Inder gathered up all his strength and ran, gasping and sobbing through the back office, out of the back door and into the waste ground behind the shop.

He ran as fast as his small legs could carry him down the lane of hardened mud to his house.

Aruna Bhati was at home with three neighbours who were sewing beads onto T-shirts for sale when she heard her son shouting 'Mummy, Mummy, Baba's dead! Those men killed him. They're smashing our shop!'

The women dropped their sewing, hitched up their saris and ran to the shop with Inder hard on their heels. A stream of concerned neighbours followed them.

Inside the shop, their horrified eyes took in the devastation. Canned goods were scattered amongst the red, brown and orange coloured spices spilt on the floor. Apples and oranges were trampled underfoot. Wooden shelves lay splintered amongst the shards of glass from the shattered fridge doors.

One of the wreckers turned to his leader, 'Is that it ...?'

'That will do.' was the reply. The men walked casually away from the wreckage and disappeared into the night.

Aruna's eyes were searching for her husband. 'Look Mummy, Baba is over there!' Inder directed Aruna as she stumbled through the debris and fell on her knees at Janak's side. She slipped her fingers in the blood trickling down Janak's neck as she checked for his pulse there. It was faint but steady. He was alive! 'Call the doctor,' she whispered to her son.

They sat on their favourite flat rock at Signal Hill's peak, the highest point in the village, drinking *chai* from a stainless steel flask.

As they chatted, Adhijat Kumar and his son Sudesh looked at their village far below. The familiar cluster of russet houses was interspersed with thatched mud huts, brightly painted homes and rusty tin-roofed shops. Dominating the scene was the pink dome of the temple that glistened in the evening light.

'Why did those men wreck Mr Bhati's shop and try to kill him?' asked Sudesh.

'They were bad men,' said Adhijat.

'But why did they do it?' Sudesh had an urgent need to understand.

'Because Mr Bhati didn't pay them. These people demand money from shop-keepers "to allow them to survive". If they don't pay, the bad men attack them. Janak Bhati refused to pay so they tried to kill him and wreck his shop.'

'Can't you stop them, Appa? You are a policeman.'

Adhijat sighed. 'I am working on that, son. I have been thinking a lot about these problems, and am trying to come up with new ideas and solutions, but I haven't tried them out yet.'

'What about the other policemen?' inquired Sudesh.

Adhijat looked at his son and spoke after a long pause, 'Are you sure you want to know?'

'Yes, Appa, tell me.' There was no limit to Sudesh's curiosity. 'The truth, my son, is that most policemen accept money from these crooks to let them have their way. It is called bribery.'

'But why don't the senior policemen catch those cops and put them in jail?'

Adhijat sighed again, 'I'm afraid the seniors also take bribes. It goes right to the top.'

'Even the Prime Minister accepts bribes?' asked Sudesh incredulously.

'Perhaps,' said Adhijat.'

'Can it ever change?'

Adhijat weighed his words. 'Only if our country gets an incorruptible Prime Minister who chooses police superintendents who perform their duties honestly, and crack down on corruption.'

'Then I will become the Prime Minister,' said Sudesh as if offering to do a household chore. 'I will put an end to corruption so that no more cruel things happen to good people.'

'Are you indeed going to do so, Sudesh?'

'Yes, I will.' The seven-year-old lad spoke with abounding confidence 'Somebody has to do it.'

Two

Hyderabad, 1990

'Dad?' called out a small girl as she wandered into a large, lavishly furnished room wherein Janak Bhati's shop could have fitted five times over.

'Yes, Vaneshri.' came the reply from a middle-aged gentleman dressed in a charcoal business suit.

'You know how Sandhi was robbed last week?' asked Vaneshri holding something behind her back. No one could resist Vaneshri, least of all her father. This six-year-old girl with her glossy black curls and bluish-green eyes looked adorable.

'Yes, Vaneshri?'

'Well, if I drew a picture of something that would catch the robbers, could you make it for me?'

Her father exchanged glances with his wife, who, immaculately dressed in a light blue sari, sat in the same room amusedly listening to the father–daughter conversation.

'Maybe, if it was electronic.'

'It is,' said Vaneshri. 'I've drawn it already.' With exuberance, she placed the drawing on her father's lap.

'You see,' she began explaining, 'it works by remote control. It sits in Sandhi's handbag and it has big sharp teeth and whenever a thief puts his hand in her bag it takes a big bite out of his hand. Simple!'

She shrugged slightly, turning both palms upward to demonstrate just how simple it was.

'But Vaneshri, how will your device know if the person is a thief or Sandhi herself?' asked her mother.

'Well, that's for Daddy to work out. That's what he does, Mummy!' And with that she turned on her heels and moved off through the house to work on her next project.

The mansion had seven bedrooms, each with a luxe bathroom en suite. There were three reception rooms, studies for Vaneshri's parents, a separate room with a home theatre system, gym and a state-of-the-art kitchen. In a separate wing was Vaneshri's suite of rooms, as well as the living quarters for her nanny, Sandhi, whose case she had just dealt with so creatively.

'That little device looks deadly,' said her mother as she leaned over to have a close look at the drawing. 'Sharp teeth! Where does she get this from?'

'I've no idea. I think it must have come from your side.'

'The more important question is, how on earth are we ever going to find this girl a husband? Who will want a wife who designs such crazy anti-crime devices?'

A hotel in Washington DC, 1990

The French ambassador slammed his fist on the table. The Dom Perignon spilled from his glass onto the floor of the room in the Washington hotel where Congressman Brad K. Henderson, Texas (Democrat) received his guests.

'We will not put up with this mad speculator interfering with our policies,' said the French ambassador.

'I agree with you, Francois. We should not allow selfish individuals to undermine government policy.'

'So, what are you going to do? What are you going to do about Upton? He is harming relations between our countries. Can't you arrest him?'

'Arrest him?' replied Henderson, his countenance affable. 'I wish we could, Francois, but what can we charge him with? He isn't doing anything criminal. We can try to introduce policies that would pronounce his activities illegal in the United States, but if we succeeded he would simply start trading offshore.

The Frenchman's face distorted with rage. Henderson looked at him apologetically.

'Ray Upton's activities are offensive. Perhaps, we should set up an international team to work on this. We cannot have individuals playing the national economies in ways that interfere with the freedom of governments to exercise control.'

A village near Delhi, 1991

Sudesh loved to go on long walks with his father. Away from the hustle and bustle, the twosome often climbed Signal Hill, from where they had the best view of the village below.

Sudesh's agile movements while climbing contrasted with his father's slow, steady pace.

'A lot of people are talking about you, Appa. They say your presence has brought down the crime rate here when it's growing everywhere else.'

'Yes, that's true. The villages in my district have less crime.'

'How do you catch the bad guys, Appa?'

'I don't, in fact I have stopped catching them. I found a way of making them stop stealing instead.'

'Did you talk to them, tell them that it's wrong?'

'No, I never get to see them. I don't even know who they are. I don't need to.'

'Then how did you make them stop stealing?'

Adhijat paused. He turned to look at the village below. Sudesh came to stand next to him on the steep hillside and saw the village glowing with lights from kerosene lamps and dung fires. They could hear the muffled bellowing of cows ready to be milked and the occasional sounds of laughter and chit-chats in the distance.

'How did you get the crooks to stop stealing, Appa?'

'Well, most criminals steal things so that they can sell them to shopkeepers or to street vendors. If the traders stop buying, then the crooks won't steal. So I got the traders to stop buying the stolen goods.'

'I see, but how do you get the traders to stop buying the loot?' Sudesh asked.

'If they can't convince me that they bought the wares from legitimate owners, I take the goods to the police station.'

'Then does that prevent traders from buying more loot from the robbers?'

'It actually does as I confiscate the stolen goods, before the traders can sell them, so the traders pay the crooks but don't get money from customers. Then, when the crooks come with more goods, the traders refuse to buy and say 'No thanks, Constable Kumar is going to take all this.'

'Wow! That means you don't have to catch crooks, which is very difficult and dangerous ...' as he spoke this Sudesh thought of the men who had hurt Inder's dad and continued, 'Why don't all cops do what you do, Appa?'

'It is not easy. It's wrong for police to take things from traders if they can't prove they are stolen goods. That worries me, so I do my best not to make mistakes. I visit all the traders in my district, even those selling from homes and pavements, and tell them if they can't tell me where they got their goods from I will consider them as stolen.

'People know that I am fair and so the policy has become popular. Honest traders, like Mr Bhati and Mr Govinder, cooperate with me, and magistrates support my decisions.

'But for my methods to work everywhere the law will have to undergo a change to prevent abuse.'

Adhijat looked down at his son who exclaimed, 'I'll fix that when I am the Prime Minister.'

'I look forward to that,' Adhijat spoke with an affectionate smile. He knew his gifted son, capable of achieving success in life, was also capable of waking upto reality.

🍂

Sudesh sat doing his homework while his dad, Adhijat, Janak Bhati and Achmad, the owner of the village snack bar, sat together gulping down salty lassi over a game of cards. The three men oscillated their attention between the card game and the news on the television behind them.

'India is facing a balance of payments crisis,' announced the presenter. The three men put their game on hold and fixed their eyes on the television.

'What does that mean?' asked Achmad.

'It means the country lacks finances,' said Bhati. Everyone laughed, except Sudesh, who was listening intently.

The presenter continued, 'India's credit rating has been downgraded and sources of external credit have dried up. This is the culmination of a deterioration of government finances that has been continuing for some time. External debt is now seventy billion US dollars, more than a quarter of the total income of the country. Prime Minister Rao today announced sweeping changes in response to the crisis.'

'So, what's happening, Janak?' asked Adhijat. Janak Bhati was regarded as the economic expert among the small group.

'We are being stupid again, trying to defend a fixed currency.'

'What do you mean?' Achmad asked, paying close attention. Janak, glad on having an interested audience, continued, 'Let me give you an example. That TV set, how much is it worth?'

'I suppose about a thousand rupees,' replied Adhijat.

'Now, what do you think would happen if I offer to buy it for ten thousand rupees?'

'I'm sure a lot of people would be more than willing to sell their TV sets to you,' said Achmad with a grin.

'Exactly. And would it make the TV set worth ten thousand rupees each.'

'Only until you stopped offering such a crazy deal.'

'Right. But that is exactly what our government is doing at the moment. Intervening in currency markets by fixing the exchange rate, that's the price of our rupees, far too high, so we've run out of foreign exchange. It's sillier and more wasteful than paying more for TV sets than they're worth.'

Hyderabad, 1991

'Dad?'

'Yes, Vaneshri.'

'Remember your electronic personal organiser?'

'What do you mean "remember", Vaneshri?'

'Do you not like me to innovate and experiment?'

'Yes my child, I do.'

'I've done an experiment.'

'Really?'

'Would you like to come and see?'

As Sabyasachi Palande and his precocious daughter moved through the house to her playroom, he tried to remember when he had last backed up his notebook. Meanwhile, she continued to talk.

'At dinner you said you want the most recent version and that Mummy won't let you buy because it's an unnecessary extravagance. So maybe, I have helped you a bit?'

He could trace a certain logic in her thought process. The device lay on the floor of her room in several pieces. Chips had been forced off the motherboard. It was irreparable.

'Vaneshri!'

She ignored his cry and continued, 'This part is a printed circuit called a "motherboard". This is RAM memory which stands for Random Access Memory.'

'Vaneshri, I run an electronics and software company; I know what a printed circuit looks like.'

'Yes, Daddy, but I didn't know, did I? This is part of my education – and now you need a new organiser.'

The Upton Corporation, New York City, 1992

'Governments are up in arms about this fund, Ray,' said the caller. 'It was okay when it was small but now money is pouring in. You're on every top ten fund performance table in the country.'

Ray allowed himself a rare smile. 'Great isn't it!'

His staff member didn't seem equally enchanted: 'I'm the one who has to deal with the French ambassador and delegations from many other countries. They hate you interfering with their policies.'

Ray had no sympathy. All the governments needed was to do the right thing which, by definition, was whatever got better results on his index.

'You're doing a great job, Frank.'

'Thanks, boss, but why can't we just run global equity funds and currency trading like everyone else?'

'With so little risk involved, would that give us a thirty-six percent per annum return for five consecutive years?' Ray grimaced. 'Why couldn't people understand that if the market rewarded you it meant you were doing the right thing?'

'Granted, government policy of a country is responsible for its financial performance,' admitted Frank.

'So, invest in countries with pro-market policies and avoid ones with socialist policies. Simple!'

'Yes, Ray, but I don't think you are taking into account other risks. You are becoming extremely unpopular in certain quarters.'

Delhi, 1992

Vasu met his gang in a makeshift office at the back side of an Old Delhi house whose cracked plastered walls had a pale green colour on them.

In the evenings he would sit in the small dusty yard between his front door and the street, sipping beer or chewing *paan*, and greeting the local passers-by. He was known as another ubiquitous *rickshaw wallah*.

His small front room had a bed, a kitchen counter and a wash basin. A back door led into two other rooms. Only a few trusted members of his gang had been through that door.

The bigger of the two rooms was Vasu's warehouse where the gang sorted stolen goods bought from petty thieves and burglars, assigning them for distribution to outlets in the district – small shops, street vendors and pan-handlers. It was the conduit through which most of the district's stolen property went across. Off to the right was the office, scarcely big enough for the four to meet.

Both rooms were dark and messy, each with a single small window behind permanently closed curtains. The warehouse had as many items piled on the floor as stacked on the old ceiling-high steel shelves. There were cookers and lamps, early and recent versions of cell phones, watches and clocks, handbags and purses, radios, clothes, cutlery and crockery, tools and torches, the usual stock-in-trade of property crime.

Vasu would have preferred to sell to the big Delhi syndicates than to the local vendors because then there would have been no risk of identification of stolen goods by former owners. But big city syndicates had their own sources of supply and paid very low prices: five rupees for a lamp, three rupees for a sari. So, Vasu had no choice but to run his 'business' locally.

Provided they were careful in not selling goods in the village where they were stolen, the gang was safe. The system was simple; many independent thieves and burglars sold to Vasu. He sold the goods on to numerous outlets selling new and used goods, none of whom would disclose their sources.

It was impossible for a handful of local, poorly trained policemen to curtail this kind of crime.

A village near Delhi, 1992

Sudesh was helping Inder stock shelves in his family shop, which had by now recovered from the attack of 1990.

A man came into the shop. He was not one of the regular customers, but Inder's father, Janak, received him warmly. The man began to examine the foodstuffs that Janak sold. He collected samples in small bags and little glass jars. A little later, Janak handed over another bag, made of brown paper and filled with notes.

Sudesh couldn't wait to ask his friend's father what this man had done that was worth so much.

After a cup of chai the man left. He's quite agreeable, thought Sudesh.

'Who was that?' he asked.

'He,' said Janak, 'was the inspector of food safety. He has the power to shut down my shop if he finds something that is not to his liking. Mostly, though, he only wants his bribe, and then everything is okay.'

'So, you have to pay to stop him from closing your shop?'

'That's right, Sudesh. He and about ten others in charge of various licensing, zoning, tax, health, building, labour, trading hour and other regulations. It's my biggest expense every year.'

'And this is happening right across the country?'

'Yes, everywhere.'

'I don't understand,' said Sudesh.

Janak paused for a few seconds, then said: 'Do you know the story of the movie called *Shahenshah*?'

'Yes, it is one of my favourites.'

'In the movie, a corrupt bank manager and a crime baron frame honest people and terrorise them to death. The police force and bureaucracy in the movie is full of corrupt people and life is miserable for common folk who are unable to counter crime.'

'Yes, the two masterminds of crime were really evil men.' Sudesh frowned.

'Shahenshah, a daring crime fighter takes upon himself the challenge of ridding the society of corruption, and becomes the nemesis for all the culprits. He smashes down criminals, bursts mafia rackets and assassinates their key members.'

'These inspectors who collect bribes each season are the evil men of today's time, and there is nothing we can do about it. Where would we get a modern-day Shahenshah to rid us of these evil men?'

'I'll do it,' said Sudesh pensively.

'It's no joke,' said Inder.

'I'm not joking,' said Sudesh in youthful innocence.

Thirty-eight thousand feet above France, 1993

In his bespoke tailored suit Ray Upton paced up and down the aisle of 'The Phantom', a Gulfstream V, as it cruised through overcast European skies. Living half of his life in a private jet didn't seem strange to Ray; he had become accustomed to it.

'Of course, I don't think it's unethical,' he said firmly into his cell phone. His deep voice had a slight Ivy League accent. 'It's those in power, who won't account for the damage they are doing, who are unethical.'

The conversation was disturbed by the pilot's announcement: 'Mr Upton, please sit down. We are preparing our descent for Le Bourget.'

Alexander Romney had executed this landing more than a hundred times before. He looked forward to visiting friends in their small flat in the Fourth Arrondissement.

'Hold on a second,' Ray spoke into the mouthpiece, 'Are we landing in Paris already?' he asked the pilot.

'We are, and not too soon. We are low on fuel.'

Ray sat down in the black leather seat and latched his seat belt with one hand while he continued his call.

Most investors concern themselves with minutiae, tiny movements over brief periods. Ray learnt from investment guru

Jim Rogers to do the opposite, to look at and understand the big picture.

Instead of choosing individual shares or commodities, Rogers saw entire countries as 'bullish' or 'bearish'. For Jim Rogers, the best way to predict a country's future was to visit it, failing which to establish whether its government was moving towards or away from economic freedom. When Botswana, China, India and Mozambique started to free their economies, he invested in them.

He also devised the famous Rogers Commodity Index to track fundamental rather than inconsequential shifts in the demand for and therefore the price of commodities. As one of the world's most influential investment gurus, he encouraged others to do likewise.

Following Roger's example, Ray ran the world's most successful investment funds, along with industries in the hi-tech sector, especially cutting-edge telecoms.

Recently, Ray had created a successful website by taking Jim Rogers' insights to 'their logical conclusion'. He started a betting service for people to place 'Rogers Bets' for and against countries. Just as George Soros, an erstwhile partner of Rogers, angered the British government by speculating against Sterling (thereby supposedly decreasing its value), Ray enraged the French government by betting against the French economy, and getting thousands of others to follow.

'Sorry to bother you again, Sir,' said the pilot, 'but the French have refused us permission to land.'

A village near Delhi, 1993

Sudesh and his father climbed steadily through the thorn trees and boulders, their feet creating small puffs of red dust as they headed to sit on the hilltop.

Adhijat looked down the hill, 'Is that Inder down there?'

Sudesh followed his dad's gaze. A blanket of smog obscured Sudesh's vision. After a while he managed to spot ten boys playing cricket down the hill. The batsman hit the ball hard – everyone could see it soar through the air.

Adhijat exclaimed, 'What a strike!'

'It must be him,' said Sudesh smiling. 'No one else can hit like that!'

They continued climbing silently for a while.

'Appa?'

'Yes?'

'Do you think we will ever catch up with America and become a rich country?'

'Yes, it is possible,' Adhijat said, 'Do you know that a few centuries ago India was the world's wealthiest nation? There was no poverty, plenty of food for everyone. India was called the "Golden Bird". Our country can be rich again if we gain an insight into the "miracle of poverty."'

'Poverty, a miracle?', asked Sudesh after a moment of pause.

'Look down there at the village, my boy. Look how industriously people work. Indians have toiled hard in every epoch. Then, what makes them so poor? Look there', he pointed to a field where the women were harvesting corn in the dim light of twilight, 'and look at those men making bricks.' Sudesh saw dust rising from quarries where clay-laden trucks groaned their way up steep ramparts. Some workers packed the clay into brick moulds, and others fed brick furnaces with tall cone-shaped chimneys.

'Look at those backyard businesses, and those shops, and there ...', Adhijat gestured along the hills to the north, '...at those children herding goats, and men ploughing fields.'

Sudesh saw every area studded with men, women and children at work.

'It is an incredible situation, my son', said Adhijat. 'They're all producing and trading wealth, working harder and for longer hours than people in prosperous countries. Our countrymen are as enterprising and thrifty as anyone else in the world, yet they're poor. I don't understand it; to me it's a mystery, a strange miracle that people putting the same amount of effort become very rich at one place, while remain poverty-stricken at other places. It's incredibly tragic and inexplicable ... the miracle of poverty.'

'Why doesn't the government find out how we were a prosperous nation back in history, and how countries like the US have reached heights of prosperity?' asked Sudesh.

'We can learn from prosperous countries, but we should not ape the West in every respect.'

'Why not?' Sudesh wanted to know.

Adhijat looked at his son. 'With new money come new ways.'

They sat down comfortably on their favourite spot of a flat rock.

'It's difficult to explain,' said Adhijat, looking at the familiar view of the busy village below. 'Our ancestors followed and preserved unique and traditional ways of doing things. We have the onus of continuing our country's rich traditions and values. We ought not to follow the western culture blindly.'

Sudesh nodded.

'Let us hope that when we embark on our journey of becoming the Golden Bird again, we learn to prosper without losing our values.' said Adhijat.

'Appa?'

'Yes, Sudesh?'

'Do you think it's possible for one person to change things in India?'

His father started to smile, and then suppressed it as he saw the intensity in his young son's eyes.

'Why do you ask, Sudesh?'

Sudesh compressed his lips. 'I want to be someone who can change things. I want India to be the world's richest country.'

'If you want to change things, Sudesh, there will be a price to pay. It will not be easy.'

'I don't mind if it isn't easy, Appa. Is this life easy?' Sudesh indicated the village below.

'It is true that many of our countrymen lead a very tough life, but changing India will be a tougher challenge. You will make enemies of people who keep their self-interest above the nation's interest. You will have to struggle very hard to rid India of numerous corrupt people who become rich by oppressing masses.'

'Appa, this is 1993. The British left over forty years ago.'

'Yes, the British are no longer our oppressors. Now, our oppressors are government bureaucrats who demand bribes for every duty they perform for the public, and who consume eighty-five percent of the taxes raised to help the poor.'

'How can they do that?' asked Sudesh, his eleven-year-old mind outraged by the thought.

'Because we let them. Because we think the government can help us better than we can help ourselves ...'

Sudesh said little for the rest of their time together. He was deep in thought.

Three

A college town near Boston, 1993

People said that Ray Upton was a hard man. Ray would have agreed to their opinion, and would have stressed that to get things done it was necessary to be tough. He was tall, a couple of inches clear of six feet. At thirty-six his hair showed prematurely grey at the temples.

Ray came from an aristocratic family of the East Coast. He had attended the best schools and aced all of his business and finance courses at Harvard Business School. At a very young age he had started applying his mind to cracking challenging projects related to finance. Not because his parents had stinted his pocket money, but because he was utterly fascinated by the risks and adventures involved in an entrepreneur's job.

Ten years ago he had married Cynthia, a beautiful blonde debutante who had desired a strong, reserved man like her father. She had achieved that but with it came disappointment. Cynthia was forced to befriend loneliness as Ray had no time for anything except his business and finance. When Ray came home he was usually focussed on the financial information that was omnipresent in his life, in his office as well as in their living room and his study.

Once, Cynthia lost her temper and shifted his computer out of their bedroom. The consequence was that he came to bed long after she had gone to sleep. She had regretted her protestation often but could never muster enough courage to apologise to him. As the frequency of interactions between the two decreased further, the distance grew.

On many occasions Cynthia had considered divorcing Ray. But then her love for him had overpowered all thoughts of abandoning him. Accepting her fate, she cultivated new interests and made new circle of friends to depend less on his companionship.

When she would look around at their luxurious house she knew that life could have been worse. She was well looked after and Ray was a wonderful company during the brief periods he was with her. He probably did love her in his own way. He just found it difficult to express. Or so she hoped.

A village near Delhi, 1993

Inder watched his father counting the stock on his shelves. There were big jars of spices, a variety of tinned foods, bottles of local *achar*, and bottles of Thumbs Up. There was a time when he had helped his father with this job but nowadays he couldn't be bothered.

'Dad, you said you would bowl for me tonight so that I can practise my batting.'

'Sorry son. The shop needs restocking. If we don't look after our customers how can we pay for you to go to school?' Inder didn't argue; he was used to his father's cast iron logic.

'Understanding this will help you in business.'

Maybe, thought Inder. But right now he wanted to play cricket.

Shakti – Inder's sister came into the shop. A quiet, gentle girl, younger than Inder, she started helping her father. As she passed bottles to her father she announced, 'Sudesh is going to change the world.'

Inder pulled a face, 'Sudesh is not going to change the world, little sister. Don't be naïve.'

'I think he will,' she insisted.

'Sudesh will spend his life reading and dreaming about changing the world. He doesn't think practically about things and he trusts too many people.'

'He's kind and he's clever. I like him.'

'He's a foolish dreamer,' said Inder. 'There's one born every minute.'

Vasu's house, East Delhi, 1993

'Who does that bastard Kumar think he is?' asked Tarun after he had explained to his boss, Vasu, that traders in the district policed by Kumar were refusing to buy their stolen goods.

Vasu was stocky and visibly muscular. He wore a black shirt with a gold-plated chain around his neck. 'Why won't those fools buy from us?'

'They say Kumar doesn't arrest them, he just confiscates their goods if they can't explain where they got them.'

'He can't do that! It's against the law! He must have proof!' Vasu raised his voice. 'What the hell are we going to do? He'll destroy our business. We'll have to set that stupid bastard right.'

'What do you want us to do?' asked Tarun cracking his knuckles in anticipation.

'What we always do with cops, pay the fucker off.'

'How much?'

'Twenty thousand rupees will do. That's what he earns in half a year. We can't afford it, but we have no choice.'

'Twenty thousand a year?'

'Yes, make that clear, annually.'

A village near Delhi, 1993

'That's the same shirt you wear every day,' Sudesh had heard this remark a dozen times with varying degrees of curiosity and ridicule.

'Why do you never come on school outings?' The answer was he could not afford them, but Sudesh often managed to find another reason.

'Always in the library – haven't you got any books of your own?'

'Where did you get that school bag? Is it a World War Two version?'

As the district policeman Sudesh's father earned little, just enough, combined with the money from Kamla's sewing, to feed the family. But Sudesh was proud of the work his Appa did, so the taunts did not intimidate or frustrate him, he usually bore all such remarks with a smile.

Ten thousand feet above Paris, 1993

'There is a fax for you,' said Ray Upton's secretary 'They must be responding to our request for an explanation.'

The plane cruised in bad visibility ten thousand feet above Le Bourget airport. Ray grabbed the fax report.

'The French government deplores the destructive and anti-social practice of those who trade on unregulated derivatives representing the national statistics of sovereign nations. Landing rights have therefore been withdrawn from the Upton Corporation and its representatives.' The fax was dated two days previously.

'What does it say?'

'Two days ago our landing rights were withdrawn because we trade social indicators.'

'Excuse me,' said Romney from the cockpit, 'I have no problem with how you run your business, guys, but if we don't get to an airport pretty damn quickly, we are going to run out of fuel.'

Upton and his secretary turned to the pilot.

'Is our fuel level dangerous?' asked Ray.

The pilot looked worried as he replied. 'By regulation all planes have to keep more fuel than they are expected to need. We are already dipping into the surplus, and we still need to find some place to land. If another country decides to withdraw our landing rights we're going to be in trouble.'

Ray appreciated rationality and objectivity. Provided people could justify their position Upton would respect them, but if their thinking was woolly, he wasted no time letting them know. This won Ray few friends. He associated with people who, like himself, could make things happen.

Ray started investing while studying at Harvard Business School. He used computers from the time PCs first came into being, and examined in great depth, through statistical analysis, each investment decision he made. He became a millionaire by the time he was twenty-three. Alexander Romney, his pilot, enjoyed a tiny fraction of Ray's wealth, but he was a happier man, and preferred not to lose the only life he had. Being refused landing rights while fuel was running low was scary.

He addressed the radio, 'Entering holding pattern.'

'Can't we just land anyway?' asked Ray. If the mogul was in any sense worried by the possibility of disaster, he showed no sign, apart from raising his eyes for a few seconds from the vicissitudes of the stock-market displayed on his monitor.

'If we do you'll be arrested and I'll lose my license,' said the pilot.

'Forget it, we'll take our chances on the fuel,' said Ray. He looked over the cockpit panel. There must have been forty instruments. 'Which one is the fuel gauge?'

'That one.'

It was sitting on empty.

Upton had full faith in Romney's capacity to tackle the situation, but he had never before flown on such low levels of fuel. He spoke into the radio, 'Is that Tag? We have been refused permission to land. Discussing with client.'

'It seems that no French airport will give you clearance to land. Where would you like to go?'

'How about the Channel Islands?' Ray asked.

'Okay, we should have enough fuel to get there but no further. I wasn't expecting this.'

A village near Delhi, 1993

'Hey!'

Tarun called to the policeman as he passed the village tap. It was already dark. Tarun remembered his meeting with Vasu with a flash of fear and knew that he could not let things go wrong or else Vasu would not spare him.

Kumar eyed the huge and sturdy man approaching him.

'Can I help you?'

'You're the local cop, aren't you?'

'I am. And you are?'

He hesitated for a second, 'Devarsi' said Tarun.

'And how can I help you, Devarsi?'

Adhijat knew this was no innocent enquiry. He could gauge from Tarun's expression what he was up to.

'It is me who wants to help you,' said Tarun.

'Help me?' Adhijat looked bemused.

'Yep,' Tarun looked around. 'Let's discuss this privately, over a drink perhaps?'

'I have to get home, and I don't drink.'

'Okay. We'll talk here. I want to tell you that some people don't appreciate your ways of dealing with shopkeepers and vendors.'

Adhijat not ready to succumb to the intimidation spoke, 'I'm sure criminals don't like getting caught or losing money.'

'That's right,' said Tarun. 'They don't. If you don't want any trouble then there might be other ways to do business, if you know what I mean.'

'Are you threatening me, Devarsi?'

'Threatening? You are getting me wrong, officer Kumar. I'm just trying to help you.'

He paused and looked about again, ensuring no one could hear, he continued,

'You see I know some people who are very keen on bringing an end to these heists. I know them through friends of friends if you get my drift.'

'I think I get your drift.'

Tarun was encouraged; they seemed to be making progress.

'And these people have arrangements with some of your colleagues.'

'Arrangements, eh?'

'I've heard. Though I can't confirm it, you understand. In your case we could arrange twenty thousand rupees a year. In cash.'

'Well thanks for your offer, Devarsi. But when you see your "friends of friends" maybe you can let them know that I don't take bribes. I joined the police to reduce crime, not to supplement my wage.'

Tarun's narrow forehead creased.

'My friends won't like that,' he said.

'You know, Devarsi; I don't think they will. But that's their problem.'

With that constable Adhijat Kumar turned away and resumed his leisurely walk around the village.

A village near Delhi, 1993

Kanak rubbed off the dust from his eyes and wiped the blood oozing out from his nose. He sobbed and felt small. Some boys had gathered to stoke Loknath's belligerence.

Sudesh pushed to the front of the onlookers and looked down at the ragged, skinny boy lying on the ground and gazed at Loknath with contempt.

'Why are you beating him?' asked Sudesh.

Loknath stared back. He was a young Goliath twice the size of Sudesh, 'Is this your business?'

'If I see a small, innocent boy being beaten up like this, yes.'

'He didn't pay.' answered Loknath.

'What does he owe you? Perhaps, he can't pay right now.'

'What's it to you, bookworm?' Loknath stepped menacingly towards Sudesh. Kanak saw the gap and tried to run, but a bruising grip on his upper arm stopped him.

'Let him go,' said Sudesh.

'Steady,' muttered Inder into Sudesh's ear, 'Don't mess with this guy.' Sudesh paid no heed to his words.

'Back off, or you're dead,' growled Loknath. Dragging Kanak beside him he stepped forward and locked his free hand around Sudesh's neck, pushing him backwards and lifting him almost off the ground.

The crowd stood there gasping, and Inder stepped forward, ready to help.

Sudesh had never indulged in a fight before. He was, however, familiar with basic self-defence tricks that his father had taught him. He drove the heel of his palm forward and upward with all the force he could muster, his fingers pulled back so the solid base of his hand hit Loknath's jaw from below. He heard the squelching crunch as Loknath's teeth drove into his own tongue.

Reeling with shock, pain and rage Loknath loosened his grip on the terrified boy at his side, and staggered, clutching his mouth.

'You baathtard!' His words were distorted by his swollen tongue.

For a moment Sudesh thought the encounter had ended, and so he turned away. Then Loknath tightened his arm around Sudesh's neck.

He knew he could not loosen Loknath's powerful grip with his hands. Instead he drew his leg forward and kicked back with full force. As his heel thudded against Loknath's shin he stamped his foot downwards, aiming at Loknath's foot. Loknath screamed and collapsed to the ground, rolling in agony.

Sudesh descended on the writhing body and wrapped his right arm around Loknath's neck. Blind with rage he gripped and squeezed until Loknath's eyes bulged and his face darkened.

'You're going to kill him!' shouted Inder, who rushed forward to pull Sudesh off his vanquished opponent. 'Come now, my friend.'

Sudesh's grip weakened. Loknath slumped back, his lungs heaving for breath. Sudesh turned and walked away from the scene, Inder at his side.

In the Gulfstream near the Channel Islands, 1993

As the Gulfstream V cruised towards the Channel Islands, Alexander Romney viewed the approaching bank of heavy black cloud with despair. 'Emma, please call the passenger.' Emma and he had worked together intermittently for many years, and shared a few tight situations, but nothing like this.

Ray appeared in the cockpit.

'Mr Upton, I am afraid we have another problem.'

'What is that?'

'Fog. I don't think we will be able to land. The runway in Jersey is short and I wouldn't want to try it in these conditions. Plus it falls under French air control. I was hoping for Guernsey. It's British and the runway is longer but in these conditions it is also impossible. We are running out of fuel.'

'What do you recommend?'

'Well, with fog as dense and as low as this, there is only one airport where it is possible to land.'

'And that is?'

'In East Anglia, Sir, but the problem is that we will have to glide most of the way. It's not easy.'

Ray took a deep breath and made a call.

'Cynthia.'

'Hey it's me. What's wrong?' she asked. He never called at this time.

'Cynthia, we're having problems with the plane. Don't panic, it will probably be fine. But just in case we don't come right, I wanted you to know that all the papers you would need are in the safe in the office.'

'Ray?' she panicked. 'Are you going to crash?'

'I don't think so, sweetheart,' he said calmly. 'We'll probably be fine.'

'I love you Ray.'

'I love you too. Try not to worry. I must go. I'll call you as soon as we are on the ground.'

He clicked off and Cynthia was left staring into the phone wondering if she would ever see her husband again.

A village near Delhi, 1993

'You taught Loknath a lesson. His foot is in plaster. Your dad taught you some pretty good tricks.' said Inder with admiration in his voice.

'Yes. He explained these techniques to me, and showed me how to respond should I be attacked. But I never thought I would behave like that. I don't believe in violence.'

'But sometimes one is not left with much choice,' said Inder. 'You had to defend yourself or Loknath would have pulverised you. You got a little carried away, but that's only natural.'

'Not natural for me,' said Sudesh, frowning. 'It shouldn't happen again.'

✿

Kamla Kumar settled into her day after her husband left for the police station and children left for their school.

She would scour her small two-roomed house from top to bottom until it was spotless, and then go out to buy groceries.

With a few basic components and twists of spices Kamla could prepare a wide variety of delicious dishes. Kamla's visits to the market and store were her time to catch up on the local news and gossip over a cup of chai, lassi or mango juice with friends.

Outside the Kumar's house was a small semicircular cooking area, enclosed by a metre high clay wall. There was a spherical clay structure in which Kamla placed the dung cakes, her cooking fuel.

As hunger drew the family members home, they would be welcomed by the appetising aroma wafting in the air, and see the familiar sight of Kamla cooking near the clay wall. She ensured that there was extra food for Inder and Shakti who visited frequently.

The Bhati family reciprocated generously, and helped stretch the Kumar budget by lowering prices for Kamla when possible, and giving Kumar's daughter Chanda packets of crayons for her incessant pattern-making activity.

Silence fell as the family devoured their meal. Kamla enjoyed the sighs of satisfaction as her husband and children ate indulgently with smiles on their faces.

Four

A village near Delhi, 1993

It was a Wednesday when three masked men entered the small brick house just after darkness fell.

'One of the men growled at Adhijat. 'How many times do we have to tell you to back off!'

'Don't do anything in haste. Let us go outside and talk about your problems.'

'We had tried doing that,' said one of the three men, 'but you weren't interested. We made an offer, but you called it "no deal".'

'I'm ready to talk now,' said Adhijat turning towards the door, eager to get these men out of his home.

'Not so fast, Mr Clean,' said the short man, drawing his gun.

Adhijat raised his palms slowly, 'Put the gun away, please. There is no need for that. We can talk.'

'Can we? I don't think so,' the man walked over to Adhijat, his gun still raised, and struck him hard across the face with the butt.

'That is for last month's interference.'

'And this,' he said striking him again 'is for confiscating goods from Hiranya Shah and Waman Mehta.'

Adhijat forced himself to remain calm.

Across the room, Kamla let out an involuntary moan. One of the other attackers looked over to see tears in her eyes.

He went and kicked her.

Adhijat gritted his teeth, struggling to maintain his control. 'Don't hit my wife. If you have any grudge, it is against me. Leave her alone.'

When Sudesh and Inder rounded the corner they were expecting to be in trouble for getting back home late. There was trouble, but they only realised how grave after entering the yard. They saw the three armed goons attacking Adhijat and Kamla.

They saw the man in blue jeans raise his gun and shoot a bullet into Kamla's thigh. The heftiest of the three heard the boys and was about to grab Sudesh when Adhijat raised his pistol and shot him through the head.

Adhijat went to his wife's rescue after firing a second shot that pierced through the chest of the man in blue jeans. He fell to the ground. Simultaneously the only remaining gangster fired two shots into Adhijat's body and then absconded.

The boys ran forward.

'Appa, Appa, are you alright?'

'Yes, Sudesh, I am, but quickly, get help for your mother.'

Inder sped to fetch a doctor.

The Health Department, East Delhi, 1993

The building was a low structure of crumbling concrete and peeling paint. It was the Ministry of Health, Maranati Division.

It was equally depressing inside as it was outside. The walls were scuffed, the floors looked dull and the ancient desks barely stood straight.

In a dimly-lit office two officials were talking.

'Four clinics in the precinct are short of supplies,' said one to the other.

'So what's new?'

'Shall I call them?'

'If you like. But nothing's going to happen until next week anyway. You know that, don't you?'

'But what about the patients?'

The other man smiled, 'How long have you been here? If you think like that you'll go insane.'

'So nothing works?'

'No, nothing. Weren't you around when there was that dengue fever disaster at AIIMS? The disease broke out as a result of mosquitoes breeding in stagnant pools of water in the hospital campus. Among the fourteen patients who died one was a doctor. They had to turn away suspected dengue cases because there was a shortage of beds.

'People were being treated in corridors and there were so few doctors in the dengue wards that patients were helping administer saline drips to each other. Believe me, we've tried to improve matters over the years, but fighting the ministry is like trying to stop people washing in the Ganges, impossible. So relax, why bother?'

East Anglia, England, 1993

The Gulfstream V dipped through the cloud towards the small East Anglian airport.

As they dropped beneath the cloud cover the outlines of runways fringed with dozens of jets, private and commercial, came into view. 'I think we might just make it,' said Captain Romney.

'Good job,' said Ray.

Seconds later he was thinking of a different matter, how to circumvent the French government. There was a satisfaction in outwitting politicians; he just needed to work out how to do it most effectively.

A hospital in East Delhi, 1993

The ward had twenty beds. Sudesh walked past the sick people, some groaned terribly with pain, while some lay so still he wondered if they were alive. There didn't seem to be many nurses around.

He reached his father's side.

'How is your mother?' asked Adhijat.

'She's in a lot of pain. The surgeon has tried to fix the fractured bone in her leg, but he says she won't walk for some time. How are you feeling, Appa?'

'Fine, my son. I'm worried about your Amma.' said his father.

'Dad, I don't think we could manage without you.'

'Don't worry Sudesh. I'm a strong, healthy man and my wounds will heal quickly. It won't be long before I am home, climbing Signal Hill with you.'

Sudesh remembered the headlines that had caught his eye in this morning's *Times*: 'Unattended dead body eaten by rats in Delhi hospital.' He shuddered. Would a hospital that left a corpse to be devoured by rats and cockroaches look after his parents properly.

A college town near Boston, 1993

Ray watched the financial news while Cynthia prepared the evening meal.

She placed sliced roasted vegetables on a platter and arranged them on the table with cooked cold lamb and baby potatoes.

Once they were both seated, Cynthia took a deep breath. 'Don't do that to me again, Ray,' she said, 'You gave me a fright. If you think you're going to crash, wait until you are on the ground before you call me. I'll hear soon enough if something happens.'

Ray looked at her with a quizzical smile, 'I am sorry, my love. I know I give you a hard time. Thank you for putting up with me.'

He changed the subject. 'There have been some interesting developments in India. I'm thinking of investing there.'

'But I thought India was a poor country with a socialist government?'

'The Prime Minister has announced free market reforms and he seems to be serious. The reforms open up a lot of scope for labour-intensive industries.'

'If that means you will be creating work for those poor people, then I am glad.'

At least I will know when he is away, thought Cynthia, and that he is doing some good, even if that is not his motivation.

A hospital in East Delhi, 1993

Sudesh felt optimistic as he strode along the now-familiar hospital corridors, climbed the stairs two at a time and entered his father's ward.

Adhijat had been recovering, but recently he had complained of worsening stomach cramps. Nurses assured him they were stress-induced.

Sudesh stopped, surprised. A stocky nurse in white and blue was changing the sheets of Appa's bed.

'Excuse me,' he said, 'where's Officer Kumar?'

'No idea,' she replied. 'Ask the duty doctor or matron. Down the corridor, third door on the right.'

He knocked.

'Come in.'

'Sorry to bother you matron, do you know where Officer Kumar's been moved to?'

Matron sat up straight and linked her hands on the desk. Why hadn't the family been informed? 'I'm sorry, I have bad news. Your father died last night. I'm very sorry.'

'What? That's impossible! He was getting better!'

Matron reached to her right and shifted papers and files until she found what she was looking for. She lifted a brown government-issue folder, opened it and removed a death certificate. She handed it to Sudesh.

Adhijat Kumar had not died from gunshot wounds. He was strong enough to recover soon. He died from undiagnosed peritonitis (inflammation of a membrane lining the abdominal cavity).

$$\mathcal{S}$$

Adhijat's dead body enshrouded in a white cloth was taken to the cremation ground on a bullock cart. His family headed the large funeral procession following the cart. Sudesh pushed Kamla's wheelchair, and consoled his weeping sister Chanda as they walked. Adhijat was widely loved and respected and people had come from miles around to attend his funeral.

Sudesh looked at his father's face and wondered whether there really was no way of bringing life back into his body.

The procession moved through the village and stopped at the temple where Adhijat had worshipped throughout his life. The priest prayed: 'This brave and honest man was a son of our village. He dedicated himself to the welfare and security of our district. He has sacrificed his life in the process of upholding honesty. We pay our tribute to him.'

At the Shmashana Ghat (cremation ground) Adhijat's body was placed on the pyre and Sudesh performed the last rites for his beloved Appa. As he walked three times round the pyre sprinkling water he prayed for his father's soul. Then, he set the pyre alight with a torch of flame and silently dedicated his life to his father's memory.

Sudesh longed to have his Appa back, alive and well, walking with him in the hills, answering his questions and explaining to him the ways of the world. As he wept he wanted to feel his father's arms tight around him.

Five

A village near Delhi, 1994

Chanda, now thirteen, realised that if her brother, Sudesh, was to continue his schooling, she must find a job.

They still had their little brick house, but her mother, disabled after the attack, was unable to make a living for the family.

After Adhijat's death the Kumars had received a small payout from the police force, but it would not last more than a few months. Either Chanda or Sudesh would have to find work.

Ashwin Lakhan was a famous owner of the carpet factory that was situated near the village. The factory, though little more than a wooden frame with a thatched roof, employed many women, girls and boys to knot carpets and rugs. Chanda had visited it a couple of times in the past. She had quietly slipped inside and enjoyed gazing at the girls as they moved their slender hands rapidly to weave traditional designs on the carpet.

Chanda had heard that the factory was looking for workers and decided to quit schooling to earn an income; there was no job she would like more than knotting coloured wool and silk to create beautiful floor coverings.

The outskirts of Delhi, 1994

Sudesh and Inder squatted beside the road as they often did, watching cars drive past. 'Are you going to play cricket for the Indian team when you grow up?' asked Sudesh.

Inder nodded his head.

'And you? What are you planning now?'

'Wait, stop, look at that car?'

They had never seen anything like that before.

The two boys were left spellbound as they saw the sleek, silver car gliding along the highway. The driver had an agitated look on his face as he manoeuvred his way avoiding pot holes on the road.

'It must be thrilling,' breathed Inder, 'to drive a car like that.'

'Yeah,' There was a pause.

'I'm going to become the Prime Minister.' Sudesh spoke with strong conviction.

'Prime Minister, still that old dream? Aren't you building castles in the air and trying to reach a bit high? Playing cricket for India is ambitious, but at least there are eleven people in the team. But there is only one Prime Minister and he stays in office for years.'

'And none of them does any good,' said Sudesh 'Look at all this around us. Slums and poverty. Useless hospitals like the one that killed my dad. People being bribed all the time and not doing things properly.'

'Nobody cares.'

'That's right. Nobody cares, but I do and that's why I'm going to become the Prime Minister.'

❦

As Chanda approached the carpet factory she saw dozens of women and young girls sitting by the roadside. Her heart sank. She wondered with so many applicants and only two empty looms, what chance did she stand of getting a job. She sat beside the last woman in line.

She opened her scuffed school satchel and pulled out a piece of paper and a pencil and started drawing. This favourite pastime of hers transported her into another world.

Chanda did not notice that another dozen women had joined the line to her right. She was absorbed in her design that was gradually taking shape on the paper. The owner, Mr Ashwin Lakhan appeared. He looked at the long line and thought that it would take most of his day to select only two new employees. As he started speaking to the candidates one by one, he was happy to see that no one bothered to ask about wages; they all seemed ready to accept whatever small amount he would offer.

By the time Chanda's turn came she had completed her drawing. She quickly put it into her satchel and went to the owner. Ashwin Lakhan looked at her and then dismissed her wondering what a girl so small will do with such large looms. As she turned to leave, the next woman came rushing in to take her place. In her eagerness she knocked Chanda to the ground. As she scrambled to her feet Lakhan reached down to help collect the dispersed contents of her satchel. 'What is this?' he asked looking at the paper in his hands. 'Did you draw this?' When she nodded her head he smiled and asked her to come back into his office.

At the end of what seemed an interminable day the exhausted factory owner came out to face the sea of faces, waiting with eyes wide in anticipation.

'The two I pick must be here tomorrow at sunrise,' he said. His arm flew through the air. 'You,' he pointed. 'And you,' his finger was pointing to Chanda. Before she could thank him he was gone.

A luxury villa in Hyderabad, 1994

In the new age of a world closely-knit by globalisation, Bangalore was booming with technological advancement. The man who had kicked off its growth was Sabyasachi Palande, the CEO of InfoSwish, the information technology outsourcing and business process re-engineering giant.

His ten-year-old daughter Vaneshri Palande meant the world to him. Vaneshri was a unique child with unique interests.

Never had she wasted her time playing computer games; at the earliest age she started to write them. She did not fancy Bollywood heroes as her dream dudes but looked up to Linux Torvel, inventor of the Linux operating system, as her idol.

It was also believed that the first word uttered by Vaneshri was 'network' and that she had often threatened to outsource her nanny, her butler and occasionally even her mother!

Vaneshri's father hadn't always run a billion dollar business. When he founded the company with six other partners he had borrowed ten thousand rupees from his wife. Before long an Initial Public Offering in India had priced the company at thirteen crore rupees.

Soon, the business moved from Bangalore to Hyderabad, India's second emerging technology hub. Sabyasachi opened offices in the United States, the UK, Canada, France, Hong Kong, the UAE and Argentina.

It became the first Indian company to list on the NASDAQ, the American technology stock exchange.

The headquarters of the Eastern Police district of Delhi, 1994

Police Superintendent Singh paced across his office floor. The desk in his office looked rickety and was cluttered with thick files. Singh was dressed in a police uniform with a light blue turban identifying him as a Sikh.

'I'm sorry Sir, but your popularity is dropping rapidly,' said the aide.

'Are people holding me responsible for the increase in crime?' Singh asked.

The aide nodded unhappily. He regarded Singh as the most dutiful, responsible and committed person in the force. But what he was saying was true. Singh was being blamed for the recent crime wave: burglaries had gone up by twenty-five percent in the last year and number of murders shot up by fourteen percent.

'Yes Sir. The increase in crime has happened since you acquired this post.'

'As if the gangs are out to make life difficult for me?'

The aide was silent.

The superintendent's eyes narrowed; his mouth set into a firm line of determination.

'We need creative solutions for this problem,' said Singh, 'and I have an idea for how we might find some.'

Srinagar, Kashmir, 1994

Vasu lounged on the front deck of his houseboat on Dal Lake. He had paid for it in cash. His business had grown rapidly over the past few years. With careful planning and ruthless violence he had swiftly eliminated his rivals one by one. He now ran Delhi's biggest stolen goods syndicate.

The girl that he had brought with him was young, perhaps fifteen, and a favourite. This was the third time she had come away with him. She lay sleeping, curled up on the banquette beside him, leaving him to concentrate on his reading.

The view of the Dal Lake from Vasu's seat beneath the intricately carved canopy of his houseboat stretched across the shimmering silver surface of the lake towards the mountains; a band of mist separated them from their snow-capped reflections.

Vasu glanced up from his book, his attention briefly captured by the dugouts carrying the lake people with their produce. Farmers, traders and school children paddled their small boats through narrow canals and across shining expanses of water, pursuing their daily lives.

Looking at the picturesque and peaceful scene one would never think of Kashmir as one of the world's most conflict-ridden and disturbed zones. Those foolish tourists lounging with their cameras in brightly coloured *shikaras*, thought Vasu, should not underestimate the threat of terrorism.

He was reading *How to Build a Nuclear Bomb and Other Weapons of Mass Destruction* by Frank Barnaby. The book though somewhat theoretical made sense to him and was helping him move closer to his goal.

The more he thought about it, the more he was convinced that a 'dirty bomb' was the way to go. It seemed easy to make one, and he wondered why no one else had done so. He smiled, and read on.

A village near Delhi, 1994

Chanda and her mother celebrated the joy with tears in their eyes. Now that the young girl had work there would be enough money for food and this also meant that Sudesh could continue his education. As they talked about it, Sudesh appeared through the door.

The skinny boy, tall for his age, approached his mother and hugged her and asked, 'What's happening?'

'Sudesh, we have wonderful news. Chanda has got work in the rug factory, so now you can continue your schooling.'

Sudesh looked at his sister, frowning. 'I'm the one who should support the family,' he said. 'Chanda should stay in school.'

'But you haven't found a job yet,' replied Chanda. 'And Sudesh, you mustn't feel bad about this. I want to learn making rugs. And the man says he might use my designs. I am so lucky to get this job, I will be learning a real skill, and doing the work I love. You should be happy for me.'

🙢

Ashwin Lakhan had chosen Chanda for her creative ability. His experienced workers taught her how to create a design for a rug in the correct proportions on a graph paper to provide a template for knotting.

Besides learning to adapt traditional carpet motifs to her own designs, Chanda was also taught knotting. She quickly mastered the skill. With her small fine-boned hands and sharp eyes it was not long before she started working on the more finely-knotted carpets with as many as a hundred knots per sq cm.

Chanda's first two designs received great acclamation by the buyers and many orders were placed for more. Lakhan paid Chanda a small percentage of the income from the rugs made to her design.

Each pay day was a day of happiness with enough to cover for Sudesh's school costs and her mother's household requirements.

৯

At the community school Sudesh had no competitors in the academic arena, so he competed with himself, aiming always to surpass his highest mark until then.

Inder usually scored well, even though he spent his spare time playing cricket. 'That boy has no application,' said his father. Nobody said that about Sudesh.

Today Sudesh was excited. 'I am going to participate in that competition the headmaster announced in assembly today, and win twenty thousand rupees as prize and give it to Amma.'

'The one about ideas to stop crime? You always were a dreamer, but I suppose you have a better chance of winning that competition than becoming Prime Minister,' teased Inder.

'Well, I have taken an entry form, and this afternoon I am going to write to Superintendent Singh about how my dad had reduced crime in our district.'

The outskirts of Delhi, 1994

One day when Chanda reached the factory, there was great commotion. Across the work area she could see three foreigners: a man, his wife and their son. Not wanting to waste her time gawking at the foreigners she got back to her work, weaving dreams along with the rug. Her small fingers meticulously wove designed patterns. This would be one of the best rugs she had ever made and would fetch a huge profit to her employer. She was so absorbed in her work that she didn't see the boy standing near her. It was only the click of his camera that caught her attention. She turned towards him and returned his smile. Then she resumed her work, proud of her design and gratified by the white boy's admiration.

The next time she glanced up, the boy was standing with his parents talking and gesturing towards her. The visitors said something to Mr Lakhan. He looked shocked but quickly regained his composure and seemed to be ordering them to leave.

Mr Lakhan's assistant came running over to Chanda. She leaned down and whispered: 'You must go away for a minute. It is important. Leave until they are gone.'

Chanda did not understand but did as she was told. When she returned a short while later, the visitors were gone and she resumed her work.

Chanda never saw the photos that were taken that day. But millions of others did. One iconic picture captured the moment when she looked up at the boy and sheepishly smiled, her eyes wide under her arched brows. Her small hands rested on her loom, drawing attention to the intricacy of her design and the richness of colours. A bead of sweat ran down her cheek. It almost looked like a tear.

This picture was published in newspapers across the globe, and used in documentaries on CNN and BBC World.

Six

Chanda enjoyed three months of grace before the consequences of the foreigners' visit to her workplace upset her routine.

Her photo was reprinted around the world and the caption beneath read 'The Face of Child Labour'. Usually her photo was accompanied by an article peppered with words like 'sweatshop', 'exploitation' and 'child abuse'.

The sixteen-year-old boy who had taken the photo was the son of a Washington lobbyist for the American textile industry. The textile industry, supported by its workers' union, was fighting the 'evils of child labour in India'. Both the union and factory owners of the US wanted to stop imports of Indian textiles, and the fact that children worked in the textiles industry provided the peg on which to hang their campaign.

As one lobbyist told a sympathetic Congressman: 'Those people are so damn poor that you know they will have their kids out there working in some sweatshop. It's not like they have much choice. And when we find them it's perfect. It's so much easier getting protection passed for our industry when we are campaigning for poor kids over there.'

The public relations firm that ran the publicity campaign arranged for the boy named Chuck to appear on the Oprah Winfrey show. The pictures that he took showing Chanda working in the small factory appeared on the screen above the stage where he and Oprah sat and chatted.

Chuck explained the evil of forcing young girls to work. This girl whose name he didn't know, he said, laboured long hours instead of going to school. He appealed to the audience to help save this girl, and millions like her, from the clutches of exploiters. As tears welled up in Oprah's eyes, the viewers around the world also dabbed their eyes in sympathy.

The labour group which funded Chuck and his parents' trip persuaded a Senator with numerous textile manufacturers in his State, to propose new legislation restricting the import of goods made through 'the sweat and blood of little children whose eyesight is ruined by close-up work done for little or no reward.'

The labour group tracked down the rugs produced in the factory where Chanda worked. They found the local wholesalers who purchased them. They discovered their international buyers and found the retail outlets in the United States and Europe that sold the carpets. They proudly published a 'List of Shame' with Chanda's face on the front, exposing the businesses that should be boycotted for exploiting child labour.

The outskirts of Delhi, 1995

This campaign did not perturb Ashwin Lakhan initially, but within some months dismay clung to him as he discovered the sales of his rugs decreasing drastically.

Lakhan hoped that the shortage of buyers would not last. He encouraged his employees to continue working for him.

He visited the wholesaler who had been his first client, and who had become his trusted friend.

'Abdul, my friend, what is happening? Please tell me the truth, why are you not placing any order for my rugs?'

Abdul looked troubled. He reached into the drawer of his desk and pulled out a coloured brochure. He handed it to Ashwin who was left numb after seeing the face on the cover. He had thought of this young girl as his daughter. He was proud of her work and delighted by her designs. She had been fortunate for his factory; her designs had fetched great sales in the market. This had brought prosperity to his family, and to his employees.

A village near Delhi, 1995

One Saturday, Inder and his sister Shakti sat chatting after breakfast. It was a rare moment as generally neither of the two had time for chit-chats. Mostly their interests diverged: in their free time, Inder played cricket and Shakti went around the village helping destitute and needy people. The conversation had turned to Sudesh, possibly their only point of mutual interest.

'Don't tell him I said this,' said Inder. 'But don't you think Sudesh is a bit weird?'

'Weird?' asked Shakti. 'How is he weird?'

Inder frowned. He wasn't quite sure what he meant himself.

'You know, most kids of our age play or just hang out with friends. If their families are poor they might work to support, or look after their younger brothers and sisters.'

Shakti nodded.

'But Sudesh,' Inder frowned, 'Sudesh talks all this stuff about helping the poor and changing the world. Who else do you know who does that?'

'No one,' admitted Shakti.

'Some people study as much as he does, but they study because they want to get a job and earn good money. They don't study books on how to make economies grow and bring people out of poverty and stuff like that.'

'Yes, you're right,' agreed Shakti.

'It is a bit weird, isn't it?'

Shakti thought about it. 'You know Inder, I do think Sudesh is different, but I don't think he's weird. I think he's special. Unlike others he doesn't think in a self-centred way. I'm sure most of the world's great leaders and spiritual thinkers were like that. And I think Sudesh is like that.'

Inder looked incredulous, 'I think you're in love!'

'Don't act funny,' said Shakti, gathering up some cups and heading towards the kitchen. She wouldn't allow her brother to see her blushing.

The outskirts of Delhi, 1995

The office of the carpet factory was functional and tidy.

'I have some bad news for you.'

'Bad news?' asked Chanda.

'Yes, I'm afraid you will have to leave our factory.'

'Leave? I am sorry Sir, how have I displeased you? I thought my work was good. Please give me one more chance, I can improve.'

She thought of Sudesh's new school, his new hopes and her mother who depended entirely on her.

'It's not you Chanda. It's not you at all. Your work has always been brilliant. Your designs are beautiful. You're a good girl and I hope you will reach great heights.'

'Well, then why must I leave?'

'People think I am exploiting you.'

'But you have always been kind to me and always paid my wages on time. Mr Lakhan, I will tell them you have never exploited me.'

'People in other countries think that it's bad that we carpet makers employ young people of your age.'

The girl looked at him blankly.

'They think you should be going to school.'

'I would like to go to school, Mr Lakhan, but we can afford to send only one person in our family to school so we send Sudesh because he is very bright. I work so that he can go to school.'

'I know, but they think you both should go to school.'

'That would be good but who would pay for our food and school books?'

'I don't know. I don't think they have thought over this carefully.'

'Can't we tell them that if I can't work here then my brother will have to quit his school? Can't we tell them what I am learning here – all about weaving and designing?'

Chanda was becoming anxious, 'Can't you tell them anything, anything that will let me keep my job?'

And with that she burst into tears.

'Please, please, Mr Lakhan, can't you talk to them?'

'I'm so sorry' he said. Tears welled up in his eyes, 'If I could do anything to help I would, but these people are too powerful and they are too many. I am helpless against them.'

Far away from Chanda and Sudesh a woman and a man sat in a television studio discussing the success of their humanitarian campaign.

'What's important to us is that we get these children back to school.'

'Children need to acquire education. Surely, we should have left child labour behind in the nineteenth century with its chimney sweeps?'

Whilst they talked Chanda was stumbling home from the factory, her head bowed and her arms hanging limply by her sides.

Seven

A village near Delhi, 1995

Kamla groaned inwardly at the downward turn of fate in the last few days. With Chanda out of work, how could they possibly afford to send Sudesh to school? Though she had regained her strength to take on some sewing work, she could not earn enough to support the family. If Sudesh didn't complete his schooling what chance did the family have of escaping poverty?

Chanda spent all of her days trudging in the heat from one place to another in search of work. 'Sorry. You are too young.' 'We can't afford to take on more people. The economy isn't good this year,' was all she heard wherever she went.

She joined her mother who was cooking beside the clay cooker.

'Chanda.'

'Yes mother.'

'You can't afford to be fussy, girl. You have to take any job you get.'

Chanda's thoughts swayed in an entirely different direction on hearing the words 'any job' from her mother. She shuddered at the thought of working as a prostitute. She remembered how disgusted she had felt looking at some girls of her age in skimpy dresses by the roadside a few days back. A feeling of horror struck her.

Kamla thought, it would be a pity to see her talented daughter Chanda labouring hard picking up bricks in the local construction sites. But Kamla comforted herself thinking that Chanda would not have to continue for too many years, soon Sudesh would take up a well paying job in a government office.

'I am proud of you, Chanda, you have been strong and have alone supported our family since your father died. You must continue to be strong for a few more years. We still need your help. I've arranged with some of the men in the village; they will see what can be done for you.'

The local men were going to find her first clients! Thought Chanda, No! She couldn't, she was saving herself for someone special. She didn't want to do it ... But she loved Sudesh dearly and wanted so much to help him reach his potential. Maybe she was being selfish. After all, people had sex every day. Some of the village girls of her own age had boyfriends who took them to Nirula's and bought them gifts, they boasted of their exploits and talked about how much they enjoy sex. Perhaps it would not be so bad. She brought herself some consolation.

'Don't look so sad. I know you enjoyed designing the carpets and you did beautiful work. But we don't always get what we want in life. Sometimes we have to do things we don't want to do.'

'But Amma!'

'I'm sorry, but the matter is settled. Sudesh must finish his education. You must be ready to take any job at this stage.'

Any job. ... Any job. ... The words echoed in her mind and filled her with panic. She leapt to her feet. 'I won't do it. I won't do it,' she cried, and ran to the other room, bolted the door from inside and spent the night alone, weeping.

It would be hard for her after all her success, thought Kamla, but she would soon understand the situation and take up the work at the construction site.

At night Chanda packed her meagre belongings in her school bag. She stuffed in a few items of clothing and shoes she had bought with the money she had earned while working in the factory.

She crept out while her family slept. She wanted to bid them farewell but chose to leave without informing them. She trembled at the thought of sleeping with the men of her own community. She would rather go far from her home, somewhere where nobody knew her. She would send money home to her mother and brother.

Chanda hastened through the dark streets. When she turned the corner, she saw a tall building in a tenement block, with huge neon signs outside. It was a bar. She stood on the other side of the street and watched for a while. Lots of men entered, some glancing around furtively as they slipped through the door. Some girls wrapped in short skirts stood outside smoking. A tall man saw her and crossed the road. 'What is a nice girl like you doing near a place like this?' he asked.

A village near Delhi, 1995

Kamla wept uncontrollably.

'I don't know what happened to her. She's been gone now for four days.'

Shakti shook her head. 'She's such a sensible girl. Why did she run away like that?'

Kamla spoke as she sobbed, 'It must have been something I said the night before she left.'

'What exactly did you say?'

'I had told her to take up some work to support Sudesh at school.'

'Go on.'

'And I asked her not be fussy and take up any job.'

'Any job? Any job at all?'

'Well, perhaps not any job.' Kamla spoke as realisation dawned upon her.

Shakti looked at Kamla with her most gentle expression, 'Maybe she thought you meant any job at all.'

Kamla choked as tears poured down her cheeks.

An apartment in East Delhi, 1995

Police Superintendent Singh looked at his twenty-two-year old wife. He had met her at an official function two years after the death of his first wife. Marrying her had brought back happiness to his shattered life.

Standing five feet ten inches tall, she was in the pink of health; she looked fit and sturdy, her deep golden skin glowed, and her black, long, pleated hair added grace to her appearance.

As a valued agent of CBI, she was more capable of exhibiting her skills at athletics than domestic chores. Today for a change she was trying to enhance her skills in the kitchen as she chopped vegetables to prepare a stew.

During her police training years, her trainers discovered that Madhumati could outperform her male competitors in every area including hand-to-hand combat (which included karate and jujitsu), shooting pistols, knife throwing or breaking into a safe. Her grasp of cutting edge technological applications was exemplary. Further, she was adept at balancing her intellect and emotions.

'Madhu, that competition I ran in my district for ideas to reduce crime,' said Singh.

'Yes?'

'There is a lot of nonsense in most of the entries, but one or two have done a commendable job. One in particular is likely to be a winner.'

'Great! Where does it come from?'

'Strangely enough, it seems to be some guy from one of the backward villages. It will be interesting to know more about him and his family.'

A village near Delhi, 1995

Inder saw his friend's mother crying and talking to Shakti. As he passed their shack, he pretended not to notice. He was going to meet Sudesh before cricket and he would ask him about it.

As he reached the cricket fields, he saw Sudesh waiting, looking grim.

'What's wrong?' asked Inder.

'It's Chanda. She's disappeared.'

Inder questioned, an intense expression on his face, 'What do you mean "disappeared", have you checked under the bed?'

'It's not funny. She's been gone since Friday, four days now. Amma is a wreck. First dad, and then this.'

'Shit, Sudesh, you don't think she's dead, do you?'

'Or almost as bad.'

'What do you mean?'

'You know what I mean.'

'Surely not. Surely Chanda wouldn't consider that, no matter how desperate the situation becomes?'

'It seems that Amma had a plan for her to work in the brick quarry. Amma didn't explain what she had in mind, but told Chanda that she should be willing to take on "any job", Amma thinks Chanda got it wrong.'

'Oh my god, we must find her!'

'I've tried. They won't let me into any of the brothels. I'm too young. And they say no one fits Chanda's description and that they don't take in girls that young.'

'But they would say that, wouldn't they?'

'Anything could have happened to her. Who knows, they might have given her an overdose of dope and kidnapped her and taken her to some other country. Sometimes the pimps also end up killing girls for not cooperating or trying to escape. I'm very scared.'

'That's terrible, Sudesh.'

Sudesh nodded.

The two boys sat brooding.

Outside a Delhi brothel, 1995

Chanda looked down. The man wore long black pointed snake-skin shoes that had white lace flaps over his insteps. She'd seen shoes like that in shop windows, but never seen anyone wearing them. Her heart thudded, she looked up slowly to meet his eyes.

'I need work,' she whispered.

'Are you sure you would want to work there?' He gestured across the road.

She was silent.

'Stand up straight, let me look at you ... you're very pretty ... turn around.'

'I've never done this before' she managed to say.

'It's no different when you do it for money' he replied, as if he knew.

'I've never done this before.' She repeated.

'You mean you've never been with a man?'

She nodded slowly, looking again at his shiny shoes.

'Now that's interesting ... hmm ... very interesting ... have you ever been in there?'

She shook her head slowly, almost imperceptibly.

'Good, that's good,' he said, 'come with me.' He took her hand firmly and walked her down the street. 'I have work for you,' he said, 'a special work, a very special work. I will provide you food and lodging, and you will be paid well.'

He knew there were men willing to pay twenty-five thousand rupees for a young virgin, and he knew where to find them.

Chanda was hungry, thirsty, tired and frightened. But she was also determined. She had come to find work and earn money to send to her mother, and here was a man willing to help her.

He was promising her food, shelter and money. She looked up for a moment when he spoke. He had a hoarse voice, red lips and a round pale face. A lock of straight black hair fell forward over his right temple. He pulled it back with a sweep of his hand as if it shouldn't have been there.

'Come,' he repeated as he led her to his luxurious car, which was bigger than the mud houses in her village. The driver opened the door and saluted. The man pushed her in and climbed in besides her. The door closed quietly, shutting Chanda in and the noisy street out.

A village near Delhi, 1995

Sudesh burst into the dark interior of the clay brick house, quivering with excitement.

'Amma,' he cried, 'I have wonderful news. You won't believe it! We won't have to worry about money ever again, everything will be fine!'

'Sudesh, you startle me, tell me what is all this about?'

'I've won! I've won the money, the competition!'

'What competition? What money? What are you talking about?'

Sudesh sat down next to his mother, and explained that he had participated in a competition organised by Police Superintendent Singh. The competition required members of the public to write about ways of reducing crime.

'You remember how Appa stopped the thieves from coming to his district, by confiscating stolen goods from second-hand dealers? That is what I suggested to Police Superintendent Singh. I explained what Appa did, and why it worked so well. Today in assembly the headmaster announced that I have won the competition, and will be given the prize money of twenty thousand rupees!

'There will be enough to live on, and to pay people to help us find Chanda.'

A house in South Delhi, 1995

Chanda woke up with a start. She looked out of the window of the car and saw a guard salute as he opened the big steel gate to a paved yard. Who was this man she had gone with and why did people salute him, she wondered. They climbed out of the car and another man with a gun opened a grand carved wooden door leading into the big white house.

Upstairs there was a small room with a huge bed and a pink marble bathroom with shining golden taps. A plump expressionless woman in a dark green sari offered Chanda a glass of sweet lassi to drink and a bowl of saffron-scented rice with lamb curry. Meanwhile, she ran a bath full of lukewarm water and asked Chanda to climb in. Apart from swimming in the river, Chanda had never before been immersed in water. All her life Chanda had washed herself with water from a bucket filled at the community tap and so this was a pleasant change. The woman helped Chanda to dress in a lacy thong and tiny red silk skirt that almost showed her bottom. Her small breasts showed through the thin chiffon blouse. The woman dressed Chanda's waist-long hair in a shining black stream. Finally, she had to put on high-heeled red sandals which hurt her feet and in which she walked with difficulty.

Then Chanda was taken downstairs and handed over to the man with the snake-skin shoes. He looked at her with narrowed eyes, and explained that he would pay, feed and clothe her if she was nice to her clients. She might be taken to these men, or they might visit her here, she was told. But her first client would be very special, a billionaire. He would spend a fortune on her, much of which she could send home to her mother.

Eight

Ratan Tata Library, Delhi, 1995

Sudesh logged in at the terminal.

'Register for Pawn Shop' he clicked.

'Please enter your address,' displayed the computer.

'This is so that we can allocate you a pawn shop not far from where you stay.'

'Preet Vihar,' typed Sudesh.

'Thank you. Your allocated pawn shop is in Krishna Nagar. Click through for full directions. Please be aware that some pawn shops and scrap yards are allocated to more than one person.'

No problem, thought Sudesh. I don't mind a little competition.

Outside a pawn shop, East Delhi, 1995

'Did you see that red Mercedes parked outside again?' asked Inder.

'That's the fourth time this week,' said Sudesh. 'Write it down.'

'Done!' said Inder pointing to the sheet. 'Plus there's the guy who parks far away and walks with his boxes to the back of the shop. I think we missed him the first few times.'

'Yes, you need to watch the back and me the front,' said Inder.

For a thirteen year old – his sister was now fourteen – catching criminals was an exciting venture.

One couldn't really tell which people were suspects when they walked up to the pawn shop. But they could be followed when they left and their car registrations were noted. Then they were on the system. All repeat visits would be recorded and eventually Superintendent Singh's system would get them.

'That's enough for today, let's go and update our report at Ratan Tata Library.'

The Imperial Hotel, New Delhi, 1995

Chanda was bundled into a luxurious car with an ankle length coat covering her skimpy outfit. Raj, the man who had brought her to the big house, instructed the driver where to take her.

She was being taken to her first man, and all she had to do, Raj told her, was to be very nice to him and do whatever he asked of her. The more obedient she was, the more the man would pay, and the more she could send home.

The car pulled up at the entrance to the Imperial Hotel. Chanda would soon enter through large glass doors that swung open as if by magic into the vast gleaming interior she saw beyond. 'Come,' said the driver. He took her arm and walked her through the colonnaded portico of the hotel where a tall handsome man in a white kurta with a maroon sash bowed and smiled in welcome.

Chanda almost forgot her fear in her wonder as she was led across marble floors inlaid with patterns of delicate designs and ceilings glowing with chandeliers. The driver walked her down wide passages past mahogany tables topped with dense clusters of crimson carnations. In the wood-panelled walls were niches displaying statues ranging from marble Greek nymphs to bronze Indian elephants and Chinese porcelain vases.

The details were lost on Chanda, but the general impression of extraordinary wealth kept striking her continuously. Finally the driver knocked and then opened the door of room 217 and pushed her in.

'Here she is,' the driver said, looking towards a fat man silhouetted in front of the tall wood-framed window overlooking the roof of the Imperial's Daniell's Tavern restaurant.

As her eyes adjusted to the dim light Chanda saw the curlicues of the oriental roof top, and suddenly seized with terror wished she could jump out of the window, slide down the roof and race back to her mother.

'Come here,' a voice emanated from the silhouette, 'Let me look at you.' The driver pushed her forward. 'Yes, pretty, a very pretty little girl, just the way I like.' The fat man reached out and stroked her shining hair. She was reminded suddenly and dreadfully of her Appa, he used to do the same. She resolutely pushed his image away from her mind. How horrified he would have been to see her here!

'Okay,' said the man. He opened the drawer in the bedside table and took out a thick wad of notes that he handed over to the driver and Chanda caught a fleeting view of his face illuminated by the light from the passage. He had a big scary face. Between his pallid cheeks was a bulbous red nose, and above his fleshy lips a thick black moustache like a big hairy caterpillar. The door was still open. She could still run. And then the door closed with a solid thunk and the latch gave a purposeful click as if it would never open again. She knew she would never forget that sound.

'Come,' the man said. 'Come, sit on my lap, pretty girl.' He sat on the bed, and pulled Chanda down firmly. 'Be nice to me,' he said. He stroked her hair slowly all the way down her back right to where it ended. 'You have beautiful hair, little girl,' he said stroking over her shoulders and hips. He stroked softly and gently, but it was the vilest feeling of her life, worse than the rat that ran up her leg one night, or the rotting corpse she found in the river. His other hand moved down her front, over her small breasts, down to her knees and back up across her tightly squeezed thighs.

The dark room swirled around her. She sat quietly like a good girl on his lap, but felt sick. The man pushed her back onto the bed, and the blood rushed into her head, preventing her from fainting. He moved away and his body was silhouetted against the window as he began to undress. She stared at his shoes. His zipper made a loud rasping sound, like a saw cutting wood. His trousers fell to his ankles. She could no longer see his shoes. He stepped towards her out of his pants and out of his shoes, which stayed beneath his pants as if waiting for him to finish with her and get back in the way he'd left them.

When he leant towards her, she could no longer see his feet or the carpet where she'd been looking. All she saw now was his belly protruding towards her as if it wanted to get to her before he did. Now every detail became sharp with heightened awareness as if the room wasn't dark and she wasn't afraid.

'Take off your clothes,' he said. She stared down at herself, but was unable to move. He leant forward and tugged at her skirt and ripped it to join his pants on the floor. He leant closer, his breath heavy with whisky, cigars and lust. He was ready to take her virginity, now. He had paid for it.

As he forced her legs apart Chanda suddenly knew with startling clarity that she could not be nice to this man. Everything she had learned from her Amma and Appa rose within her and shouted 'No!'

'No!' she cried, 'No, stop, let me go!'

'You have to be nice to me,' he said. 'Be a good girl now, be nice.'

'No!' she cried loudly.

Suddenly she mustered some courage and tore herself from his grip and ran to the door, but it would not open. She banged on it with her fists, screaming. He grabbed her from behind and pulled her back to the bed, one great gnarled hand clamped over her mouth.

She broke free again and ran to the window, but was confronted by solid glass, too thick to crash through. He grabbed a fistful of her long black hair and dragged her kicking and screaming to the bed. Her scream was cut short as his big wet mouth closed on top of hers and his bulk descended onto her, pinning her down like a butterfly crushed beneath a jackboot.

She jerked violently, searching frantically in her mind for some means of defence. He had forced her knees apart with his huge leg, and now his hand was gripping her mouth to stop her screams. She dug her sharp teeth deep into his palm. He ripped his hand away and flung it behind him as if he were trying to shake it off his arm. He bellowed and blood spattered across the white sheets of the bed.

As she again opened her mouth to scream, he covered her face with the pillow. She could not breathe with the pillow squeezed firmly over her face. Nor could she move her head under the weight of his arm. Flashes of light danced through the darkness before her eyes; all she could think about was the need to breathe.

In the few seconds it took for the man to force his way into Chanda and ejaculate she began to lose consciousness.

Then the pillow slipped off her face and her lungs involuntarily sucked in musty air in great shuddering gasps. The man was done and rolled over onto his back.

Chanda slid off the bed and lay on the carpet curled in a foetal position, shivering and gasping. As her breathing steadied she became aware of the pain that shafted up from between her legs deep into her belly.

As soon as she could stand, she stumbled into the bathroom. Blood trickled down her thighs. She cleaned herself, washed her face and drank a glass of water. Then, slowly and methodically, moving like an automaton she found the coat she'd been given to cover herself. She considered leaving through the hotel corridors and lobby, but couldn't face the prospect of watching eyes. So she struggled with the window latch until it opened.

As Chanda climbed out of the window she heard the fat man's loud rumbling snores. She shuddered and clambered quickly across the tiled roof of the famous Daniell's Tavern restaurant beneath where diners talked softly against gentle strains of music. She climbed down a big tree adjacent to the restaurant, one of many magnificent trees in the manicured Imperial gardens, and crept through the shadows until she reached the gates and ran past the guards into the night.

*

Tired and sore, Chanda looked for a place to sleep. The streets were full of life. Cars, motorbikes, and rickshaws hooted and jostled. Chanda wanted to be alone. The buildings around her were dark, with only a few lights glimmering behind shaded windows. Litter backed up against the crumbling pavement. She noticed nothing. She was looking for a dark place to curl up where no one would see her. She passed a house that seemed to be abandoned. No light showed and no people moved. She spotted a shadowy place in the corner of the doorway under the overhang. Almost as soon as she lay down and curled onto her side, she fell asleep.

She woke up suddenly, aware of a figure approaching her doorway. The tall man's face was not visible in the dark. What now, another assault? she wondered. Chanda cowered into the corner of the alcove seeing behind the man's shoulder the clear outline of a rifle. Then she breathed again, relieved, there was a woman at his side.

The woman came closer peering down at her, when she spoke her voice was kind. 'What are you doing here, girl? You shouldn't be out here on your own.'

'I ran away,' whispered Chanda. 'I was trying to find work to send my brother to school. Please don't hurt me.'

She could see that the woman was smiling, 'I am not going to hurt you, but please move aside so that I can get into my house.'

'I'm sorry,' said Chanda as she slithered from the door.

'You may sleep on a mat inside. It will be safe.'

An Ashram in Rishikesh, 1995

'This is it, Chanda, they will be expecting you,' said Janardan. He was the man who had found her at his sister's house, and he was a soldier. 'I need to go now, I need to visit my family and then head back to Kashmir.'

'Thanks for all your help,' she said and hugged the young man who had become her friend.

She watched him as he disappeared around the corner, then turned back to the elaborate wrought-iron gate.

The gate opened onto a steep flight of stairs flanked by banisters. Chanda joined the other people wending their way up as she climbed in the oppressive heat.

At the top she gazed around in wonder. She was standing in a large paved courtyard surrounded by a complex of white-washed buildings. The most imposing was an elaborately decorated temple, with a row of elephants, freshly painted in bright colours, marching along the lower façade whilst reliefs of the Hindu gods stood out vividly against the white of the upper façade.

There were big shady trees, and a bookstore called 'Sivananda Bookshop'. Amongst the people walking around she saw monks with bald heads, wearing orange robes.

Chanda walked over to a column covered with engraving and read across on a side 'Be Kind. Be Compassionate.' She walked to the other side and read 'Seek. Find. Enter. Rest in God.'

I am in the right place, she thought, and a woman wearing a blue sari and an orange turban walked up to her smiling, 'You must be Chanda.'

Nine

Ratan Tata Library, Delhi, 1997

Sudesh was at his desk in the Ratan Tata Library serving the Delhi School of Economics on the Delhi University North Campus. It had been his habit to come here since the early days when he had used their computer to log in to Crime Stop.

He had long since stopped attending the village community school as his knowledge far outstripped that of his teachers. Now he studied alone, working his way through various economic texts that filled the shelves around him.

The librarian, Miss Raman had been watching him for a long time. She had often helped him locate books, and explained how the library system worked.

For past few days, she had been mulling over an idea that might help both of them. The library needed to be computerised. All books, magazines and academic papers had to be categorised and entered into a computer software program to give the students easy access.

Miss Raman did not have the time for the job, but she guessed that this boy would be efficient at it. She had a small budget to upgrade library facilities. She could use it to pay him a stipend for this job. But she knew that she could not employ him legally as he appeared to be around fifteen years in age and would be regarded as a child labourer. The librarian decided that hiring Sudesh would be too risky.

A village near Delhi, 1997

'They are saying on TV that India is in the grasp of high consumerism. Amma, is that why our country is declining spiritually?'

Kamla smiled grimly, 'I'd like to see someone who lives from hand-to-mouth like us and is not materialistic. Every poor person is materialistic, Sudesh, otherwise he would die.'

Sudesh nodded, he knew the realities all too well. The twenty thousand rupees he had won in the police competition had been banked in a savings account, and he drew money for his mother every week. The prize had seemed a huge amount but their daily needs rendered it meagre. His Crime Stop work brought in a little but he would have to find another source of income while he continued to study.

'Okay, so poor people need to worry about material things, but can't we be spiritual as well?'

'As your father used to say, in India we have lived by strong traditions and ancient values. We honour our religious teachings whether we are Hindu, Muslim or Sikh. We have strong family and community bonding. India is spiritually sound, Sudesh. It's the material condition that causes us to suffer.'

An internet café, Delhi, 1997

The internet café's building with unfinished concrete walls and old computers was Sudesh's techno city. He sat down on a rickety chair and logged in. The news was good.

'Congratulations,' said the e-mail. 'This month you have entered the largest amount of workable information on Crime Stop. In addition to your fees you have won ₹ 10,000. Scroll down for details.'

'Yeah!' exclaimed Sudesh, punching his arm into the air.

He would pay some to Inder and Shakti who had helped with his Crime Stop work. The rest would go to his mother, for their living expenses, and towards his search for Chanda.

Police Headquarters, Delhi, 1997

The boardroom of the Police Headquarters in Delhi was messy. The central table was old and the walls were a grubby dull beige colour. To Sudesh, however, it could have been the Oberoi. The mens' uniforms reminded him of his father. He would have been proud of his son now. Sudesh smiled.

The Sikh man who seemed to be in charge raised his hand and the room fell silent. He started to speak. 'Ladies and gentlemen, when it comes to crime prevention, not only in India but in many parts of the world, there is little to boast of. Policemen are not well paid, and are expected to work from a sense of service. For some this is sufficient motivation, but many become disillusioned and cynical, and end up taking bribes, turning a blind eye to crime.

'Today, however, we have a happy story to narrate. This is a story of communities and individuals banding together to fight crime with great success. Today we are here to honour somebody who has helped us in this endeavour. Not only did Sudesh Kumar win the competition which gave us the idea for Crime Stop two years ago, but he has also been our best performer in keeping track of hot spots for the trafficking of stolen goods.

'Mr Kumar, please join me here at the front.' Police Superintendent Nanek Singh was left astonished as he saw a teenager walking towards him. He had expected Sudesh to be a grown-up man who had business and organisational experience. 'Well done, young man. How have you managed to report so much activity?' he asked Sudesh.

'I have remained alert and have been a keen observer all these days. My friends have also aided me in this task.'

The police superintendent smiled, 'You are likely to become very successful in life. Thank you for your contribution, here is your cheque for the best Crime Stop performance for 1997. Is there anything you would like to say?'

'Yes Sir. The idea behind Crime Stop, which I sent you in response to your competition in 1995, was an idea brought up by my father. He was a constable in the village in the Delhi 5 district.

'My father, Adhijat Kumar, was an honest policeman. Being an upright man, he served his community to the best of his ability.

'My father used to discuss his methods for stopping theft in our district with me while I was still a child.

'My dad died because he wouldn't give in to threats or take bribes, and wouldn't stop confiscating stolen goods from dealers who couldn't tell him where the items came from. He was shot by a local crime chief and died in a government hospital as a result of inadequate facilities and improper treatment.

'The success of Crime Stop is the best possible tribute to a village policeman who gave his life for the sake of his values and beliefs. I would like to accept this cheque in his memory, and dedicate the rest of my life to advancing his values.'

Ten

The suburbs, East Delhi, 2000

The Superintendent of Police slumped down in his soft blue sofa, tired but elated. He watched his daughter playing with their fox terrier. The dog's compact, wiry little body pranced across the lawn between their frangipani trees in response to Devika's equally energetic play.

'Good news, I read, property crime is down by forty percent since your initiative started,' said Madhumati.

'Good news indeed.'

'How precisely does it work, my love? I know you have hundreds of people out there watching street vendors selling used goods, scrap yards, second-hand car dealers and pawn shops, but how does that reduce crime?'

The Superintendent smiled at the opportunity to describe his strategy.

'We have worked it out in a number of ways. We have computer software that InfoSwish designed for us which correlates the serial numbers and descriptions of goods on the shelves in the outlets. We match those serial numbers from people who have been burgled.'

'Serial numbers for radios, TV sets and so on?'

'Yes, serial numbers for electronic goods which are the most popular targets of thieves, as well as engine and chassis numbers for cars.'

'Okay.' Madhu was thoughtful.

'We also check the car registrations and take photographs of people who go in and out of any particular dealership frequently. Our guys on the street keep tabs on the shops allocated to them and correlate vehicle visits across the city through the computers.'

The ringing phone interrupted his flow. 'It's for you, sweetheart,' his wife said, passing the phone to him.

'Who is it?' he asked covering the mouth piece.

'He said it was private.' she replied.

'Hello, how can I help you?' he spoke into the receiver.

'You can help me by ending your campaign against organised crime, today.'

'Who is this?'

'That is not important. What is important is that we know where you live, where your wife works. And we also know which school your cute little daughter studies in.'

'We do not respond to threats.'

'I think you will, Police Superintendent. Most people do in the end.'

'Who was it, Nanek?' enquired Madhumati as her husband slammed the phone down.

'Some thug who wants me to end my anti-theft programme. He's making threats against you and Devika.' He looked worried.

'Well, I can take care of myself, but Devika is another matter. I will organise a guard to watch our gates and accompany her and her ayah to school.'

A village in Delhi, 2000

Inder waved the letter at Sudesh triumphantly as he spoke,
'I've been called for an interview!'

'Great! Which company?'

'JTH, that big American computer company.'

'Well, you got great results at school; you deserve to get a chance. Or, do they have a cricket team?'

Inder smiled, and the two friends sat down together on the old, wooden chairs outside Janak Bhati's shop to talk about their future.

A pawn shop in East Delhi, 2000

Anwar Patesh entered Quick Cash Enterprises as usual by the back door.

'Got some good stuff for you here. Cell phones, TVs in the van, couple of CD players.'

'Sorry Anwar, but we can't take your wares anymore.'

Anwar's heart sank. He had heard the same story everywhere today.

'Look, man, we know the score, but we've lowered our prices and we've told the guys that they need to lower theirs too. We can do a deal.'

'Anwar, I've had half my stock confiscated this week and sold at auction to fund the little rats that sit outside my shop and visit to check my serial numbers.'

'Half?'

'The half I got from you. I can sell goods that have been pawned and second-hand clothing shipped out from America for charity, but your goods have become a liability.'

'Well boss, you make a much bigger margin on my stuff, so why not buy some more to make up for your confiscations? They can't catch you twice in a row.'

'Sure they can, Anwar, and they will. The game's up man. I've paid more in fines this month than I've made in the last six months. I've had to take a loan to pay the fines. I'm going to diversify into something else, maybe new goods rather than second hand. Honest-like.'

Anwar took a deep breath. Same old story. He'd need to sell his wares down in the slums; he'd get a quarter of the price he was expecting and fifty percent less than he'd paid the bloody burglars for it. And he might also be caught there because one can't sell contraband without being visible. Maybe, he thought, he should diversify too.

New Delhi, 2000

Inder strode confidently into the square, and stopped short. The whole area around the offices of JTH was full of protestors, many of whom were not Indian. The placards read: 'Against the Exploitation of Workers'; 'Localisation'; 'Fair Trade'; 'Same Job, Same Pay.'

He worked his way through the crowd, hoping that he should not be late for his interview.

As he approached the main entrance, he could see that his way into the building was barred.

'Excuse me,' he said. 'Can I come through?'

The men at the barricade eyed him suspiciously.

'Why would an Indian want to visit JTH?' asked one.

'I have a job interview,' he said innocently.

One of the comrades spoke: 'Are you sure you want to work for JTH? Do you know that the company will pay you less than it pays Americans for the same work?'

Inder was confused. 'But isn't that because we are poor and willing to do the same for less.'

'It's not fair. You should be paid a decent wage.'

Inder started to squeeze through the crowd, as he replied. Actually, it is quite a decent wage. It's about a third more than anything else I saw advertised.'

'That's not the point. They pay us less than they pay their own people, they exploit us, they are a threat to our economy!'

'But don't we want more jobs to come to local people?'

'Not if they exploit employees – exploitation is a crime!'

Inder had by this time managed to squeeze through the crowd and was edging towards the company's main doorway.

'Well, it was nice talking to you guys,' he said out loud.

'Imagine trying to protect me from getting a job,' he muttered under his breath. 'Thanks for nothing!'

'Fair trade! Fair trade!' came the outcry.

The InfoSwish head office, Hyderabad, 2000

Vaneshri was five feet seven inches tall and beautiful. Her thick hair was naturally wavy and hung below her shoulders when it wasn't tied back in a pony-tail. At seventeen, she was extremely smart, sharp and well-versed with open source, XML and the vagaries of object-orientated programming. Being fully aware of her capabilities, she walked with a lofty, proud gait commanding adequate respect from all in her office. Everyone told her that she was remarkable and that she would be still more remarkable some day. And she agreed. She knew she was an amazing human being; she just wished there were a few more like her on the planet.

Her pony-tail whip-lashed as she turned her head to examine who had entered the new, post-modern office. Four waterfalls cascaded down the central well of the four-storey building providing a background of white noise.

'I've a question about this job for US Enterprise Solutions.' Vaneshri turned around and looked scornfully, as she saw a young lad voicing this query.

'What is it that you don't get? We need the interface ready by Friday for the client.'

She's had nothing else to do for the last three years but read our code, thought the young man. That's why the boss is so enchanted with her.

He looked at the floor, 'I just don't see why we can't have more resources on developing the distribution here in India. It's still a vast untapped market.'

'The future lies in taking on processes outsourced to India by the West. We can often do the work at half the US cost. That means potentially huge profits for us and them.'

'I see that, Miss Palande, but why can't we expand here as well?' He spoke nervously as he started regretting challenging the boss's precocious daughter.

'We cannot expand here because we have limited resources to invest and if we invest them here we have less to use in the potentially much more lucrative business process outsourcing unit.'

'Well, maybe we can discuss it?'

'We cannot discuss it further. The issue is closed.'

'There's no getting round a seventeen-year-old who thinks she's always right', said an employee who heard the verbal exchange between the two.

Another employee nodded, 'Especially when she usually is.'

An anti-globalisation rally, New Delhi, 2000

Great cheers resounded around the stadium.

'Up with fair trade, Down with Upton.' the crowd roared.

'No!' Sudesh shouted.

A few people near him turned round and stared for a while. They started yelling the slogan again, ignoring Sudesh's sole voice that eventually faded in the hullabaloo.

Enraged, Sudesh worked his way to the front. Large, muscle-bound men barricaded the steps leading up to the stage, but the number one bouncer leaned forward to hear his request.

The bouncer shrugged his shoulders. But the message was communicated to the chairman.

'There is a guy who wants to speak something in public here.'

'That could be fun,' muttered the chairman; after all, the crowd was clearly on his side and he didn't have a whole lot more to say. It couldn't hurt to have someone to ask questions or put forward weak arguments for him to demolish ... someone perhaps to educate or humiliate.

His eyes scanned through Sudesh. 'Looks harmless,' he said to the bouncer. 'Bring him on.' The bouncer returned obediently to the steps.

'Come on then. Quick now, we haven't got all day,' said the bouncer as he almost dragged Sudesh up the stairs to the platform.

'Ladies and gentlemen,' said the chairman. 'We have a question from one of the audience for our esteemed speakers.'

'What is your name?'

'Sudesh Kumar.'

'Well Sudesh Kumar, welcome to Indians for Justice.'

'Thank you,' said Sudesh into the megaphone.

'What did you want to ask?'

'I don't care about Ray Upton and he doesn't care about us. He cares about profit not people!' Sudesh began.

'Down with Upton!' came the answering roar of the crowd.

'That's why he exploits workers.'

'Down Upton, down,' protested the crowd.

'I don't care about people who have jobs,' Sudesh continued. 'They're the lucky ones, the people we don't need to worry about.'

The 'Down Upton' chorus faltered. What on earth was this guy saying?

'The one thing worse than being exploited by Upton is not, I repeat, not being exploited by him. I don't care about Upton, I care about half a billion destitute Indians. If you care about them you would want many people like Upton to exploit many crores of comrades.'

Sudesh was surprised by his own words, and by the silenced audience.

'We don't want Upton to care about us, we want him to employ us; we don't want his charity, we want our wages, we want him to bring wealth from his rich country into our country.

'We have been poor for a hundred years. We remain so because our government drives people like Upton away. We want them here, comrades. We want rich men to build factories and employ us.

'Upton doesn't invest here because he wants to enrich us, but that is the result. We want, no we demand ...'

The chairman snatched the megaphone from Sudesh. 'Sorry comrades, I didn't realise this man was a capitalist stooge,' He was breathing heavily. 'Don't listen to him, we don't want Upton getting rich from the sweat of our labour ...'

'Let him speak,' someone shouted from the crowd.

'Yes, let him,' more voices joined the demand.

The chairman turned to his colleagues sitting behind. They shrugged, unsure how to proceed. He returned the megaphone to Sudesh reluctantly.

'We don't want Upton to care for us, comrades, we don't want his feelings, we want his money, that is what we want, his money in the form of our wages and his investments to bring more jobs.'

'Up with Upton!' shouted a lone voice.

'Up with Upton, Up with Upton ...' began a slow chant from the far side.

'Upton offers us jobs, comrades. We don't have to accept the jobs, it is our choice – are we too stupid to decide for ourselves? Let us call on our government to invite all of the Uptons of the world to India, to invite them and welcome them with open arms so that we can exploit their wealth.'

The new slogan grew in volume.

Sudesh returned the megaphone to the chairman and left the platform to the swelling sound of 'Up with Upton, Up with Upton.'

Suburbs of New Delhi, 2000

Superintendent Singh drove his car into his driveway. His daughter ran to meet him, tears flowing down her cheeks.

'What's wrong, Princess?'

He hugged her as he closed the car door behind him.

'It's Bella,' she burbled, her breathing hysterical. 'Somebody killed her.'

Madhumati appeared on the porch looking grim.

He hugged her longer than usual realising the gravity of what had happened.

'Someone broke in today when we were all at work.'

'Yes?'

'And shot Bella,' added his daughter, her eyes swollen from weeping. 'She's in the back garden.'

'Let me go and see,' he said. 'You stay here with Madhu.

'The white and brown fur of the animal was stained red with blood.

He bent down to look. This was no amateur job.

He used the quick-dial feature on his cell phone,

'Forensics, please.'

'Peter Duncan.'

Peter was an expat doing research in India. Nanek trusted him.

'Peter, I know it's late, but could you come over and take a look at this. Someone has shot our dog.'

Eleven

The Upton Corporation, New York City, 2000

Ray Upton's assistant moved to and fro on the cream carpet of his large office, lifting papers from one table and placing them on the other. Ray sat near a big glass window working on his computer.

'Have you heard you have a new admirer?'

'A new one? I didn't think I had any.' said Ray.

'In India, haven't you read the papers?'

'In India! Wonders will never cease, I thought I was a persona non-grata in India.'

Ray's assistant looked thoughtfully out of the window, towards the Brooklyn Bridge.

'This young man addressed a huge crowd at the anti-globalisation rally and gave a rousing defence of you and your investment in India. He did more good in ten minutes than the five million dollars we wasted trying to improve our image!'

'Hmm. Find out more about this boy. He sounds interesting.'

'Okay Sir. Do you have any plans for him once he's found?'

'Maybe we should offer him an internship.'

'That's a thought.'

'Do a background check before you talk to him, will you?'

I'll be thorough.'

The residence of the CEO, InfoSwish, 2000

Being the CEO of InfoSwish didn't make the task of finding a suitable match for his daughter easier. He glanced through the marriage adverts in the classifieds section:

'Fair, Brahmin, Harvard educated, 23, sweet temperament, tall.'

Hmm.

'Parents invite alliance for their 27-year-old daughter. She is fair, slim, beautiful, homely and talented. She is intermediate and has good computer knowledge. We are Marwari (Khandelwal) Digamber Jain from Bangalore.'

He looked at his daughter working on her laptop, concocting some new 'killer app' he presumed. How would a matrimonial advert for her look in the newspaper.

'Fair, slim, 17, fiery temper, not to be messed with,' he wrote on the margin of the Matrimonial section.

'No, that wouldn't work.' he said to himself and scored it out.

'Beautiful, lively, an expert in creating fully-functional java programs in half the normal time, doesn't bear fools gladly, has been known to cause employees nervous breakdowns.'

He shook his head. That was just not going to cut it, even with today's men.

'Looking for a knight in shining armour with the guts to beat into submission a woman whom no one has conquered before. A thousand lakhs to the man who can tame the shrew!'

Maybe not.

He tilted his head and looked at Vaneshri, fortunately she was only seventeen, there was still time.

'What are you doing, Daddy?' she asked.

'Oh nothing darling,' he said hurriedly closing the newspaper. 'Nothing at all.'

An office complex, Eastern Delhi, 2000

Despite Crime Stop, Vasu's graph of gangster activities was moving up.

He was working day and night to expand his activities. Cirincione's *Bomb Scare: the History and Future of Nuclear Weapons* had come in handy to him as it guided him in his mission. He read such books in private.

Now Vasu focussed on four of his men who had joined him at a small round table to discuss new developments.

'How did you get on with that fool of a police superintendent?' asked Vasu.

'I think he'll back off now. We killed his dog.'

The others laughed.

Tarun's laugh was the loudest, as always.

Vasu turned to the man on his right.

'Update, Chandresh?'

'Not a bad week, boss. Cars are selling well, except in East Delhi.'

Vasu nodded and Chandresh continued.

'We have over a hundred dealers in the network now.'

'Good work, Chandresh.' Vasu remarked.

'Doesn't sound like much to me,' a voice growled from across the table.

'A hundred primary dealers,' said Chandresh impatiently, 'Our primary dealers buy directly from the operators. Then the dealers have numerous guys who purchase goods and sell to the public. Work it out for yourself! It comes to plenty.'

'Go on with the update, Chandresh,' demanded Vasu.

'Electronic goods continue to rise. Up by twenty percent from last year. Electrical equipment is up by five percent, and the car market has grown by ten percent.'

'Thank you, Chandresh. Vikram? What's happening at your end?'

'You know we pulled off the Jaipur road deal. It cost $50,000 bribes to officials and our MP friends, but we got the tender for the boys at Antron Construction with a guarantee that no one is going to be checking the quality of the cement. Antron is paying us $135,000 for our services, so a nice little earner there – the third big deal this year.'

'And what's in the pipeline, Vikram?', asked Vasu sipping tea.

'There is an airport deal coming up. It should be a big one. New terminal. Lots of bidding. But we'll get it.'

Vasu nodded. Vikram was good at his job, that's why Vasu had brought him into his syndicate.

'What about me?' said Yashpal. 'Don't you need anyone killed? I need work.'

Vasu frowned. 'My friend, you are on a good retainer. Do not be greedy for bonuses. There will be plenty of work, I'm sure. We'll let you know when we need you.'

A village near Delhi, 2000

Sudesh and Inder sat at the top of Signal Hill looking at their village below.

'I think those fellows must be lost.' said Sudesh pointing from the hilltop at the two men standing on a street in the village below.

The western gentleman in a grey business suit looked singularly out of place in the village. He was accompanied with a well-dressed Indian who was trying to figure out something from a piece of paper he held in his hand. Sudesh thought it should be a map. Sudesh and Inder tracked the two men with their eyes as they moved between the huts fishing for their destination.

The teenagers looked on for a while and then decided, 'Let's go and help them.'

They descended the hill past the brick works and the clay huts and headed towards the lost strangers.

'Do you need some help?' asked Sudesh.

'That would be very kind of you,' answered the European man, 'I wonder if you could tell me where I could find Sudesh Kumar.'

Sudesh smiled.

'You're talking to him.'

The headquarters of the East Delhi Police, 2000

Police Superintendent Singh sat at his desk with a heavy heart brooding over the attack on Bella. His phone rang:

'Superintendent Singh, Can I help you?'

'Maybe you can, Mr Singh. Maybe you can. I am very sorry to hear about your dog ...'

Nanek Singh waved frantically to his assistant, indicating to him to trace the call.

'How do you know about my dog?'

'Well, it was not very difficult to find that out, Mr Singh.'

'So, how can I help you?'

'Just want to offer some advice.' The man continued, 'if you want your wife and daughter to be safe, you must bring your Crime Stop programme to an end.'

'So which syndicate are you calling from?'

'I don't think it's necessary to discuss that, Mr Singh. I'm sure you understand me. I hope we will not need to continue this conversation in the future. It has been very pleasant getting to know you.' The line went dead.

&

Vasu was a Muslim with a Hindu name. Things had taken a tragic turn for his family in 1947 when eighteen million people underwent mass migration at the time of India-Pakistan partition. His family was one of those unfortunate ones that were forcibly relocated from India to Pakistan. His grandparents contracted typhoid on the journey and lost their lives. Left alone, his mother, Rabia, turned for support to a young activist with whom she fell in love. The man brought Rabia back to India and married her. Vasu was their only child. Rabia died when he was very young and he grew up under the sole influence of his father's fundamentalism.

As the years passed Vasu's faith in the superiority of Islamic fundamentalism increased. Simultaneously he became involved in violent crime. The people he knew from the mosque urged him to turn away from his criminal ways, but he was attracted by destructive force in all its guises.

'It is time Islam took the Holy War seriously and makes every effort to win it,' he would say to his radical confidantes. 'There is no point in fighting a war unless you fight to win.'

At other times he would say, 'I will single-handedly terrorise Hindustan and precipitate a nuclear war between India and Pakistan.'

The radicals listened tolerantly to his ramblings.

A village near Delhi, 2000

'Mr Kumar,' said the American stepping across the uneven ground with his hand held out, 'my name is Brad Robertson and this is my colleague Jay Naidu. I have a message for you from Mr Upton.'

'Ray Upton? The man who's investing in India?'

'That is correct.'

He paused for a second.

'Mr Upton was very impressed with the impromptu speech you gave the other day at the rally. It is most unusual to find someone who understands the consequences of his business policies in this part of the world, or for that matter in any part of the world.'

Sudesh said nothing and kept listening intently.

'Mr Upton would like you to come and work for his corporation.'

Sudesh was puzzled, 'Mr Upton wants to employ me? Here in Delhi? In what capacity? I am not trained enough.'

Brad Robertson smiled, 'Not in Delhi, Mr Kumar. He wants you to work in his head office in New York, and he will start you off as an intern and decide to which aspect of his business you are best suited.

'Naturally, there are conditions. You will have to undergo financial market training, commit yourself to a three-year term, and sign a loyalty agreement. When you leave the company you will have to return to India and be a spokesperson for it for another three years. You won't have to work for it, only represent it when required. You'll get a generous retainer.'

'Thank you', said Sudesh formally and decisively. 'It is a wonderful offer, but I have to say no. Mr Robertson, Mr Naidu, please come to my home for some tea.'

Inder gasped in disbelief. He could not understand Sudesh's abrupt response.

Brad Robertson and Jay Naidu exchanged glances.

Sudesh led them down the rutted track running between the painted brick houses of the village. Inder made polite conversation as they walked, telling the visitors about his job as a rookie programmer for JTH.

On arriving at Kumar's place, the four men hung around the surrounding clay wall, whilst Kamla boiled water over her clay stove and listened with mixed feelings to their discussion with her son.

'Thank you for the offer, but I'm an Indian, my family, my life and my future belong to this country. I have to support my mother and find my lost sister. I'm not interested,' Sudesh explained. 'Most importantly, I can't undertake to represent a company when I might not agree with something it does.'

'Let me assure you, Mr Kumar, that there is no company with more integrity than Upton Corporation,' said Naidu. Mr Upton believes deeply in honesty and objective truth. It's his philosophy of life, and he demands the same of everyone in the company. I should add that all expenses will be paid, travel and accommodation. You'll have enough money to support your mother comfortably.'

'Please,' said Sudesh raising his hand to stop him, 'please thank Mr Upton on my behalf. The future is unknowable, so no one knows what the company will do and no one with integrity can agree to represent it. I also don't want to be absorbed into a big corporation. I want to work here with people in my community.'

'Here, take my card,' said Naidu as they departed, 'and call me if you come to your senses. Everything is negotiable.'

'Including the loyalty agreement?'

'Not that,' said Brad. 'Loyalty is a standard employment condition.'

Twelve

The Singh household, 2000

Nanek Singh was home for no more than ten minutes before Madhumati joined him on the terrace looking tense.

'So what are we going to do?' she asked.

'About the attack on the dog?'

'Yes, of course.'

'I've been talking to a lot of people and reading up on ideas from South America, where they face similar problems.'

'And?'

'The best way to deal with organised crime is through informers.' he replied. 'You pay for information or you give some people lower sentences if they incriminate their bosses.'

'We're already doing that in the force.'

'It works. We've arrested a number of people.'

Madhumati raised her voice and gestured to her beloved step-daughter, playing with her doll beside the lily-pond. 'It obviously doesn't work well enough; we still have crime lords and syndicates. And they are threatening our family. Look at her!'

Nanek watched the child cautiously as he shared her anxiety. 'I'm trying to get an increase in the budget so we can put more informers out there.'

'Nanek, we both know it can take years for that to happen and by then we will all be dead. We need direct action.'

Nanek frowned:

'You want me to go out and shoot them all? You surely don't want that.'

'That is exactly what I want you to do. There is no point in being a police superintendent if you don't get rid of the scum, particularly when they threaten your own children.'

'What, without proper arrests, fair trials and so on? What about the protection of the innocent?'

Madhumati narrowed her eyes as she spoke, 'I'm also a police officer, I know all about this crap of protecting the innocent. We all know that most of the time it is the guilty who get protection.'

Nanek started to speak but Madhumati interrupted.

'I know what you are going to say: Without a trial we can't be sure who is guilty. That might be true for ordinary people but it doesn't apply to crime lords. Everyone knows they are guilty, and it's our job to stop them or get rid of them. Otherwise we fail in our duty.'

'We can only act according to the rule of law.'

'Bullshit, Nanek. You play by the Queensbury rules, but the criminals play dirty. No wonder they win. If you were half the man I married then you would make it your business to defend us and get rid of them. You could if you wanted to and you must!'

Madhumati turned and walked back into the house.

Nanek sat deep in thought. He and Madhu had never before argued like this, but she was so much younger than him, and saw matters in black and white, whereas for him there was an infinite range of greys. Madhu was brilliant and single-minded, which was why she was rocketing up the promotional ladder at the CBI. She still lacked a clear insight.

Nanek sighed and waited for Madhumati to calm down, as he prepared to break the news of his abandoning the Crime Stop programme.

A village near Delhi, 2000

'You have done a right thing, Sudesh, by rejecting Upton's offer,' said Kamla as Sudesh walked with her to the store. 'Appa would have been proud of you.'

'It was the right thing to do,' he said.

'But you should think over it again, the way Appa would'.

'What do you mean?'

'Well, working for a big company doesn't mean you will be swallowed by it. 'You'll obviously have the choice of quitting the company if you don't like it. And you don't have to be here for me; our neighbours will take care of me. All I'll want from you is to pay me visits whenever it'll be possible for you.'

'I belong here.' Sudesh frowned.

'Many great Indians spent some of their lives abroad. Mahatma Gandhi was a lawyer in South Africa, Muhammad Jinnah was a lawyer in London, and Lakshmi Mittal is still living in London. Would going to America not help you understand why they're rich and we're poor?'

'I'll think it over, Amma.'

ॐ

Sudesh called up Jay Naidu from Janak's shop. 'Tell Mr Upton I'll take the job if he drops the obligation on me to speak for the company.'

'That would defeat the object of the offer, said Naidu. 'The whole point is that he wants you because you did such a good job at the rally.'

'Okay, then there's no deal, I won't sell my soul to anyone.'

New York City, 2000

'Did you find that Indian boy?' Ray asked Brad.

'Yes, we found him, but it was a waste of time, he refused to accept our offer.'

'Did he give reasons?'

'He just said he wanted to base himself in India. Naidu said he called to say he'd consider it if you drop the condition about speaking up for the company.'

'That's a pity', said Ray. 'What progress in the anti-trust case?' asked Upton changing the subject. He never knew how they could call a law that says in effect "compete but don't win" competition law.

He stood up and paced around the office as he briefed Brad on things he wanted done. Then he paused, and suddenly sat down.

'What I liked about the Indian lad in the first place was that he was a man of principle, and now we're about to lose him for that reason. Tell him the deal is on. And add a clause to all your contracts saying a condition of employment is that no one will compromise their principles for the company.'

The Singh Household, 2000

Being an unconventional wife, Madhu's demands to Nanek were never for diamonds and gems. But an exclusive studio to practise combat skills was at the top of her wish list.

Along with the usual training in firearms and close combat she had also acquired espionage skills, like breaking, entering and code cracking, from the CBI. She was determined to hone these skills, and add to them.

Nanek's love for her made him fulfil his wife's desire without delay. He had a studio built for Madhumati near their house.

The studio was equipped with a wide range of devices constructed according to her specifications. The CBI's top field agent enhanced her fighting and defence skills here. She practised knife throwing techniques, hand to hand combat and acrobatics. Eventually, the studio also became a centre for competitions as she invited Delhi's top martial arts instructors to pit their skills against hers.

As a little girl she had read the Modesty Blaise adventure thrillers with great interest. She owned Modesty's favourite weapon, a yawara stick which she had learned to use in a fashion similar to Modesty.

'You look tired and worried,' she said as she returned home from her workout session at the studio.

'These threats have started bothering me.'

She gave him a bear hug. 'I'm sorry I shouted at you the other day, darling. I realise that it really isn't possible for you to take the law into your own hands, and descend to the level of these rogues.'

Nanek eased himself into a chair and said, 'Thanks my love, I know you can look after yourself, but if anything happens to Devika I will never forgive myself.'

'No, Devika must not be hurt,' she nodded thoughtfully and spoke with grave concern, 'Did you get to know who is making these calls?'

'We managed to trace the last call. But these people seem least bothered about us finding that out.'

'Pretty brash.'

'I am closing down Crime Stop, there are plenty of other criminals to catch and I can't be risking our little girl's life.'

A village near Delhi, 2000

Sudesh sat resting his back on a boulder in one of his favourite haunts half-way up the hill, reading *Upton Guide to Investments and other Alternative Investments* by Ray Upton and David Park. Pleasantly surprised to see Shakti approaching him, Sudesh yelled from the distance, 'Hi, Shakti! Nice to see you!'

'Sudesh, are you going to New York?' asked Shakti.

'So, the word has spread. Yes, I am.'

She stood facing him, blocking out his view of the village. 'You can't go, Sudesh. You had different plans, didn't you? What about changing India?'

Sudesh could see the spark in her eyes. 'Listen' he said. 'I'm not giving up. I need to learn the ways from a developed nation. Sit down here.' He patted the ground at his side.

She sat close to him, becoming more thoughtful.

'Shakti, I need to learn ways of making our country prosperous. India needs capitalism, liberty, prosperity. The Upton Corporation has knowledge that is far in advance of even the American universities.'

Shakti's heart sank. What Sudesh said was making sense to her, but she could not imagine life without him.

Sudesh put his arm around the young girl, 'I'll miss you.'

Sudesh felt tear drops moistening his arms as Shakti rested her head on his shoulder.

'Don't worry, Shakti,' he said, stroking her hair. 'I'll be back.'

New York, 2000

Brad Robertson looked cross as he waited for Sudesh to clear the gruelling passport controls of JFK. Sudesh was gazing around awestruck. He had spotted the World Trade Centre among Manhattan's sky-scrapers from their plane when it was just about to land. The long lines of parked jets on the runway left him astonished. He couldn't take his eyes off the cutting edge mobile phones and palmtop computers he saw all around him.

'You are very fortunate,' said Brad as they sat waiting.

'I know it, Brad,' said Sudesh, dragging his attention away from everything that was new and different about this place.

Brad smiled. 'What I mean when I say you are fortunate is that Ray Upton doesn't often take on the role of mentor.'

Sudesh nodded politely.

'Time is money, but you seem to have caught his attention. Sudesh, you need to survive in this corporation on pure merit. You will not find Ray Upton asking for favours or granting them. But if you perform you will earn his respect.'

'Does Mr Upton believe in "corporate governance", "codes of conduct" and other concepts like that?'

Brad smiled, 'I would advise you not to think on these lines until you get to know him more. He says that's for stupid people who only see initial consequences and can't trace things through to their final result.

Sudesh raised his eyebrows as Brad continued,

'In his view it is more important to look after shareholders so they have an incentive to invest in the future. More investment leads to more jobs and better and cheaper products which is good for the poor.'

'So he does want to help the poor?'

'In a way, but he achieves it by being the sharpest, shrewdest capitalist you can imagine.'

As they exited the airport, an enamelled black Lincoln Continental drew up at the curve.

'This is our car,' said Brad.

'Upton stays downtown, that is to say near Wall Street, the financial district, so most of us in the senior ranks also live in that area,' said Brad. 'He likes to have us close by should he need us.'

'You mean after office hours, or during the night?'

'Sometimes,' nodded Brad, 'the world's economy never stops so we have to be available in person when major events break. But we are paid well. We don't complain. We're paid for performance, and if we don't perform we're out.'

Sudesh looked at Brad as he spoke. By the time they crossed the Williamsburg Bridge into Manhattan, it grew dark and the cluster of sky-scrapers that dominated the southern tip of this remarkable island were lighting up like Chandni Chowk at Diwali.

After some time as their car halted near a pavement, a lobby attendant came and carried their luggage to the elevator.

Brad took Sudesh to the thirty-third floor and showed him his large, luxurious apartment. 'This is where I live, Sudesh, you'll stay with me for some days until we find you a place of your own.'

Part Two

Part Two

Thirteen

New York City, 2000

The Upton building, formerly the Squibb building was a twenty-eight-storey Art Deco building on Fulton Street, with the higher floors designed in typical 1930s style. Its powerful elevators transported Sudesh from the restored 1932 lobby up to Ray Upton's offices on the top floor, decorated in minimalist style.

The investment guru's desk faced a wall-sized window with magnificent views of South Seaport and the Brooklyn Bridge.

'So Mr Kumar, how do you like New York?' asked Ray Upton. His blue eyes were direct and penetrating, creasing slightly at the corners in the smallest of smiles.

Sudesh answered seriously, 'It's amazing.'

'What is amazing is that Congress has been able to prevent America from being much richer and more advanced than it is. That has taken some doing, Mr Kumar.' Upton looked out of the window over the Manhattan skyline and down to the street to where yellow cabs and pizza delivery bikes vied for space with high end limousines. Then he smiled.

'What do you mean?'

Upton shook his head decisively.

'It will all become clear with time.'

He walked to his floor-to-ceiling book-case and selected a book, which he handed to Sudesh, 'Read this.'

He started to walk off. 'Brad will look after your arrangements.'

And Sudesh was left alone in the office looking down at the title of the book in his hand, *Atlas Shrugged* by Ayn Rand.

The next day

'Sudesh, I am giving you an opportunity. I won't stand indolence and disloyalty. Is that understood?'

Sudesh nodded.

Ray walked around the office as he talked, his hands behind his back.

'We will teach you how to trade the markets in poor countries that are abandoning socialism. Your goal will be to make money for us. I have a team of traders working round the clock watching sixty indicators in two hundred countries. You will join this team.'

'Yes Sir.'

'The information and techniques we teach you are proprietary. They do not leave this building, is that clear?'

'Of course, Sir.'

'I will discuss principles and strategies with you. If you are not satisfied with my arguments, say so.'

'Okay.'

'First lesson today.'

Sudesh listened attentively.

'There is no place for emotions in investing markets, Sudesh.'

Sudesh's eyes widened slightly. His feelings played a huge role in his life, they motivated him and guided him. He trusted them. This was not going to be easy.

'If you don't apply an objective insight into your trade or stock, you will have to move out of it. Don't fall in love with your strategy. Don't rely on being "lucky". If you don't have a valid reason to expect a price movement, don't take a position on that movement. Otherwise you will be gambling and casinos are rich because gamblers lose.'

An office block, North Delhi, 2000

Mukul Sharma left his office at his usual time, long after the sun had set. He had started losing interest in his work now. Earlier – before liberalisation of trade in the 1990s – it simply involved smuggling ordinary goods that had been banned, taxed or restricted by the government. After trying his luck in the business of prostitution and drug smuggling, he now took to bribing judges and policemen to keep murderers and rapists out of jail. It left a bad taste in his mouth.

But then, he lived well these days. It would be difficult to give up all of that. Two tall men in dark coats followed him, more to warn off people who didn't know who he was than for those who did.

Mukul didn't have any fear of being attacked as he was walking in a safe zone where organised crime divided the territories by agreement and none of the gangs liked to kick off tussles with each other. Budding goons on the block who challenged a mafia boss were instantly eliminated. The biggest threat to any leader of the mafia gang came from within, and that was why, like most other bosses, he had kept his business mainly in the family. You could trust family.

He would have been much less confident had he been aware of the long range rifle pointed at him from the other side of the highway.

The traffic on the highway, which had been very sluggish during the rush hour, started moving at a fast pace now. But eventually it allowed several seconds with no obstacle between the marksman and his target. One bullet drove into Sharma's heart, one to his brain.

As he fell to the ground one of his bodyguards dragged him back into the building, rapidly tapping a number into his cell phone. The other man ran fast in the direction of the rifle shot. He quickly identified the vantage point in the building from which the shots had been fired, but the assassin was long gone.

The Upton Investment Corporation, 2000

Sudesh was trying to understand Ray Upton and his company. He was receiving a lot of information. It took time to grasp the facts. More difficult was to come to terms with the implications.

Initially, Sudesh thought Ray was being provocative, but he was beginning to realise that his new boss was serious.

'What you are not getting, Sudesh, is that greed is good.' said Ray one evening.

'Is greed good?' asked Sudesh.

'Yes,' said Upton, teasing.

Sudesh looked worried, 'I can't accept that.'

Ray looked at Sudesh and softened slightly.

'People confuse motive with effect. It was Gordon Gecko, the leading actor of the film *Wall Street* who said "Greed is good".'

Sudesh recollected how the film had enthralled him and Inder with its high-powered stock market deals and the fast paced world of high finance.

'I saw the movie in India. Gecko's the one who breaks up the company and thousands lose their jobs.'

'You got it. And that's good.' Ray smiled at Sudesh.

'How can that be good?'

'Just think and tell me what do you feel?'

'It's not good, it's bad. People lost their jobs.' Sudesh was sure of his ground here.

Ray took a new approach: 'How many people across the world were farming three hundred years ago?'

'Most of them, I suppose.'

'Right, more than ninety percent. And how many of them had to quit farming between then and now?'

'Again, I suppose most of them. Ninety percent don't work in farms anymore.'

'And now, tell me was it a bad thing that people lost their jobs, and should we think of returning to a time where everyone does farming?'

Sudesh frowned. 'No ... but ...'

Ray smiled and raised his eyebrows, 'But what?'

'But we worked out how to farm effectively with fewer people involved.'

'Aha, I think you are getting the drift.'

'As technology enables us to produce more with less people, then the cost of products, be they food or anything else, becomes cheaper and everyone becomes richer ...' Sudesh explained logically.

'Good! Go on.' Ray was genuinely impressed.

'And people can now spend the money that they have saved on other things...'

'Right.'

'Which creates new job opportunities.'

'Correct. So all the people who were once working in agriculture now work elsewhere. Unemployment isn't much higher than it was a hundred years ago. People keep entering into different job markets. That is in fact what progress is!'

'So progress is when people walk out of one industry because it has become more efficient, and move to a new one.' Sudesh said slowly.

'Right.'

'So when Gordon Gecko asset-strips his company and closes it down, he tries to pave way for the progress of his nation?'

'Yep. If the company is worth more divided up than in one unit, then splitting it will release wealth into the economy to create jobs elsewhere.' Ray leaned back in his chair and folded his arms, satisfied.

'But he wasn't trying to help the economy, he was just trying to get rich.' Sudesh found this difficult to accept.

'That doesn't matter. It had a good net effect, regardless of the fact that people lost their jobs.'

'But he wasn't trying to help people,' Sudesh insisted.

'You are confusing motive and effect again. Did you read *Atlas Shrugged*?'

Broadway Street, New York City, 2000

Sudesh meandered through the city sidewalks for hours anguishing about his future. After the promise and excitement of being found and employed by Upton, he no longer had direct contact with Upton. Sudesh was seconded to low-level staff whenever he asked to see Upton. He felt rejected and dejected.

He was deep in thought when he reached Strand Book Store. He entered unthinkingly. It had become one of his favourite places in Manhattan. He was drawn inexorably to its comprehensive range of topics, and its eighteen miles of shelves filled with raggedy rows, piles and boxes of rare, used and discounted books.

Americans, Sudesh realised, take Christmas seriously. Last-minute shopping and mailing of gifts and cards had hectic crowds rubbing shoulders in shops and post offices. Stores dealt with the Christmas rush by hiring extra staff, post offices by having extra queues. He'd heard an anecdotal story about the divergent attitudes in private and government operations, and decided to test it.

'Someday, isn't it?' he said to the shop assistant, gesturing at the crowded aisles full of busy shoppers as he presented the books he had bought as gifts for mailing to Shakti and Inder.

'Yes, wonderful! It's the best day we've had this year!' the cashier replied with a huge grin.

Sudesh made his way through the crowded pavements, buttoning up his jacket and pulling his hood over his head against the blast of icy air. Besides gifts for Shakti and Inder, he had an important letter to mail. He was sending information to an elite Delhi detective agency, whose services he could not have afforded previously. Perhaps they could locate Chanda. It was over five years since she had disappeared.

At the post office, Sudesh joined one of the lines that snaked its way beside others, making it difficult to decide which queue to join. He waited patiently.

'Someday, isn't it?' he commented to the woman behind the post office counter when he finally reached the front of the queue.

'Terrible, worst day of the year,' she muttered, avoiding eye contact.

It had been as predicted by the anecdote. That's odd, thought Sudesh as he made his way back to the office. Two young cashiers, on the same day of the year; one thinks being busy is splendid and the other thinks it's terrible. Why the difference? The answer and significance of his question dawned on him at a critical moment years later.

Connaught Place, New Delhi, 2000

Rajan Mistry was a creature of habit. Every Thursday between noon 12.00 and 1.00 p.m., he enjoyed a lavish lunch at Le Canard near Connaught Place, one of the best French restaurants in Delhi. Italian would have been more appropriate, he sometimes joked, proud of his mafia connections. But he found himself incapable of resisting French cuisine at Le Canard. 'As usual, Sir?' asked the waiter.

'Yes. The duck.'

He pondered over the events of the week. He was an expert at bribing politicians and judges. The situation also demanded him to threaten them and occasionally, if necessary to kill. It was easier to kill a politician than a judge because killing judges resulted in major reprisals. He didn't understand the reason behind it but that was reality.

The restaurant was off the road, secure from the danger of drive-by shootings that had recently upset the town. It was a gangster-friendly arrangement, and Mistry made sure the owner benefited from his diligence.

The crisp roasted duck a l'orange arrived accompanied by a robust Pinot, and Rajan savoured every morsel.

Twenty-five minutes later he was ready for his coffee. As he nodded, the waiter brought his filtered Brazilian roast.

Leaving the restaurant Rajan felt strangely dizzy. As he walked towards his car with faltering steps he wondered if he had overdone the wine.

When Rajan Mistry's driver stopped the car outside his office complex and opened the door to help him move out and walk to his office, he was shocked to see his boss lying on the back seat, breathless and lifeless.

The Upton Investment Corporation, 2001

'Sudesh, glad you came by. There is someone I want you to meet.' said Ray with a smile, 'There is a young lady from your country, over here with her father. She's only happy on her laptop apparently. I thought having her on your laptop might be better.'

Sudesh was disappointed that he'd not been summoned for a meeting with Ray. 'I'm really not much of a Casanova.' He muttered.

'She's pretty,' said Upton, clearly enjoying tormenting his protégé. 'Clever too, according to her father. I met her with him at the Manhattan Institute on Saturday. He's one of India's top IT guys, started off in Bangalore, but now runs his business from Hyderabad. Interesting fellow, rags to riches. She, on the other hand, is a bit of a princess, born with a silver spoon in her mouth, I think the two of you could relate.'

Fourteen

The Empire State Building, New York City, 2 September 2001

Sudesh had resigned himself to returning to India as soon as he'd fulfilled his contractual obligations to the Upton Corporation. He felt as 'used' by Ray as a woman who was abandoned after a one-night-stand. He could not explain the feeling logically to himself. He'd been offered the job, the corporation's side of the deal had been fulfilled, he'd learnt a lot about life, and understood why some countries were 'winners' and others were 'losers', including why some changed virtually overnight from being one to being the other. He'd discovered the 'applied relevance' as Ray Upton called it, of abstract values and principles, and knew how wealth is earned and lost. But there was something missing.

Long after Sudesh had accepted that he would never be a special person in Ray's universe, Ray surprised him by taking him on a tour of New York, which turned out also to be a tour of Ray's philosophy of life.

From the viewing platform of the Empire State Building Sudesh and his mentor gazed at the Twin Towers.

'They are beautiful,' said Sudesh. 'Yes,' replied Ray 'simple, but perfect, a wonderful exemplar of human ingenuity.'

'Look around you,' he continued. 'The glory all around you is the result of capitalism. Every prosperous city and country is the result of capitalism. Capitalism offers prosperity and liberty.'

'But what about the poor?' Sudesh said reverting to his basic concern. He wondered whether challenging Ray's beloved capitalism would offend him. He no longer cared.

'They're the ones who benefit most,' said Ray. Capitalism has given the world all its technology, especially what the poor need: medicines for diseases; building material for low-cost housing; mass transport and affordable energy.'

'But since India's pro-market reforms in 1993,' argued Sudesh, 'the rich got richer and the poor got poorer. The same happened here. During high rates of sustained economic growth following Reagan's free market reforms the income gap has grown.'

Sudesh was sure of his facts. He was not going to say what Ray wanted to hear. Although he was in America because he stood up for the right of Indians to work for Ray's company, he wanted a system that created and distributed wealth more equitably.

'Yes and no, Sudesh.' said Ray. 'The gap may have grown, but the poor got richer faster.'

'You're contradicting yourself.' Sudesh had discovered that Ray preferred him to be open and straightforward in their discussions. At home he would not have challenged an older man so directly, particularly not his employer.

'No, the arithmetic is simple. Add ten percent to the income of a rich person earning ten thousand dollars a month, and five hundred percent to a poor person earning one hundred dollars. They now earn eleven thousand dollars and six hundred dollars, respectively. Even though the low earner's income increased fifty times faster, the so-called "gap" still widened. It increased to ten thousand four hundred dollars instead of nine thousand nine hundred dollars. The income gap is irrelevant. It can be closed only if everyone becomes poor. The poor person's income would have to grow at one thousand percent merely to maintain the gap. Don't fall for the disinformation of anti-liberty and anti-prosperity fundamentalists who promote the lie that a growing gap during high rates of economic growth means the poor are getting poorer.

Sudesh grappled with Ray's simple yet not simplistic logic as they moved on to locking horns on other issues.

'The real irony is that American capitalism is being smothered by a deluge of interventions whereas India is moving in the right direction. If India keeps growing at ten percent, it will overtake America in a generation.'

Sudesh took his time to assimilate that argument.

'Hmm, I like that thought, India issuing Green Cards to Americans, in search of the promised land, your politicians begging us for aid, pirated Bollywood movies on your sidewalks, and Americans visiting Indian gurus to confront their karma and gain enlightenment, wearing kurtas instead of denims.'

Ray smiled. They gazed again, deep in thought, in the direction of the World Trade Centre. 'Interesting,' mused Sudesh, 'the two symmetrical towers look like a giant eleven.'

Neither Ray nor Sudesh could foresee that nine days later, suicide bombers would fly passenger-laden planes into the twin towers unleashing a tsunami of global fear that would be felt even in India.

ॐ

Her introduction to Sudesh Kumar jolted Vaneshri Palande out of her boredom. So far few people had interested her in New York City, but this man was different. He was very young, perhaps no older than she, but he had 'presence'.

He was different from the hordes of high status suitors her parents invited to meet her in Hyderabad. They were polite, self-deprecating and excessively friendly. They seemed scared of her, she thought, like rabbits caught in headlights. Such was not the case when Sudesh Kumar was introduced to her. He was polite, but didn't seem unduly interested in her and certainly not scared

of her or enraptured by her zippy presence. That, in itself, made
him interesting.

He was tall and lean, with large eyes for a man. He had a rather
long, narrow bridged nose and a wide mouth. When she looked
into his eyes, she found them profound, something that Vaneshri
had difficulty relating to. When he smiled, which he did not do
often, his face lit up, and so, for Vaneshri, did the room.

He'd been introduced to her by one of the world's biggest
investment gurus, so he was probably in high finance. She speculated
that perhaps his family owned an Indian financial services company
and he was expanding their interests into the US as she was doing
with technology.

She also thought he was probably a descendent of a Maharaja,
which meant he might have princely estates back in India.

When he asked for her cell number, her heart fluttered.
Maybe he liked her? Of course, he liked her she reassured herself
remembering that there was no reason why he shouldn't be in love
with a brilliant and gorgeous girl like her.

Southeast Corner, Washington Square Park, New York City, 2002

'What are you doing?' demanded Sudesh.

'What's it to you?' snorted one of the two burly New York
Police Department officers.

Sudesh stood his ground. 'Why are you arresting this woman?
Why are you taking her goods?'

'Look here', said the cop grumpily. 'If you don't get outta here,
I'll arrest you too.'

'What for?'

'For obstructing us in the course of our duty.'

She was a black woman, with short grey peppercorn hair, wearing
a maroon floral dress and orange sandals that she'd procured from
a rubbish bin. This woman who seemed about his mother's age,

submitted passively to the police as if she'd expected the arrest and knew her crime.

Sudesh had often seen her across the road from New York University's Elmer Holmes Bobst Library where he had been doing research on the unique Swiss system of direct democracy and intensive devolution of power to cantons and communes.

Usually he would recognise her presence from the aroma of her roasted sugared nuts. He spent many of his free hours at Bobst, which was one of the world's largest academic libraries and was the hub of academic luminaries. Occasionally he'd meet one of his intellectual heroes, emeritus professor Israel Kerzner who'd specialised in entrepreneurship. Maybe he could explain the 'miracle of poverty' to him; maybe he knew why enterprising Indians were so poor. And why the roast nut lady was poor despite selling delicious snacks to students and academics.

Sudesh was creating a scene.

'Why are you arresting her and not those buskers?' he asked pointing to a saxophonist, drummer and double bass player beside the Garibaldi Statue at the Execution Site, beneath the infamous Hanging Tree.

'She's trading unlawfully on a city sidewalk,' one of the policemen answered grudgingly.

'Now get lost.'

'Where are you taking her?'

'We're taking her into the police station. She has to pay a fine.'

'What about her things, her gas cooker, folding table, packets, nuts …?'

The taller officer put his face close to Sudesh's and said as if stating the obvious. 'She's committing a crime; she loses them.'

'I'll see you at your station,' said Sudesh as he hailed a taxi to follow them.

'No need', said the second officer. 'We're arresting you too.'

He took a firm grip on Sudesh's wrist, spun him around, pinned him against the roof of the police car, and frisked him for concealed weapons. He pushed his head down, and bundled him into the caged back seat alongside the nut lady.

The Suburbs of New Delhi, 2002

Singh shook his head as he entered the mansion tucked away behind long-established trees at the end of a winding driveway.

'I must admit I find this hard to take in.'

The other man nodded. He knew exactly what his boss meant. This was the third crime boss to be murdered in a year.

They walked down the corridor and into the living room where the dead man lay on an expensive Persian rug. Singh wondered idly whether the blood could ever be removed from this work of art representing thousands of hours of the finest knotting.

White tape outlined the body. Forensic experts had already done their work and left the body for Singh to inspect before it was moved to the morgue. He glanced about the room with high ceilings, white walls, heavy blue velvet curtains, elaborately draped and trimmed with silk fringing. The air scented with the fragrance of fresh roses was smothered by the stench of death.

'It's difficult to feel sorry for him,' Singh commented.

'Yeah. Having this bastard out of action will make our job easier.'

The eyes of the two men scanned the body for clues.

'Small bullet hole. Must have been shot from the garden, straight into the heart. From the barrel's groove pattern on the bullet, forensic experts identified the weapon as a Bernadelli 22, the 100 model. We'll do the checks.'

The second-in-command scanned his boss's face for clues.

The peaceful neighbourhood reflected nothing of the violence this man's life had generated.

Singh looked at the grey face, slack and empty and wondered if they should be spending their time tracking down the killer of a man whose life revolved around robbing and terrorising others.

Ray Upton's Office, 2002

'Where have you been? It has been reported to me that you were expected at a meeting, that you made no advance apology and that you simply never arrived.' said Ray, indicating displeasure.

'Well, I saw these cops arrest an innocent old lady for selling nuts, then they arrested me because I protested. They took both of us to the police station where they released me on bail. Then they arrested me again because I wouldn't leave until they released her and stopped eating her nuts', said Sudesh with a straight face.

Ray could not believe his ears. He had never heard of an employee with the gall to spin such an absurd yarn. He wondered if Sudesh was drunk or drugged.

'Let's start again,' said Ray as he straightened his torso to his full height. He repeated and articulated each word slowly and firmly as if to ensure that he was understood. 'Where were you?' There was an unfamiliar tremor in his voice.

Sudesh repeated himself, changing the form but not the substance of his story. He told it as diplomatically as he could.

Upton was bewildered. Could Sudesh be telling the truth? 'Are you being serious? Explain yourself. If not, you're fired.'

It dawned on Sudesh that the reaction of the police, bystanders, Ray and even the nut lady had a common thread: incredulity. Without understanding it, he proceeded as cautiously and articulately as he could. 'In India', he said in a matter of fact way 'people trade everywhere, it's taken for granted. Traders provide goods and services desired by pedestrians. They serve everyone and harm no one. That's what this woman was doing. She was earning an honest living selling nuts – here have some – and these cops just arrest her for no reason, some or other stupid city ordinance they said after my arrest. Naturally, I intervened and couldn't understand why her other customers didn't join me, and ...'

'What's it got to do with you?'

Sudesh paused, 'Nothing. It's just wrong ... like those guys at the rally against you investing in India.'

Suddenly Sudesh's story no longer seemed so crazy. It hit the right spot with Ray. 'Umm, well yes. Okay, so you're out on bail. That means you're facing criminal charges.'

'Yes, for obstructing the police in the course of their duties, creating a public disturbance, and trespassing in a police station.'

'Do you realise how serious that is, Sudesh? A decent defence will cost you at least twenty thousand dollars and another fifty thousand if there's an appeal. You don't have that kind of money. You could be jailed and have a criminal record. That means you'll never come back to America.'

New York City, 2002

Sudesh chose Saravana, a South Indian restaurant on Lexington Ave, for dinner with Vaneshri.

Unlike many men who had grown nervous and uncomfortable in her presence, Sudesh had only grown curious.

She looked around, enjoying the familiar atmosphere with unfamiliar faces. People looked back at her, some staring openly, others glancing furtively. She was used to being admired; at least she assumed it was admiration.

Sudesh scanned her face. Her eyebrows arched like a bird's wings above her radiant sea-green eyes. Her full lips parted into a slight smile beneath her aquiline nose. He had never seen such a beautiful woman.

'So, where do you think is India headed?' asked Sudesh. He was bad at small talk.

'It will be fine if we just keep freeing the economy.'

'Many Americans would agree with that. Privatise telecoms, electricity, roads; Ray Upton thinks that even the education, health and welfare should be privatised. "They should privatise the ocean, the ozone layer and the Presidency" he once said with such a straight face that I thought he might not be joking.'

'The evidence shows that the private enterprise under conditions of free competition is twenty to forty percent more efficient.' said Vaneshri. 'But you must know the figures, working for Upton, making money out of emerging free markets.'

Sudesh stiffened slightly. 'For me it's not about making money, Vaneshri. I want justice and prosperity not just for the rich, but for all. I want to make things better, for the poor especially in India.'

Vaneshri wondered what was wrong with him. She hoped he wasn't a bunny-hugging do-gooder. She found such people ignorant, irrational and tiresome.

'Let's start with a *thali*,' she said, placing the order without referring to Sudesh for any input.

She turned back to him, 'I can't believe it is so easy to access the internet here, even in public places. The speed is breathtaking, and bandwidth is uncapped. I can download all the new shareware and freeware I want.'

'The open-source revolution is changing things fundamentally.' said Sudesh. 'It challenges the capitalist concept that everything should be for profit. Everything should be open-source.'

'Do you realise how far it can go? Ultimately everything involves information technology,' said Vaneshri.

'But not all products are information based, I'm sorry.'

'But they are.' She insisted. 'The internet allows thousands of people to collaborate online and design everything from software to cars, they can do their shopping and get married; already people have collaborated to build design, finance and market a car at sixty percent of the normal price.'

'Okay, but you can't say the same for real wealth, for what people really need, like land and houses, things that make use of physical goods or involve physical labour.'

'I'll concede that for now, I want to eat my dinner.' she said as if food for one mattered more than food for all.

As Sudesh watched Vaneshri dig in to her *appams* and fish curry with coconut, he felt amused at her unusual appetite.

E-mail to Inder Bhati, 2002

Hi Inder,

They heard my case – the one about the nut lady. For creating a public disturbance, I was fined $2,000 and ordered to attend special classes on civil conduct. It's absurd. Police who harass innocent traders should be attending those classes. For obstructing police officers, I was fined $5,000 and sentenced to one month in the county jail followed by six months of probation. For trespassing in a police station I got a cautionary discharge. Now I know what they mean about 'zero tolerance' law enforcement in New York City!

Ray Upton was surprised to see me at work, "How come you're here? You're supposed to be in jail," he asked with a withering look.

"I noted an appeal, but I can't afford a decent lawyer, so I'll have to represent myself, or get a cheap backstreet lawyer. Maybe the nut lady knows a good one!" I quipped.

"Do you understand American courts, Sudesh?" he asked. "This is no joke. Their job is to decide who has the most expensive lawyer!" That's one of his favourite lines. He hates the system. America doesn't have the loser-pays principle, so even if you win, you pay through the nose. Another of his lines is that in American courts everyone loses, winners just lose less. I'm learning it the hard way.

He said he'd lend me the money to get a top lawyer and will deduct instalments from my salary.

Ray is fed up with me and I will be cash-strapped for some time. I will have less money to send Amma. It's a financial disaster. You always said I was crazy. Maybe this time I have to admit that you were right!

How's your cricket?

Sudesh.

A village near Delhi, 2004

Shakti and Inder were trapped inside due to the rain. Thunder struck the tin roof of the house making it almost impossible for them to hear each other.

'Have you heard from Sudesh?' asked Shakti.

'Yes,' spoke Inder while doing bicep curls with 10 kg dumbbells. 'I'll take a printout of his e-mail and give it to you.'

'I'd like that.' Shakti gathered most of the news about Sudesh from his letters to Kamla, but there were some things he did not tell his mother.

Inder gave his sister a quizzical look.

Shakti looked away.

'Does he have a girlfriend?'

'Do you feel that he is incapable of getting a girl?'

'A sensible individual he is, not a player like you.'

Inder smiled. What his sister meant as an insult but he took it as a compliment.

'I think he's met someone but I can't recall the details.'

'Inder!'

'Oh, yes. Not an American chick though; she is an Indian girl and you'll never guess who.'

Shakti's heart sank. 'Who?'

'The daughter of the InfoSwish chief. Vaneshri, I think is her name. I saw her on TV once. She's hot.'

Shakti looked grave. How could she even think of competing with a beautiful girl who had a billionaire father?

'The rain has stopped, I must go. I have important tasks to finish.'

And Inder was off, sloshing through the puddles swinging his bat in his hand.

Shakti looked at her feet, deep in thought.

Her mother looked up from her needle-work, 'Never mind, sweetie, they're not married yet.'

Shakti hadn't realised her mum was aware of her attraction to Sudesh but she was glad it was so. She had always been close to her mother.

'What should I do, Mother?'

'There's nothing to do now, Shakti, except to be patient. If Sudesh had stayed here maybe your father could have spoken to Kamla.'

'It's what I have always hoped for.'

'I know, my love, but be patient, you are good at that. Sudesh was never one to rush into things, I don't expect he will get married soon.'

New York City, 2004

The apartment in Greenwich Village near the Hudson River reverberated with the tinkling of glasses as the guests attending the cocktail party raised toasts.

Though unaccustomed to such parties, Sudesh was finding the entire scene. New York was full of smart, successful people who could speak engagingly on their area of expertise. Across the room Ray chatted to another successful entrepreneur. They were perhaps considering a billion dollar deal, Sudesh thought, or possibly discussing baseball.

As he turned, looking for other familiar faces, a glossy magazine on the glass table captured his attention. It topped a pile that included *Architects' Digest* and *Harpers Bazaar*. His heart jolted as his eyes took in the familiar, beloved face gazing up at him. He felt dazed, the sounds around him receded and time seemed to have come to a standstill.

Vaneshri tugged on his arm, 'Sudesh, what is it?'

As Sudesh regained his normalcy, a man standing nearby spoke 'that was the first magazine to feature the iconic "Face of Child Labour" from our successful ad campaign in 1995.'

'Ad campaign?' Sudesh sounded as if he was sleep-talking.

'Yes, let me introduce you to John Medley. It was his brainchild. We were proud of the project. We managed to put an end to the use of child labour in carpet factories across most of the world.'

'Oh yes, I remember,' said a lean tall man, 'you used that pretty little Indian girl to rally support, I saw the feature on Oprah. It was heartrending.'

Sudesh turned and stumbled out of the room, Vaneshri close behind him. He sat down on the top step of the staircase leading to the apartment, his head between his knees.

'What is it? Please, Sudesh tell me, what has happened, are you alright?'

'That photo, that child, she is my sister Chanda. She disappeared in 1995 after she lost her job in the carpet factory. I have been searching for her ever since.' He raised his face, his eyes unseeing, 'Maybe she is dead.'

Fifteen

A village near Delhi, 2005

Shakti walked through the village to Kamla's house to see how the renovations proceeded.

Since Sudesh had received his first pay-packet he had been transferring dollars into a savings bank account in Delhi for his mother.

Shakti had helped Kamla in her bank transactions. She took her to the nearest branch of the Bank of India, taught her the way to access her money, and then persuaded her to get some renovations made in the house using the extra money left with her. Kamla insisted that she would get the new rooms built only with the help of local people. She agreed to a simple tiled bathroom with a flush lavatory, hot and cold running water, and a hand-basin and shower. As for the kitchen, an electric oven with four hotplates, a wooden worktable and double sink were also added.

When power-cuts interrupted, she took pleasure in cooking in her old clay oven, the one Sudesh had built into the clay wall surrounding her yard soon after Chanda went missing.

Both Shakti and Kamla took great delight in reading Sudesh's letters over a cup of tea. Sudesh wrote to his mother in long hand, at least twice a month, relying on Shakti to read to her since he knew his mother was barely literate.

He gave detailed descriptions of his life in New York and wrote about his adventures in the city so that it would make her smile.

The Upton Investment Corporation, 2005

Ray's time was valuable. When he set aside half an hour for Sudesh he was being generous, and Sudesh acknowledged his generosity.

Today Ray made himself comfortable in his original Corbusier LC2 armchair, upholstered in rust-coloured leather, and gestured for Sudesh to take the matching two-seater. The chairs were placed to take advantage of the view from Ray's office.

'So, what exactly do you do in India?' asked Sudesh, 'All I know is that you are investing there.'

'We have begun to invest in countries that liberalise, cut taxes and privatise. Since Rao's pro-market reforms in 1992, I have been keeping an eye on India. A short time after his reforms, the country's economy began to move upward and I started investing. Now, Manmohan Singh is considering free enterprise zones, based on China's incredibly successful Special Economic Zones. People live and work there, but don't pay tax,' said Ray.

A young woman slipped quietly in with a tray carrying Ray's favourite Columbian Arabica coffee, freshly ground and served espresso.

'If there is no tax, where does the money come from for education, health and roads?'

'People pay for them as they use them, like anything else, food and clothes for example.'

'What if they can't afford it?'

'The key point to understand here is that the service can be provided privately and the users who can't afford it can be subsidised by government.'

'You mean all schools and hospitals can be private and the poor can be given financial assistance to make use of them?'

'Exactly, if that is what you want to do. The best way to help the poor is through charity, which is given voluntarily and supplied efficiently. Charity is enough for the few needy people in rich countries with full employment.

'In poor countries like India some taxation would be necessary to subsidise the poor, but far less than the taxes required for government to run everything. When services are delivered by the private business, it doesn't mean the poor are ignored, it means that service providers must compete for the business of the middle class and government supported poor. Competition drives up performance. The main problem with governments supplying services is that they have no competitors.'

'So you believe cities could work entirely on this principle?'

'Indeed and I am not the only one. Many people think this is the way of the future.'

Sivananda Kutir, Uttarkashi, 2005

At Sivananda Kutir, Chanda learned meditation, which she found therapeutic, for both her body and soul. She had lost the desire for all worldly attachments and led a life of contentment. There came a change now. She had developed a fascination for Janardan.

The two sat on large stones at the edge of the Ganges discussing their lives.

'So are things going fine with you?' asked Janardan.

'Yes, especially since I completed my training with the Divine Life Society in Rishikesh. I feel so fortunate to live amidst these wonderful mountains and to learn from Swami Vishnudevananda. You know I have completed my basic training as a teacher now, and I share discourses with the devotees who visit during the season?'

'It must make a change of pace when the visitors arrive. Where do they come from?'

'Yes, it is different from winter months, much noisier. Most of those who come are women, but there are men too. A few Indians, but the majority from China, Japan, the USA, European countries, South Africa and Australia. We limit the numbers and they have to fit into our normal daily routine, so although it is busy, it does not get chaotic.'

Janardan looked at her, smiling. 'Over the years you have changed significantly from a timid little girl whom I had brought to Rishikesh to a confident, brave, cheerful young lady.'

'Thank you. I have acquired peace of mind after coming here. Sometimes I wonder what might have happened if you had not rescued me and brought me to Sivananda.'

Janardan nodded. He took her hand in his.

Chanda's eyes filled with tears, 'How could I go back to my family after that horrifying incident in the Imperial Hotel?'

'It wasn't your fault.'

'It was partly my fault, and my actions would bring shame on my village. You know, I have realised that my mother would have never expected me to take up prostitution. My parents were upright people, full of integrity in every way. I must have misunderstood my mother. That is the only explanation I can come up with. But whenever I think of my folly, I feel deeply ashamed.'

Janardan nodded, 'But I know you miss your family; don't you want to see them again?'

Chanda's eyes welled up with tears, 'I think of my mother and brother every day, and pray for them. But I can never return to the village. I have lost my honour and my right to live among decent people. My foolishness and irrational behaviour have made me unfit for that.'

Janardan put his arm around her and she collapsed against his chest, breaking down. 'I try to overcome these traumatic thoughts by meditation.' He could hardly hear her muffled voice. 'But I feel so sad at the thought of Amma and Sudesh. I feel terrible that I will never see them again.'

Janardan embraced her and rocked her gently in his arms, 'Come now my love,' he said, 'you need to think this through more carefully. From all you have told me about your mother and brother they would forgive you and want to see you again.'

New York City, 2005

Vaneshri and Sudesh walked through Central Park. They both wore woollen hats, gloves and padded parkas. 'While we are here we must do things we can't do in India,' she said. They walked together between the bare trees.

'Don't you think that people are not very bright?' she asked him.

'Well maybe, compared to you,' he replied.

'No, I know I'm cleverer than most,' she replied cheerfully, 'but none of the people I work with, here or in Hyderabad, seem capable of a single original thought. Even the qualified ones just reiterate what they have been taught.'

'You might be right,' said Sudesh. 'But everyone has a place in society and a role to play.'

'Yes, but it annoys me when people are incompetent.'

Sudesh nodded. He didn't share her feelings, but he had become used to her extreme views; they didn't make him like her less.

The two wandered on.

'Don't you think politics is so far-gone, we need to replace it with a different system? Maybe, go back to having kings and nobles, maharajas and maharanis?' said Vaneshri.

'No, I agree with Winston Churchill, "Democracy is the worst system except for all those others that have been tried."'

'Churchill said that in the mid-twentieth century. Since then things have deteriorated. No one has respect for politicians any more. Government is a racket, and it wastes so much money.'

'I agree but I think the system can be reformed.'

'So what would you do, Mr Let's-Change-the-World?'

'If democracy is going to regain any legitimacy, governments have to stop most of their current activities. They are involved in the direct provision of hundreds of thousands of unrelated products and services. No private corporation would ever attempt such diversification.'

'That makes sense, so get the government to focus on a few things it does well?' said Vaneshri, turning her head. Her lustrous dark hair cascaded over her shoulders.

Sudesh paused for a second, momentarily enchanted, before he continued, 'Ninety-five percent of what the government does at the moment, should not happen. Everything should be privatised.'

'What do you mean? Education, health, roads, policing, courts and stuff like that? You can't privatise all that. Poor people wouldn't be able to afford it.'

'I used to think that way, but I see now that when you have many companies competing to provide schools, clinics, roads and so on, then the price goes down and the quality goes up. Then if you want to help the poor further, you can give them vouchers that they can use for a wide range of things, I was thinking maybe in the form of smart cards. Then they too could shop around for the best services. Unlike at the moment, when their education and health facilities are mostly neglected by the government.'

'Smart cards? Sudesh, that's brilliant! That's why I like you, you think out of the box. Hey, why don't I start working on that? Software for a smart card that can be used for hospitals, schools, even to buy food from street vendors. Wow! Great idea!'

Sudesh loved watching Vaneshri in her animated spirit. There was a spark in her eyes, a glow on her face. Overwhelmed by his love for her, Sudesh embraced and kissed her. When he released her she said batting her lashes at him, 'I'd been wondering when you would get around to that.'

The Upton Investment Corporation, 2005

As Sudesh walked into the Upton Building his mind was elsewhere.

'The boss wants to see you urgently,' said Linda, when he reached his floor.

'Really? What have I done now?' he smiled at her. Passing down the corridor he knocked gently and walked in.

'What's up?'

'Ah, Sudesh, I have something for you to do,' Ray paused, 'in your own country.'

Sudesh listened, 'Something related to India?'

'That's right. I want to discuss a privatisation matter with you. The Indian government is outsourcing telecom assets to strategic investors. We've done a lot of the groundwork and filled in all the forms.'

Sudesh nodded, feeling interested.

'But what we need now is the trust factor.'

'Okay.'

'So I'm going to send you, if you are willing to talk to your government and persuade them to give the concession to us. There will be a bonus in it for you if you succeed.'

Sudesh frowned slightly, 'I'm not really bothered about the bonus, Ray. Helping Indians to get better telecommunications is good enough for me.'

Ray smiled indulgently, 'Whatever makes you happy.'

'So where and when do I start?'

'Get your tickets from Linda. You'll be leaving for Delhi on Wednesday.'

Sudesh's heart leaped. Back to India to make a difference!

The Singh household, Delhi, 2005

Nanek Singh relaxed at home after another hard day.

His wife sat behind him on the couch, massaging the knots out of his back. Devika was asleep and the house was quiet.

'So the crime stats are down again, you're winning,' she said.

'So it seems,' he replied. 'I'm happy. Our policies are working and we seem to be getting help from god. Five crime bosses down so far, and the only thing they have in common is that we can't find who killed them, despite our best efforts.'

She smiled, 'Help from anywhere is good.' She moved her hands down to the middle of his back and pressed deep into the muscles adjacent to his spine.

'And how was your week?' he asked.

'I'm getting closer to finding out the people who master-minded the December attack on the Parliament. Been in and out of Kashmir and Pakistan all week, following leads.'

'It's good to have you home again.'

They drifted into a contented silence as she continued to knead the tension out of his back with her strong fingers.

A government office, New Delhi, 2005

'We didn't expect to have an Indian endorsing the Upton Corporation,' said Pachauri, the man in charge of government owned telecom giant, BSNL. 'We thought only heartless capitalist Americans worked there.' He smiled briefly.

The round table was too small for the six people seated around it. The five officials flipped through the pages of the documents piled up near them sipping their chai side-by-side.

Sudesh smiled, 'Some of us have other aims than money.'

Pachauri brought the meeting to order. 'Your comment brings us straight to our concern, Mr Kumar. We aren't sure whether the Upton Corporation is interested in the welfare of the Indian people. It is most likely out to make money.'

Sudesh gave a short version of the story of his life thus far, explaining that Upton was aware that he intended to come back to India and use his skills.

He concentrated all the strength of his personality into persuading the officials that the Upton Corporation was the best option for India. Better than the French consortium or British Telecom. 'The Upton Corporation,' he explained, 'understands the nuances of the Indian market, and the social responsibilities inherent in any Indian investment.'

After nearly two hours, Pachauri leaned back in his chair. 'I must admit I feel a lot more comfortable after our discussion.'

The other officials nodded their heads in consent.

'Upton's bid is the best on price. Our doubts regarding the company ethos and its attitude to India have been reduced by talking to you, Mr Kumar. Thank you.'

'My pleasure.'

'It seems the great Upton Corporation is not as ruthless as we have been led to believe.'

'I'd say it has not only a great mind but a great heart too.' said Sudesh.

New York City, 2006

It was a dull, drizzly day. Sudesh emerged from the subway and saw the headline: 'Upton Corporation rapes third world company.'

Just newspaper superlatives, media exaggeration he thought, yet there was a sinking feeling in his stomach.

He bought the paper from the news stand and scanned the article. After reading a couple of paragraphs he leaned against a pillar to steady himself.

'Are you okay, bud?' asked the vendor.

'On January 3, 2006, two-thirds of the Upton Corporation's Indian Telecom staff will receive notice. The Upton Corporation, who recently bought the switching and maintenance division of BSNL, said that the workers are not required since the Corporation is introducing sophisticated switching equipment that makes manual operations unnecessary. Mr Pachauri, Permanent Secretary for Indian Communications, said the Indian government was outraged but contractually bound not to intervene. The labour union, of BSNL, is up in arms.'

In his mind's eye Sudesh saw tens of thousands of workers leaving through a factory gate; hopeless, forlorn, without marketable skills. Going home to families that would never be as happy as before. Sudesh fumed with rage and betrayal.

Sudesh rushed into Ray Upton's outer office.

'He's busy,' said Linda.

Sudesh ignored her and burst into the inner sanctum.

'How dare you! How could you sack all those people?' he shouted, 'You used me!'

Ray was calm and spoke quietly, 'Sudesh, modern digital telecoms equipment is more productive than manual labour. I have to bring the business into the twenty-first century.'

'Why didn't you tell that to me first?' Sudesh yelled, 'I would never have put myself on the line for you.'

Sudesh had lost all control. He grabbed Ray's in-tray from his desk and sent it hurtling across the room.

Ray moved out of the way.

Peter Drake, who was in a meeting with Ray when Sudesh burst in, sat agape wondering why Ray didn't throw this young man out of the room.

'What will the Indian government think of me now! How can I ever go back?' Sudesh's face turned red.

'Calm down' said Ray, still reasonable, 'What has happened to BSNL is what is happening to telecom companies all over the world. In India they just do it slowly and waste money that could be put to better use. I'm amputating the limb instead of cutting it off in pieces. It's better for India.'

'Don't tell me what is "better for India". You don't care a penny about what's better for India.'

'True,' said Ray, 'but you do. Right?'

'You lied to me.'

'No I didn't.'

'You gave me the impression that everything would be fine. That's what I told the Indian government and that's why the deal went through.'

'I gave you no such guarantees.'

Sudesh tried calming down, his rage expended.

'You used me.'

'We all use each other every day. I am not your father. You must make your own decisions. I won't look after you and I don't expect you to look after me.'

❦

Sudesh felt tormented. He left the Upton Building and walked slowly towards Battery Park. He had felt forlorn and trivialised when Ray ignored him for so long. Now he felt betrayed. He resolved to resign from the Upton Corporation, but return to India with blood on his hands? He sat down on a bench in the manicured gardens of the Battery Conservancy.

Lost in thought, his body folded unconsciously into the posture of Rodin's 'Thinker.' He mused intently on the dark side of liberty. He wondered if human suffering was the price of freedom. Perhaps this was why radicals are hell-bent on driving capitalists from the third world, he thought.

He considered the words of his mentor who had morphed into a tormentor. The many things he had learned from the books and journals he'd bought at Strand Book Store and ordered from Laissez Faire Books clouded his mind. His inner turmoil deepened.

He remembered the story of an American engineer who visited a communist Chinese dam site, and asked the reason for using so much manual labour when machines could do the job in less time at a lower cost.

'To create jobs,' came the reply of the Chinese site manager.

'Oh, I thought you wanted a dam,' said the American. 'If you want jobs remove the shovels and wheel barrows, and let them dig with spoons and carry the stones and soil by hand. You can create more jobs like that.'

He recalled the silliness of Luddites rioting against technology because it supposedly destroyed jobs, and Adam Smith's celebrated description of a few highly paid workers using machines to make millions of pins. Smith observed that to match their production by hand, England's entire workforce would have to be pin-makers, rolling and cutting wire, and hammering pinheads one-by-one.

Sudesh swung helplessly between heart-wrenching visions of his destitute countrymen losing jobs at the behest of a selfish Upton, and prosperous visions of full employment in a booming free market. He thought of a billion humiliated Indians begging for aid under socialism, and contrasted it with the prospect of a nation walking tall amongst the worlds' best.

He wondered if his decision to stay or leave was any different from the 'investment' decisions he made at his work every day. Did Upton's 'don't make any investment decision with your heart' mantra apply here too? Thinking about his long-term plan of helping India, he felt that staying, learning, and saving money in the US would make more sense.

The free market injunction that 'there ain't no such thing as a free lunch' known by its acronym, TANSTAAFL, was the economic equivalent of his gym instructor's warning, 'no gain without pain'. Must that also be true for his country, he asked himself.

Sudesh's head and heart were in unison about wanting what was best for India. He would urge Upton to seek a third way, a golden mean, between economic sense and human decency. And he would re-dedicate his life to the transformation of India.

He decided to go back to the office and apologise for his behaviour.

Sixteen

New York City, 2007

Sudesh had been at the Upton Corporation for seven years now. Work took up most of his day, and he used his spare time reading on social and economic issues. Mentoring conversations with Ray Upton were infrequent. Vaneshri's intermittent visits to Manhattan allowed for some pleasant socialising.

But today Sudesh's day kicked off with a surprise. Inder's mail in his inbox read:

Dear Sudesh, I am coming to New York! I'm bringing Shakti along. She would not let me survive if I didn't give her this opportunity to see her old friend.

Sudesh was surprised to read the mail. He was partly joyful and partly disturbed. He thought it would be wonderful to see Shakti and Inder after a long time but could not understand what disturbed him. Not choosing to think more on this, he turned his attention to the day's workload.

The Brooklyn Inn, New York City, 2007

Sudesh, Inder, Shakti and Vaneshri had a tiring yet delightful time sightseeing. Taking a break now, Sudesh and Shakti seated themselves comfortably into bar chairs in a dark pub of the Brooklyn Inn on Hoyt Street.

Sudesh turned to Shakti, 'So how is Amma doing, Shakti?'

Shakti looked at him; not the skinny boy she remembered, still slim but a man now. His crisp yellow cotton shirt and navy pants looked dear. His spruced hairdo added a touch of sophistication.

'She misses you,' she replied, 'she invites her friends for tea and shows them around her fancy house. She basks in your reflected glory,' she laughed.

'I know you are there, taking care of her. Thank you, Shakti!'

'No word of Chanda?' Shakti knew the answer, but she asked Sudesh hoping he could tell her something different.

Sudesh's face fell, 'No, it's the same story. I try different detective agencies and at first they're enthusiastic, they come up with a few look-alikes, but after a while they tell me the trail is dead.'

Shakti reached out and touched his hand. She understood and shared his suffering. No words could change the situation.

'Sudesh, maybe I am out of line, but I can't help wondering. You have a very comfortable life here. Do you still plan to return to India one day? Do you still dream of changing the lives of the Indian poor? What has become of your ideals?'.

Sudesh hesitated, 'Thank you, Shakti, for asking me that. We are old friends. You have the right to question me and I want to give you an honest answer. I do want to dedicate my life to transforming India, but so far I haven't come up with any ideas about how I could do it. Meanwhile I'm learning and saving money.'

For a moment, as he looked at her, he felt a pang of longing. He felt at home with Shakti. He loved her for her simplicity, sincerity and humility. These qualities brought an unusual radiance to her face and made her adorable.

Suddenly he checked his fascination for Shakti. He reminded himself that he was in love with Vaneshri and she meant the world to him.

Inder and Vaneshri rejoined them for a drink. Vaneshri sat beside Sudesh and responded with a smile as he slipped his arm around her waist, 'Inder has been telling me about your ill-spent youth,' she said and they all burst into laughter.

Shakti felt coy sitting in the company of the other three who were splendidly dressed and had illustrious career reputations to boast of. Inder played cricket for India's second team. He was over 6 feet tall. His broad shoulders balanced his height, and his body rippled with the long, lean muscles of a sportsman.

Shakti was awed by Vaneshri's charisma. Sudesh also seemed smitten by her. Looking down at her turquoise salwar kameez she felt small. 'I can still be his friend, and I can help his mother.' she told herself.

New York City, 2007

Inder invited Vaneshri for lunch at Lombardi's in Little Italy. Sudesh was at work, and Shakti was shopping for her and Sudesh's mother.

Lombardi's was crowded but Inder was determined to try the legendary pizzas from the brick oven.

'We've been friends all our lives,' said Inder. 'He's a great guy, but remains a bit serious.'

'Yes,' said Vaneshri, 'and obsessed with economics and politics.'

'And how to get rid of the Indian bureaucracy?'

'Well, he is not wrong there!'

They smiled.

'And you, Inder, how are things going at JTH? I learnt you are a systems analyst there.'

'Yeah, work is good, but now I've been selected for the Indian cricket team so I'm strictly a 9.00 to 5.00 guy. All my spare time is for practising.'

Vaneshri smiled, 'Then I won't try to poach you for InfoSwish. We are supposed to work forty hours a week, but it's the mythical man week as we say in IT. We work seventy.'

'Sudesh and I had these dreams when we were kids,' Inder told her. 'He wanted to be the Prime Minister of India; I set my sights lower at being the number one batsman of the India team.'

'Well you are close to your goal. Sudesh's dream sounds interesting, though he's never mentioned that to me. I wonder if he has grown out of the idea. Seems like a long shot!'

'I always teased him about it, told him he was a crazy dreamer. Maybe that's why he keeps quiet. Are you going to settle in New York?'

'No, I've nearly finished setting up our American operation. Soon I'll be heading home to Hyderabad.'

'When you visit Delhi, give me a call. We can meet over lunch?'

'Sure, that would be great.'

As Vaneshri left the table, heading off to a meeting, Inder's eyes followed her, admiring the swing of her hips in the close-fitting fuchsia skirt. He smiled and thought that Sudesh was a lucky man.

Sudesh's apartment, New York City, November 2008

Vaneshri and Sudesh were breathless and excited as they headed across the small, grubby entrance lobby of Sudesh's apartment building, situated beneath the shadow of the Brooklyn Bridge in South Seaport.

They had been in Times Square, watching the vote count on CNN with thousands of other people. They had shared the thrill of the crowd when the Californian polls closed and the camera swung from the announcer to the words flashing across the screen, 'CNN projection, Barack Obama Elected President.'

They had listened to and watched Obama's victory speech, moved to tears by the passion underlying his seriousness, and joined the applauding and cheering crowd at the end. They, like millions of others around the globe, had been filled with wonder at this momentous event.

When they entered his apartment, Sudesh headed for his small kitchen to make Kashmiri green tea with cardamom and cinnamon while Vaneshri collapsed into one of his comfortable brown corduroy armchairs.

Vaneshri often visited Sudesh here during her business visits to New York. She was reflecting on the high points of the evening, and thinking about the ways in which Barack Obama reminded her of Sudesh.

As Sudesh came to join her, bearing a tray with a teapot and two mugs, she said, 'Inder once told me you used to dream of becoming the Prime Minister of India.'

'That's true.'

'Do you ever think about it now?'

'Yes, occasionally. I'm older and wiser now,' he smiled.

'I don't know. No one is a greater cynic than I, but as I watch Obama on TV I am reminded of you, despite the differences you have on economic policy. You have a similar presence, a similar aura – no, its not funny, for once I'm serious. If he can do it, why can't you?'

'To begin with, as you know, the political system is different in India. Also neither Congress nor BJP has policies that I can support. Further, Obama raised his funds through small donations on the internet, and from Democratic Party supporters. That would be impossible in India.'

Vaneshri nodded slowly, 'But what about Upton? He has the money to get you going. Ask him to help you.'

Police Headquarters, Delhi, 2009

In the last two years three more mafia dons of organised crime had been murdered in Delhi, and Nanek Singh had no idea who the perpetrator might be. That brought the total to ten upto now.

Nine years ago, in 2000, he had closed down Crime Stop. He had done so to protect his daughter. He was a committed policeman but he was also a committed father. Fortunately, god had been with him. Despite his lack of direct action against them, these mafia dons were being shot down.

He joined twelve other officials around a large conference table. They were the best detectives in Delhi.

The Chief Superintendent for Delhi opened the meeting.

'What progress do you have to report on the Mafia Murders?' asked an official.

'We thought it might be a turf war between mobs, but none of our intelligence reports support that theory. It could be Vasu's network; he's still around, though I don't see a motive. He has always dominated the stolen goods market in Delhi, and nobody has ever tried straying onto his turf. Our sources indicate that Malhotra's people are not responsible, but we will keep them under surveillance.'

Another official spoke, 'As you know, Sir, the murders are no longer limited to our jurisdiction. ... Mafia dons have been killed in Mumbai, Kolkata and Bengaluru.'

'The bottom line is that we have no idea what is going on here. The suspects are either dead or appear to have no connection with the deaths. We know from security camera footage that a different murderer has been at work in each case. All have been experts in different fields: a sharp shooter, a martial arts expert, someone with advanced knowledge of poisons. One killer scaled down the side of a building and cut his way into an office with a glass cutter.

'We have no knowledge of any organisation that could have so many experts at its disposal. The irony is that if we, as the police, had accomplished this clean-up we would be cracking open the champagne.'

'It's a serious problem,' said Singh.

'I don't think so,' said one of the others. 'I vote we spend less time and energy trying to track down these killers, and concentrate on other areas.'

'No' said Singh. 'Regardless of how welcome it might be to us when these mafia dons die, the law is applicable to everyone equally. We cannot ignore the murders of Indian citizens however disreputable they might be. We must track down these killers.'

New York City, 2009

Vaneshri was on her next visit to New York. She was there to market InfoSwish's new software that was designed to monitor the values of underlying assets of securitised derivatives. InfoSwish was making profits from the global collapse of financial markets.

She met Sudesh for a drink at a bar around the corner from the Metropolitian Museum of Art. Both of them planned to attend a special exhibition of contemporary Indian artist, Rawib Shaw, and then they would head for Sushi Sen-Nin on the Upper East Side.

Vaneshri looked fabulous in her black silk attire. Her hair swept up and back in a classic chignon, showing off her long neck studded with a gold chain and an emerald pendant which must have cost her father at least five lakh rupees.

'Darling, I think I have the solution for you,' she said.

'About what?' he asked, settling down with his scotch.

'About getting Ray to fund you.'

'He won't do it. He hates politicians and governments. He has no place for compassion. And most importantly, he believes everyone must make it alone without taking any help. He is an Ayn Rand fanatic,' said Sudesh.

'Exactly,' she replied, delighted with her idea.

Sudesh narrowed his eyes, 'What have you come up with now?'

'I am going to tell you how to get Ray to fund you because he loves Ayn Rand.'

'Okay, go on.'

Smiling at her own ingenuity she continued, 'You know Ray's passion for *Atlas Shrugged*, his all-time favourite book?'

'Yes, he made me read it as a condition of employment. But I didn't agree with Rand's arguments against helping others.'

'No, you wouldn't,' she smiled. 'But anyway, remember at the end all the top business people leave their positions and move to a hidden valley, Galt's Gulch, where they start a new society, free from government interference, and create huge wealth?'

'Yes, that's where she was off track. It's an unworkable idea.'

'Exactly! You are thinking along the same lines as me. A single valley couldn't be viable, but an entire country could. You persuade Ray to turn India into a Galt's Sub-continent!'

Sudesh paused for a moment to let the thought sink in, 'But people from all over the world would not move to India.'

'They don't need to. All they need is the economic conditions of "Galt's Gulch" to apply in entire India. That way the world's innovators and entrepreneurs will be attracted there, if not physically, at least in terms of investment.'

Sudesh nodded slowly, 'Yes that sounds good. We don't even need more people. We have enough of our own. All we need is their technology, capital and markets.

Vaneshri smiled and continued, 'But wait, there's more to my idea. If Ray invests in selected real estate in India and you succeed in transforming the economy, then the value of his investments will sky-rocket.'

'Vaneshri, I think you're onto something. Ray just might go for that. It would create unique opportunities. He would be funding me to transform India into a rich country by freeing up the market, and he would be doing himself a favour because he would make a fortune in the process!'

'Yes, you've got it!' her eyes were shining.

'Vaneshri,' said Sudesh. 'Have I told you how beautiful you look tonight?'

She grinned, 'I can't help being a gorgeous genius.'

Sudesh turned to a passing waiter, 'A bottle of Dom Perignon, please, I have a remarkable woman to celebrate with.'

The Upton Building, 2009

It was late evening when Sudesh entered Ray's office for their scheduled appointment. Ray stood at his bookcase flipping through some pages that glistened with the lights of New York shining through the window.

'Ray?'

'Yes, Sudesh?'

'You are interested in India, right?'

'I am interested in India because it is reforming and I have interests there. That is correct.'

'I have something to ask you.'

Ray looked at Sudesh, 'Let's sit down.'

He pulled out a chair at the round table he used for small meetings, and Sudesh sat down opposite him.

'Would you consider supporting me to run an office in India?' he blurted out.

'Of course I would, I would vote for you too, if I could.'

'But would you support me financially? If I was able to gain political influence in India, and use it to implement the ideas you believe in, to create the freest economy in the world and transform India from its present poverty to the world's freest and richest country ...' His words were running away from him.

'If I could become the Barack Obama of India, but with the right policies, the ones that encourage innovation and reward productivity, this would attract world's top entrepreneurs and investors and result in an explosion of wealth on a scale the world has never seen. If I could create a Galt's Country, would you invest in me?'

Ray looked at Sudesh. In the silence that lasted perhaps thirty seconds, Sudesh felt as if a life-time passed.

'Sudesh, you have many compelling qualities. You have the same priceless blend of charisma and eloquence, combined with a genuinely deep concern for your country that Obama evinced in his election. More importantly, you have a clear and hard-won understanding of the nature and virtues of true liberty.

'But you are still young, only twenty-six years old, if I am not mistaken. And although your idea is inspired, I doubt if you have given serious thought to the details of its implementation.

Ray rose and paced slowly back and forth, his hands behind his back. He seemed to be looking at something in the distance. Then he turned once more to Sudesh.

'You will have to wait four more years for my answer. Come to see me on your thirtieth birthday, 18 March 2012, I believe.' Ray's eyes twinkled. 'When you come, bring along a detailed plan of action sufficiently compelling to convince me that you can turn this daring dream into a reality. If you succeed I will provide you with the financial backing you need.'

But long before Sudesh could present his plan on his birthday four years later, Ray called for him and said he'd changed his mind. 'I'm told by my Delhi lawyers,' said Ray, 'that Indian parties cannot be funded from abroad. They say the law is unclear, but it doesn't matter because Indians would never support a party funded by foreigners.'

'I know,' said Sudesh, 'but you can fund us exclusively from your Indian investments.'

'No, that would be seen in India as the same thing, as foreigners interfering in domestic affairs. I'm sorry, but you must abandon the idea of starting your own party. Politics is a waste of time anyway. It's inherently evil. Give up the idea and use your talents to make money instead.'

Sudesh was visibly stunned. After a long silence, he spoke slowly, almost inaudibly. 'I will,' said Sudesh.

Ray sensed something more resolute than anything he'd heard Sudesh say before. 'I will make money,' continued Sudesh as if speaking to himself. 'Yes, that's what I'll do, make money ...'

'Thank you, Ray,' he said raising his eyes to meet Ray's and projecting his voice as if he'd had an epiphany.

Part Three

Part Three

Seventeen

Delhi, October 2012

Sudesh reached India and this time he was there to stay. Before he settled down to the serious task of building a political party, he decided to spend the first three days with his mother to reconnect with her, to ensure that she was properly provided for and that she was in good health.

He spoke to her about Chanda. He explained that he had commissioned the best detective agencies to search for her but that they had found no trace of her. Many false leads had come to nothing. He assured Kamla that he would keep searching.

Whilst they were sitting in the small yard on comfortable moulded plastic chairs, Shakti joined them.

'When are you going to start your new work, Sudesh?' she asked.

'I intend to leave the day after tomorrow. First, I must find a place to make my office, and then an apartment to live nearby,' He smiled. It was a smile she knew well, it reminded her of when he felt especially happy and fulfilled as a boy.

Shakti looked at him, her face turned serious, 'I have been thinking, Sudesh, that perhaps you need a helper at your office for doing little chores. Someone you could ask to do all the mundane yet essential work, such as finding office furniture, organising phone lines, making chai, and so on.'

'Yes, if I can find a person I can trust to get on with the job, that would be great,' Sudesh replied.

'Would you trust me to do it?'

'You Shakti? Of course I would! It would be wonderful! But what about your life here? Your mother? The people you take care of? Your friends? I don't want to take you away from everything you know,' Sudesh looked into Shakti's eyes questioningly.

'Since our childhood days I have seen you cherishing your dream of transforming India one day. Now when you are really going to make it happen, I want to be part of it. If you permit, I want to work with you.'

Central Delhi, 2012

Registration of the Liberty and Prosperity Party, under section 29A of the Representation of the People Act, 1951, took two days. The forms were forwarded to the Electoral Commission of India along with the fee of ten thousand rupees. Now the party existed, at least in name.

Sudesh had laid the ground-work for his core team. He did not intend to employ a large workforce, but was keen on having a handful of qualified, specialised and capable people who shared his dreams.

Sudesh's journey from India to America and now back to India had also been a journey of intellectual progress. His father's words of wisdom had given him a fillip to see such dreams and his stay with Upton had made him smart, and tactful enough to realise the dream.

Sudesh had listened carefully to, but had not been convinced by Ray's dogmatic arguments for the philosophy of Objectivism. He remained skeptical of Objectivism's insistence on atheism and pure logic, and questioned the assumption that conscious reason was necessarily more reliable than spontaneous emotion and intuition.

He had read widely delving in diverse schools of thought, and was outraged by how universities brainwashed students with the views of their tutors. He dreamt of an India in which people were exposed to and could make informed choices between alternative world views. Of all the alternatives he'd encountered, he found libertarian arguments for unambiguous liberty and prosperity for all, most convincing. This demanded a minimal role for the government with maximal emancipation and empowerment of individuals.

He was converted, but not yet fully informed.

There remained, for Sudesh, many unresolved issues and contradictions: the need for government intervention to protect destitute and unemployable people, especially tens of millions of orphans and street children in India. He was also concerned about the environment, endangered species, protection of animals from cruelty, police protection, national security, justice, basic infrastructure and much more.

He'd learned from the scores of books and from visits to free market think-tanks in North America such as Cato, FEE, Fraser and Reason, that there were good answers where he expected none.

During the preparations for his political career he had harnessed the formidable resources of their Indian counterparts and formed a brain's trust with pro-liberty Indian intellectuals like Deepak Lal, Parth Shah, Barun Mitra, and Bibek Debroy.

Though they greeted his plans with varying degrees of scepticism, they offered advice willingly. In addition, they came up with practical solutions to complex challenges.

With their assistance, Sudesh lined up a PR and marketing manager who would identify and communicate with Delhi's top PR agencies. He chose a Press Officer to generate daily press releases and develop relationships with journalists and decision-makers in the media.

Vaneshri had allowed him to poach one of her top internet specialists to set up his computer systems and run the party's website.

His fourth core team member was an administrative manager, an extremely competent woman who was picked up from a top management position in a major corporation, her bait being a lucrative package that was more than what she could expect, and tremendous opportunities for completely new challenges. She would coordinate the activities of the team and employ an accounting firm to take care of the finances of the venture. She would also be responsible for establishing party offices in other cities and towns at a later stage.

Shakti was settling in as an efficient office manager. But her tenure would be short-lived. One of her early duties was to be the bearer of bad tidings. She had to give Sudesh the shattering news that their newly-formed party had been banned and deregistered. She handed him the documents served on them by the Election Commission.

Panaji, North Goa, 2012

Vaneshri put on a silvery black head visor as they climbed into their rented car.

'What on earth is that for?' asked Sudesh.

'Wait and watch,' she replied, with a coquettish smile. 'Let's head for Old Goa and check out the churches and cathedrals.'

'Will you navigate?'

'Sure,' said Vaneshri, 'two-hundred metres from the hotel's entrance gates, you will come to a road on your right, turn there.'

Sudesh cast a curious glance at her, 'Have you ever driven on this route before?'

'No,' said Vaneshri, her face broke into a smile, 'you have just experienced GPS tourist navigation, another Indian product from InfoSwish.'

The couple had flown in to Goa for a romantic weekend and a well-deserved break at the Taj Exotica.

'So your visor can tell exactly where you are?'

'And which way to go and what you are looking at. It shades your eyes from the sun as well. It's clever. Looks cute, too,' she said glancing in the car mirror.

'How does it work?'

'It accesses a data source, in this case the solid state hard drive on my phone, but the information could be beamed wirelessly from the Goa Tourist Board, for example. It collects the information associated with your geographical position. When we reach old Goa and walk around the churches it will provide precise information every step of the way like when was the church built, a description of the architectural features, religious history and so on.'

'Do you have a second ear-piece so I can tune in, too? Or, are you going to be my tour guide?'

'Second ear-piece, of course. We've also designed a headset for doctors to use during surgery. It gives them X-ray vision which makes it easy for them to navigate inside the body.'

Sudesh smiled and shook his head. 'Awesome!'

She smiled back, 'Straight ahead for the next five kilometres then turn left!'

❧

Sudesh and Vaneshri were strolling down the hotel's private beach, enjoying the cool evening breeze.

'Do you think our policies are good enough?'

'What do you mean?'

'Well, I know the policies are good, but do you think they are saleable? People are used to politicians promising free electricity, welfare programmes, housing and so on. Will we win over them without making promises we can't fulfil?'

'I don't see why you can't make promises too. You say that your policies would deliver education, housing and a chicken in the pot for all, so promise those things during your campaign. Unlike other politicians, when you take over the show you might even deliver!'

'Now that I'm in a position to put my ideas into practice I wonder if I actually can. For years when I was reading I wondered if I was wasting my time because I would never get a chance to apply the information. Now I wish I'd spent more time reading so that I don't miss anything when I try to influence policy.'

'Sudesh, you don't need to worry about insufficient information. You have your experts to help you, should you need to brush up on a quick response. Your most attractive quality is your honesty. It shines through.'

'Even if you make mistakes, you are genuinely trying to improve the lives of ordinary people.'

Office of the Election Commission, Delhi, November 2012

'I am afraid, Mr Kumar, that your party has been deregistered because it is funded from abroad, specifically by the Upton Corporation in New York,' said a representative of the Election Commission in monotones sounding more like a computer text recognition program than a person.

'I can contest your interpretation of the law, but I won't,' responded Sudesh.

'Good, then why are you here?'

'To have my party re-registered.'

'I don't understand.'

'What don't you understand?'

'Well, you said you won't contest deregistration on account of foreign funding.'

'No, I said I won't contest your view of the law. I don't need to because we have no foreign funding.'

'Our information, Mr Kumar, is that you worked for a modest salary for the Upton Corporation, that all your party's money was earned from or donated by their American head office and that there are no significant funds from elsewhere other than a donation from Vaneshri Palande. I know I shouldn't say this', he added gratuitously, 'but the Upton Corporation is not popular in this office.'

'You are mistaken,' said Sudesh calmly. 'None of the money is from abroad and none is from Upton.'

This was the moment the official had been waiting for, time to deliver the *coupe de grace*. "You're lying. We know how little you were earning, yet you have millions in your bank account, all of it from Upton. We used our investigative powers to get bank deposit details. Upton paid massive amounts into your personal account with Anand Rathi Securities who, in turn, paid it into your private bank account. Did you really think we were that foolish, that laundering forex through a local broker would disguise the foreign source?"'

'Speaking for myself, and off the record,' he added furtively, 'I regard donations from Upton as particularly vulgar additions to his exploitation of our workers and subversion of our policies.

'I'm surprised at you, Mr Mudraj. I did not expect you, with your jaundiced view of corporations, to assume payment of a large sum to be a donation. Do you want me to explain, or do I have to take you to court?'

He interpreted Mudraj's silence as preference for the former.

'Don't get me wrong, I wanted Upton's money, I asked for it, but he rejected me. All the money in my account is mine, earned by way of foreign investments made from India.'

'How so, you were abroad?'

'Since you ask, which you should have done before jumping to conclusions, I'll tell you. Apart from creating jobs for Indians, the Upton Corporation pioneered the idea of policy bets, whereby people could bet on the success or failure of countries and their policies. When Upton refused to help me, he told me to get rich instead of going into politics. I took his advice.

'Well, half of it. I decided to make money and go into politics. I did the obvious thing. Since he'd taught me how to predict the effects of policies, I started betting on the Upton Exchange, always with my own money, all of which I transferred to India, and always through my local broker, Anand Rathi Securities.'

'I would hardly call gambling an investment', said the official disparagingly.

Sudesh ignored him and carried on. 'I always bet that pro-market policies would succeed and anti-market ones would backfire. I seldom lost. I'd started with what little was left of my salary and commissions after basic living expenses, I borrowed from anyone who would lend to me, and I reinvested everything I won into more bets.

'If you understand the power of compound interest,' said Sudesh auto-suggestively, you will understand what followed. Albert Einstein called compound interest "the greatest invention of all time" and Benjamin Franklin called it "the eighth wonder of the world". Basically, if you keep adding interest to interest the original sum grows faster than people expect.

'Anyway, the amount soon built-up. Winning bets beats compound interest because you can place bets frequently. I always bet at the last minute and only on bets where the outcome would be known soon, such as whether a new tax-funded rapid transit system would cost more and yield less than budgeted, or whether new credit legislation would be followed by fewer defaults. The value of my investment multiplied at a massively accelerated rate.'

'Did you pay tax on your profits?' asked the official in the vain hope of finding a basis for saving face.

'Yes. On the other hand, no,' said Sudesh, He was beginning to enjoy this one-sided cat-and-mouse game with obstructive officialdom. 'I wanted as much as possible for my party, and I hate high taxes – ridding over-taxed Indians of confiscatory taxes is one of our central planks.

'Of course, I expected the likes of you to search for ways to thwart our democratic right to contest elections, so I bet through countries with which we have double-tax agreements and where the proceeds of policy bets were untaxed, usually because they hadn't worked out whether the Upton Exchange was an exchange, a kind of casino, or something not yet provided for in tax law. And I instructed Anand to ensure that every cent was properly audited according to Indian tax law.'

Sudesh smiled, not because of his triumph over officialdom, but because of how much he expected policy bets to continue earning for the party, and how much more he expected Vaneshri's hi-tech plans to earn.

Liberty and Prosperity Party, Delhi, 2012

The party's website was designed not only to provide brief and detailed descriptions of policies, but also to encourage private donations.

Vaneshri arranged an online payment system whereby people could pay small amounts at no cost. One of her innovations was a tele-payment system, whereby people could make contributions by using their mobile phones. She arranged a system with phone companies whereby people could use their phones as if they were wallets. They could maintain surpluses in their accounts with which they could make any payment to any other mobile phone, any other phone account, or an account in a bank or other financial institutions.

There was also easy access to conveniently circulating mobile branch offices where supporters could make contributions, however small, and where they could support the party in kind by registering voters, canvassing and getting people to polling stations when the time came.

Upton added a significant amount of material to the website. Apart from locality and subject-specific Google options, there were links to the world's best websites on all relevant issues. Unlike other parties, the L&PP ran un-moderated blogs where anyone could debate any subject. With Upton's help Sudesh gained the right to have many important classical liberal texts freely downloadable from their website. It soon had a reputation of being the first port of call for anyone looking for information. Thousands of copies of the UK based International Policy Network's CD containing a 'mini library' of classical texts on the nature and benefits of liberty were distributed via party branches and internet orders.

All this was being put in place by Vaneshri's computer wizard, Jaival Garodia. Jai, as he was known, could install state-of-the-art computer technology, and establish the hub of a system that would eventually network wirelessly with millions of computers and cell phones across India.

InfoSwish offices, Hyderabad, 2012

'Your father wants to speak to you; he is calling you inside his cabin.' said Vaneshri's secretary.

'Oh, good,' thought Vaneshri, 'maybe he has an answer to my proposal.'

She entered her father's office and dropped into one of his armchairs, 'Hi Dad.'

Sabyasachi Palande picked up his desk phone and asked his secretary to bring coffee for two, then sat down beside his daughter.

'Hello, my dear. I have a serious matter to discuss with you.'

'What?' I hope Mummy isn't ill, she thought.

'This young man you've been seeing in Delhi; it is time to give him up. You are twenty-nine years old and need to think seriously about marriage. Kumar is unacceptable for a girl with your background.'

Vaneshri's heart sank.

'Dad, he worked for Ray Upton, the investment guru, and was the best financial trader Ray ever had. Now he is starting a political party.'

'Vaneshri, I know about his crackpot scheme to enter politics. It is another strike against him. He doesn't even have a university degree.'

'He is self-taught, Dad. He is always reading. He knows much more than most of the people who hang around our circles in Bengaluru and Hyderabad.'

'That may be so, but our family has a reputation in the market and we are expected to maintain our standards. Our business is not only about quality and price, it's also about maintaining the respect of our peers.'

'I know, Dad.'

'What I don't understand is why you have shown no interest in the genuinely eligible young men who have been introduced to you in the last few years, but instead have developed an unsuitable crush on this Mr Nobody.'

'Dad, he is going to be the Prime Minister of India.'

Her father laughed, 'Don't be ridiculous, girl, he'll burn his fingers and run back to that dubious investment cowboy who will probably soon be expelled from this country. You are the heiress of one of India's most successful companies.'

'I am nearly thirty years old. You can't be stopping me from seeing Sudesh.'

Sabyasachi looked at his daughter sadly. 'I know I have spoiled you, Vaneshri, you have always had everything you wanted, and I knew you would be stubborn about this. So, I am going to make you an offer.'

There was a knock on the door and Palande's secretary entered to place two Rosenthal china cups and a bodum of coffee on the table between them.

Sabyasachi continued after the secretary left, 'I have thought about the unsuitability of this young man, and I have thought about the proposal you made for me to finance your own company.

'I will provide the necessary funding for your Security company, Vaneshri, and let you break free from InfoSwish. I will give you full independence and control of your business.

'In exchange you must stop seeing Sudesh Kumar.'

Eighteen

Delhi, 2013

The Liberty and Prosperity Party's first goal was to achieve a foothold in India's national Parliament by fighting the 2013 elections.

The L&PP would contest all seven of the constituencies allocated to "the National Capital Territory of Delhi" for representatives to the Lok Sabha (lower house).

Their candidates would be competing with 136 others, sixty-three of them representing registered parties and the remainder running as independents. Such an abundance of candidates was a common scene in Indian politics. Usually all seven Delhi seats were shared by the INC (Indian National Congress) and the BJP (Bharatiya Janata Party).

During the weeks after his return, with the help of his libertarian advisors, Sudesh had persuaded six candidates to join him in his first campaign.

Sudesh's team worked at full steam. His marketing manager, Kaamini Upreti, employed a young and dynamic marketing company to work for the publicity and promotion of the L&PP. Designers set to work on leaflets, brochures and posters, a team of young innovative minds worked to create newspaper and TV ads.

Sudesh's press officer, Anil Gupta, kicked off with a press conference. It had not been an easy task to persuade representatives of the major national and local dailies and financial journals to attend the press conference. They had seen too many new parties appear on the scene only to fizzle out. Many small parties and independent candidates contested India's national elections, but few ever came close to winning a seat.

Press Conference, Delhi, 2013

The party's lawyer, Das Gupta, of Gupta, Singh & Associates, sat alongside one of the journalists, an old friend. He whispered, 'We lawyers call this sort of thing "the art of the losing case". This happens when you know there's no chance of winning but proceed because you want to make an important point.'

Sudesh strode to the platform facing the journalists. Behind him sat his six candidates. He confidently faced his audience, his only notes a small mind map on an index card.

'Our post-1992 reforms made India one of the great success stories of modern times,' he said. 'Instead of capitalising on our achievement and driving our reforms through to their logical free market conclusion we let the pace slacken. Instead of resisting the crazed orgy of interventionism that followed the 2008 subprime crisis, we joined it.'

As Sudesh spoke he made purposeful eye contact with each journalist so they felt that he was speaking to them personally.

'Research spanning more than thirty years shows that countries that offer economic freedom, prosper and ones with restrictions lose out. Prosperity and poverty are matters of choice not destiny.

'The Liberty and Prosperity Party has been formed because time has come for India to choose prosperity. We have detailed policies on every major issue. You can find these on our website or the DVDs in your media packs.

'For our first election, we are focussing on four main issues. First: welfare of the poor, second: end of corruption, third: privatisation and fourth, reduction in taxes.'

Sudesh smiled, 'Any questions?'

ॐ

The journalists stared at Sudesh. They had not thought any politician was capable of a short speech. The silence extended until it seemed that there would be no questions. Punita Banerjee of *India Finance* broke the silence. 'You appear to be confused, Mr Kumar. You favour free enterprise, yet your first priority is welfare!'

'Our long-term goal is to eliminate the need for welfare by replacing poverty with prosperity. However, until we are able to take full control of the Lok Sabha and introduce the necessary reforms, we intend to make use of India's IT technology to ensure that existing welfare money goes directly to intended beneficiaries. This can be done through smart card technology.

'At present most welfare is welfare for the well-to-do; it supports the bureaucracies who run the programmes.'

'Under our scheme,' he continued, 'the welfare budget will be credited to personalised cards with built-in fingerprint identification to prevent theft and fraud.

'The cards will be debit cards which allow the money to be used freely, as with pensions. Some of the funds will be earmarked for specific benefits such as education and health care.

'Instead of inefficient and wasteful government delivery, people will be empowered to buy what they need from freely competing suppliers. The Care Cards will double up to serve other official and private purposes.'

The journalists leaned forward, some interested others surprised. 'Privatisation is somewhat an outdated and a discredited system,' said Mahala Patel of the *Delhi Times*, 'It has no popular appeal, yet you elevate it to one of your main policies.'

'We expect that our concept of People's Privatisation will stand hugely popular when the public will see through the big facade of government ownership. The voters have been told that what belongs to government belongs to them: "public" schools, "public" transport, "public" hospitals. We will restore the family silver to the family, and revive the correct meaning of the word "public". The proceeds of the sale of government assets will be given directly to the people.'

Banerjee responded to this instantly, 'Your party's propaganda appears to be very materialistic, obsessed with economics,' she said.

'On the contrary, it's our adversaries who are obsessed with materialism,' replied Sudesh. 'We are concerned about liberty and direct grass-roots democracy. Our opponents are obsessed with regulating and redistributing wealth. They disguise an insatiable appetite for plundering wealth by hiding from their constituencies the fact that most of the citizens' hard-earned money finds refuge in their own pockets. They allow people to control non-material, personal choices regarding voting, marriage, the number of children they have and so on, but deny them freedom when it comes to simple material choices, like what to buy, from whom and on what terms.'

The press conference lasted for an hour, leaving some of the audience dismissive and some entertained. Howsoever, the journalists had received straight answers and had plenty to think and write about. Just as everyone was preparing to leave came another question.

'You speak persuasively about India becoming the world's richest country, but economic miracles like the Asian Tigers, post-war Germany and Mauritius are rare. They're recognised thanks to effective government interventions,' asserted Bibek Raju of the *Sunday Times*.

'The rise from destitution to prosperity in a generation,' responded Sudesh, 'in those countries is no "miracle". This is what happens when people are free – freer than elsewhere – to work naturally: produce and trade. And yes, prosperity is the result of effective policies, specifically those that liberate enterprising people and their customers and employees.'

'Why are you so concerned about freedom?' asked Rangarajan of public radio. 'We are a free country, the world's biggest democracy. Freedom is constitutionally guaranteed.'

'We say we're a free country,' said Sudesh, exuding confidence, 'yet we violate the rule of law constantly by endowing officialdom with discretionary power – that's the rule of man, not the rule of law. We violate the separation of powers by transferring law-making and adjudication functions from the legislature and the judiciary to an increasingly bloated and omnipresent executive. Every statute compromises personal liberty. In fact, that's the purpose of most laws. We override due process, civil liberties and natural justice by shifting the burden of proof to the accused, and imposing so-called "administrative penalties" instead of properly adjudicated fines in criminal courts. Our government schools misguide our youth by teaching them that control is freedom. It's funny that the government gets away with it.

'By the way, Mr Rangarajan, you're in public broadcasting. That's one of the misnomers to which I referred. To be frank, there is no such thing as "public" broadcasting. It's what the public doesn't want and something that politicians want. It's that for which no one is willing to pay, except looters using someone else's money.'

There was an audible intake of breath in the auditorium. Rangarajan smiled briefly then became uncharacteristically quiet, concentrating on the quality of his recording.

Punita Banerjee tried to consolidate the mood of scepticism.

'Why are you so anti-government? she asked. 'Everything you say insults millions of dedicated decent civil servants. You portray them as evil demons.'

'Quite the contrary, Ms Banerjee. No one is more on the side of the civil servants than the L&PP. We'll rescue them from being victims of the system. I'll give you an example.' Sudesh recalled his last-minute Christmas shopping experience in New York the significance of which suddenly dawned on him.

'Once I was shopping for gifts and greeting cards during New York's frenetic Christmas season. "Someday, isn't it?" I said to the lady at the till. "Yes", she agreed. "It's the best day we've had this year."'

'When I went to mail the cards at the Post Office I repeated the words to a clerk. "Someday, isn't it?" "Yes," she agreed, "It's the worst day of the year."'

'The point is,' Sudesh explained, 'that people in the private sector regard busy days as good days and people in government regard busy days as bad days. Nothing, absolutely nothing, can change that. It's an inherent feature of the system. Our policies will have all those decent diligent civil servants – the ones who really are civil and are servants – doing what they like doing in the private sector, where they will not only be paid but will be given due respect and become aware and proud of their true worth.'

Many thought, that this good looking young man with his clarity and integrity was unlikely to survive the political scene for long.

The Sheraton Hotel, New Delhi, 2013

Sudesh joined Vaneshri at her favourite South Indian restaurant. She hadn't visited him in Delhi for several weeks, and today had persuaded him to take a break from his campaign. She had something important to tell him.

He turned his attention to her and asked 'What's up?'

'Let me get to the point,' replied Vaneshri, 'Our relationship – the romantic part – cannot continue.'

'What's wrong?' he questioned.

'My dad,' she said. 'feels that we're not "socially compatible".'

'But he's never met me.'

Vaneshri shrugged. 'You know how it works, Sudesh. Dad is hung upon stupid issues like family background and caste. So, he thinks you are not the suitable guy for me.'

Sudesh looked at her for a long while. 'And since when have you begun acting against your choice and following your dad's orders?'

'Since he offered me a deal I can't reject. Sweetheart, he will give me all the financial backing I need, and cut me loose to do my own thing, on condition that I stop seeing you.'

'I see.'

'Do you? Do you understand that SecuriTech is my dream, like being Prime Minister is yours? I have been working towards launching my own hi-tech security business since I was twenty. It is the most important thing in the world for me.'

'Your dad understands that, even if I don't.'

'Don't look so sad, Sudesh. I hope you will continue to see me as a friend. Though I will truly regret the fact that we couldn't be together in life, but I have thought about this long and hard and in the end I have chosen my dream and the goodwill of my family. And you should understand it because if you had to choose between me and your dream, and your family, you would do the same.

Joint Meeting of Lawyers' Associations, Chennai, 2013

Das Gupta walked rapidly towards Sudesh through the milling crowds of lawyers. 'Bad news,' he whispered furtively. 'It's a disaster. There's an application before the High Court to declare the L&PP unlawful and its policies unconstitutional. I'm afraid, Sudesh, they have a strong case.'

'On what grounds?' asked Sudesh as his mind raced.

'Two. Firstly that your pro-market policies are unconstitutional because India is constituted as a socialist State, and secondly that your party is unlawful because it does not have socialism as one of its principles as required by the Act under which parties register. It's unlikely that anyone at the meeting today will have heard about it yet.'

❧

Sudesh had prepared well to address the legal community of Chennai. Mindful of their profession, he avoided economics and explained his party's understanding of and commitment to the Constitution, principles of good law, the rule of law, property rights, due process, natural justice and personal liberty.

After some general questions, Punita Banerjee, the journalist, fired her first salvo at Sudesh. 'Mr Kumar, have you read our Constitution?'

Sudesh was beginning to recognise Punita at a distance now, with her cloud of wild black hair and petite frame.

'Of course.'

'Oh, really?' Punita smirked. 'Then you must have skipped the pivotal provision, the very first sentence, the Preamble. And many other provisions, including the whole of Part IV. For your information the Preamble reads "We, the people of India, having solemnly resolved to constitute India into a ... socialist ... republic ... give to ourselves this Constitution..."'

The young lawyers leaned forward, intrigued by the unexpected line of questioning.

The Madras Bar Association, formed in 1862, was one of India's oldest and most distinguished association of lawyers. Some of its members had been Ministers of State; one had been a central government minister. Another host organisation was the Madras High Court Advocates Association. In 2009, it had been at the centre of a scandal in which lawyers had behaved, according to the Supreme Court, 'as hooligans and miscreants' when they attacked the leader of the BJP in the court house and boycotted court proceedings. Sudesh knew that the meeting would not be dull.

'Our entire Constitution,' Punita continued, 'echoes our collective commitment to socialism, Mr Kumar. Clause 36, for instance, requires the government to provide everyone with an adequate means of livelihood, and to ensure that ownership and control of our material resources – all of them – serve the common good. In other words, that they should be nationalised, not privatised. According to section 38, the government has to promote equality, in other words, socialism. Given your policies, Mr Kumar, surely we must conclude that you cannot be familiar with the Constitution.'

'You are mistaken, Ms Banerjee. I have read carefully through the three hundred and ninety-five Articles, twenty-two Parts, twelve Schedules and ninety-four Amendments of India's Constitution, a total of nearly 1,20,000 words. It is the world's longest Constitution.'

Laughter ensued and the lawyers settled back to enjoy the debate.

'Mr Kumar, your party and your policies are unconstitutional.'

Sudesh often relied on humour to relax his audience. Now, he hoped it would help him. 'Brilliant exposition, Ms Banerjee, brilliant,' exclaimed Sudesh with a disarming smile. 'Are you a socialist?'

'Yes, of course.'

'Good. Please swear before the lawyers here present that you will permit your own nationalisation and redistribution once we come to power.'

As the laughter subsided, she persevered. 'Please answer my question.'

'Oh yes, are we constitutional? We are a lawfully registered political party.'

Sudesh wondered why she pursued this line of questioning.

Punita's moment had arrived; her face wore a self-satisfied expression and there would be no more laughter.

'Apart from the fact that you do not seem to realise it would be unconstitutional to implement your policies, there's something more fundamental you don't yet know. It is my pleasure to inform you that as we speak a High Court order is being sought to have your party deregistered. The Election Commission registered you erroneously under the Representation of the People Act. It should have refused registration just as it refused to register the Swatantra Party during the late 1990s because it never had socialism as one of its principles.

'The fact is that you will not be in this election, nor in any other election, not with your policies.'

There was an audible gasp from the audience.

Sudesh had his back to the wall.

Gurgaon, South of Delhi, 2013

Vijay Malhotra did not like moving in crowded public places. The armoured limousine in which he travelled had thick, tinted windows, constructed from blackened steel. The outside view was relayed to Vijay from the cameras set into the roof that provided images on his laptop and phone and the online screens in the car.

A combination of sensors and cameras gave the driver a 360 degree view of surrounding traffic. Between the back and front seats was more reinforced steel.

Despite such measures for security, Vijay Malhotra seldom left his home office that he felt was safer than his car. Encased in reinforced concrete that could have survived Hiroshima, it would have taken the Indian army weeks to get him out. During this time he would have had food to spare. His three-year supply of canned goods meant that whilst he may have become bored he would not have starved. Vijay was aware that medieval castles had often fallen as a result of starvation rather than through a breach of defences.

Malhotra was filthy rich. He had no desire for people to admire him. He detested the company of weak men.

He reserved his respect for the military powers of the world. He admired the American military though he pitied their need to put up with weak politicians and a liberal press. He approved of the Russian military too, they had lesser capabilities nowadays but a better attitude than the Americans. Even the Muslims had some spunk, he thought.

People approached him to carry out assassinations. He was well known in the Middle East where he had many clients. He did not meet people in person to discuss business for that would be dangerous. He had skilled men working for him who communicated on his behalf through encrypted messages.

His survival in India was easy. Ample money was showered on corrupt policemen and lawyers to keep trials and arrests at bay. He paid his taxes on time and saved himself the trouble of being scrutinised by the government.

Malhotra trusted his wife as much as he trusted anyone. She was the only person who handled the purchase and preparation of his food. She was pretty, though not very clever and derived immense pleasure in flaunting her husband's wealth.

She was subjected to constant monitoring and all her movements and interactions were tracked.

The entire staff that worked under Malhotra was subjected to psychological scrutiny as well as lie detection checks. The disloyal members were tortured and then executed. It had now been many years that Malhotra enjoyed a disciplined and loyal workforce.

Despite these measures Malhotra chose to remain a paranoid for he felt that 'only a paranoid could survive in his world'.

Malhotra was legendary in the security industry well beyond the criminal underground. Not much detail was known about his security systems, except that he was probably the world's most effectively protected individual. An article in *Security Magazine* called him 'Mr Safe'. He had employed or consulted the industry's top experts including a former Director of Homeland Security from the USA, a German Professor Emeritus of Security Studies, leading personal protection firms, and a host of security technology geeks. His home and office were 'as impenetrable as Fort Knox' according to the article.

Joint Meeting of Lawyers' Associations, Chennai, 2013

Sudesh had to think on his feet. There would be no time to consult with Das Gupta or to re-read sections of the Constitution. The hours he had spent studying it had to give him the answers he needed.

'Ms Banerjee, we are aware of the Commission's refusal to register Mr Raju's party in 1996. More importantly, we know that our country's great leaders, like Nehru and Ambedkar, considered entrenching socialism in the Constitution because they were socialists, but they decided not to because it would be anti-democratic. It would curtail political freedom.'

'That's irrelevant, it's there now, introduced by Nehru's daughter, Indira Gandhi, when she served the country as Prime Minister.'

'Curiously,' Sudesh responded, 'the addition of socialism to the Preamble might itself be unconstitutional. During the 1975 State of Emergency Indira Gandhi pushed through a raft of socialist amendments, including the addition of socialism to the Preamble.'

'It's constitutional; she had a two-thirds majority.'

'That's not the point. The amendments may be unconstitutional,' argued Sudesh, 'not because of insufficient votes – there were enough – but because the Supreme Court ruled three years before that the Preamble was part of the Constitution's "basic structure" and therefore not subject to amendment.'

'Yes, but her successor and son, Rajiv Gandhi, amended the Representation of the People Act in 1989 to require all political parties to include socialism in their party platforms. That,' proclaimed Punita triumphantly, 'is your nemesis.'

'There are few people,' he said with sincerity, 'more reluctant than I to amend our Constitution, but if my party or policies are considered unconstitutional by the courts, we will have to get the Preamble restored to democratic neutrality and have that obviously anti-democratic requirement removed from the Act. If we claim to be the world's biggest democracy we have to start by being a democracy.'

'How will you do that without a two-thirds majority, in fact with no votes at all, considering that you won't be contesting the election?'

The Chair invited others to ask questions, but it was decided by general consent to let the heated debate continue.

'Further,' Sudesh continued, 'the courts have not found that the single word, "socialist", precludes pro-market policies.'

'Oh, come on,' Punita interrupted, 'what about all the other provisions?'

'Okay, let's examine supposedly socialistic provisions beyond the Preamble. Under section 38 the government must strive to promote welfare by securing a social order in which social, economic and political justice governs national life. The L&PP is for welfare. That's why it wants policies that ensure prosperity. And we are for justice, by which we mean the right of consenting adults to interact freely in all spheres of life.'

'You mean the right of the rich to exploit the poor, and to destroy the environment …?'

'And what about the State's constitutional duty to promote income equality?'

'That's in sub-section two,' Sudesh pointed out. 'The government must minimise specified forms of inequality, not all inequality. We agree with that. That's why we'll scrap interventionist policies, such as licensing laws, that impact disproportionately on the poor. More equality and less poverty will be the outcome of our policies.'

The Chairperson was delighted by the increasingly sophisticated encounter. The lawyers regarded this as the most successful of their series of meetings with politicians. At this point he made an unusual suggestion. They, as lawyers, would vote at the end of the meeting on the chances of Sudesh surviving the High Court challenge. The debate continued, with Sudesh arguing that every socialistic provision referred to ends, not means, and that L&PP's policies were the best for achieving those ends. Punita, whom the Chair had invited to join them at the main table, countered by pointing to the inescapable tenor of the Constitution, the explicit Preamble, the unambiguous Act, and India's universally recognised anti-colonial and socialistic legacy.

'Is that not just another way of saying you want to leave the poor at the mercy of the rich?' Punita asked pointedly when Sudesh said he was for liberty.

'Absolutely not. I would never leave the poor at the mercy of the rich. There's no such thing; the rich have no mercy.' A few anti-business lawyers applauded. 'At least that's what government policy should assume. I want to subject the rich to the merciless market where suppliers and employers get hired and fired on a daily basis by merciless consumers and workers.'

Sudesh returned to the kind of jurisprudential point that clearly impressed his audience. 'In Nakara versus the Union of India,' he explained, 'the Supreme Court held that the principle aim of socialism is to reduce inequality of income, status and standards of life, and to provide a decent living. In the Samantha case, the court declared that the purpose of socialism is to establish an egalitarian order through Rule of Law. In the Kesavananda case the Preamble was found not to be a binding provision, but merely a guide to interpreting ambiguous provisions. Other cases ruled that the purpose of socialism is social justice, a fair distribution of material resources, and an end to poverty, ignorance, disease and inequality of opportunity. We are for all that, Ms Banerjee.'

Voting at the end of the meeting was informal, by a show of hands. By this time constitutional specialists were admitting to themselves that Sudesh seemed very thorough with the Constitution. Nevertheless, the law was clear and most of those present there agreed that the L&PP would and should be deregistered. 'That,' wrote Punita the next day, 'can be regarded as conclusive. It marks the end of Sudesh's political career before it has started.'

Nineteen

L&PP office, New Delhi, November 2013

Sudesh and his team, glued to the television screens, waited in their boardroom for first results of the election. The long hours of campaigning were over. There was a lot of commotion around as Sudesh's party sat, analysing the day and attempting to predict results. Electronic voting machines had made the counting process speedy; however, for Sudesh and his party, it seemed to be taking too long.

Fortunately for the L&PP, the High Court judges had not agreed with the Chennai lawyers. They found in a series of urgent resource-depleting applications and counter-applications brilliantly orchestrated by L&PP's legal advisor the provision in the Representation of the People Act making socialism obligatory was unconstitutional, that the Preamble was indicative, not binding, and that India was a modern democracy with the freedom of political organisation and expression. The L&PP was still in the running for the election.

Our chances are so small, thought Sudesh. Those who believe in true freedom are a tiny minority. So he had been told and he knew it was true. If the L&PP didn't win any seats they would have to give up. He would not only have disappointed Upton but all the people in this room. They had trusted him and his new party to break the mould. For months they had worked round the clock. It would be the death of their dream.

'Look,' exclaimed Shakti, 'the Delhi results are coming in.' As the announcer listed the outcomes for the various constituencies, the pictures of the winning candidates appeared on the screen: New Delhi: BJP, South Delhi: INC; Outer Delhi: INC; East Delhi: L&PP.

London, November 2013

'With great pleasure we welcome Mr Ray Upton to the board of Asset Finance International.'

The ten conservatively suited men and women around the table clapped, smiling at Ray.

'Ray has an interesting proposition for us,' said Damian Knight.

'Thank you, Damian. I look forward to working with AFI.

'For those not aware of our products, they involve betting on government performance. These are my ideas on future strategy:

'At the turn of the century, with the rise of globalisation the tendency of investors to focus on countries with open economic policies became increasingly marked. But since the financial collapse of 2008, it has become difficult to find attractive markets. As you know, the response of western governments to the crisis has massively increased spending, nationalisation and regulation, particularly of financial markets.'

Heads nodded.

'You may be familiar with a book by Ayn Rand called *Atlas Shrugged*?'

People nodded again in positive.

'The top entrepreneurs and executives, in the book, resist exploitation by the government.'

'That's right,' said Ann Ruthers, one of the two women on the board, 'they all go on strike, don't they, and the USA collapses?

They go to a settlement in the mountains – John Galt was the leader – wasn't it called Galt's Gulch?'

'What does that have to do with us, Ray?' asked Damian.

'What I suggest, ladies and gentlemen, is that we do the same.'

'What,' said Ruthers, 'leave all this and go to the mountains?'

'No' replied Ray Upton 'leave all this and go to India.'

L&PP Headquarters, New Delhi, November 2013

The room was in an uproar. Of the seven Delhi constituencies the L&PP had won only East Delhi, Sudesh's constituency, by a tiny margin, but that was enough.

Shalini congratulated everyone, some danced on the table, Sudesh spun Shakti around in the air and everyone cheered together loudly.

Shakti, rejoicing and breathless, headed for the kitchen and returned with a tray of glasses and two bottles of Moët. She had them on ice, 'just in case.'

Sudesh raised a toast.

'To our first victory,' he said. 'Thank you for your hard work and dedication. This is only the beginning but it proves that we can achieve the "impossible." This is our first milestone on the long journey of freedom and prosperity that India is bound to witness in the near future. Cheers – to India!'

Sivananda Kutir, Uttarkashi, November 2013

In the shadow of the great mountains, life was simple and disciplined. The daily routine included *satsang* (meditation); *karma yoga* (which entailed the cleaning and general care of the Ashram), *aasana* (exercise) classes, and discourse sessions between April and November when the visitors came.

Now that Chanda was a senior teacher at the Ashram she undertook advanced teacher training primarily in satsang and aasanas. Her days were rigorous yet balanced, and most of the time she felt at peace.

As she watched the holy Ganges flowing downstream, her thoughts drifted to Janardan.

During his last visit he had talked to her about the war. He was based at the Siachen glacier since 1992 and had described the great beauty of his surroundings. He had spoken at length about the two contrasting situations that he encountered there. He experienced serenity and closeness to god when he stood on watch, while the horrors of violent death and destruction haunted him during the short periods of conflict.

'The politics of power is so complex,' he had said. 'I know that the Pakistanis on the other side of the border are similar to me. We grew up poor but ascended the social ladder because of this job. We didn't join the army because we believed in war.'

Chanda had said nothing.

'We didn't believe in anything then. Now, over the years I have learnt that there are no easy solutions of the Kashmir issue. Meanwhile, terrorism is on the rise, and the possibility of a nuclear war is growing. And there is nothing we, high up in the mountains, can do about it.'

Chanda knew that Janardan would be back. He had been visiting her regularly for nearly twenty years. Over those years they had become close and she had learned to love and trust him. Often they had sat together, his arm around her, and she had felt her heart thudding as she longed for him to kiss her. But he never did, and she could not understand why.

She knew that he did not hold that terrible night in the Imperial Hotel against her. She knew he wasn't married and that he cared deeply for her. She was thirty-one and he must be over forty now. What was standing in his way, she couldn't gauge.

London, November 2013

'India! Why India?' Damian Knight of Asset Financial International asked Ray.

'I have an inside track there. You may have read the article in this month's *Economist* about Sudesh Kumar, the budding political star who has just been elected to the Indian Parliament. The extraordinary thing about Kumar is that, despite representing a new party with a radical *laissez faire* agenda, he has managed to win a Delhi seat in the national government. Furthermore, for ten years he worked for me, I trained him.'

Knight raised his eyebrows.

Ray continued, 'It may take a few more years, but I predict that Kumar will exert a great influence on India's economy. The country has been growing for the past two decades, but still has a huge poverty problem, as well as its on-off war with Pakistan. India doesn't want to follow the lead of the struggling economies of North America and Europe, or China for that matter. It is looking for different solutions.

'Kumar has got the same appeal as Barack Obama had when he was elected in 2008. He is an outstanding communicator and comes across as honest and caring. He has a great team and adequate funds.

'Plus he has a couple of advantages over Obama: first, he understands what makes an economy grow, and second, India is lesser developed than the USA. This gives India an opportunity to achieve explosive growth from a low base.

'In *Atlas Shrugged* the innovators and entrepreneurs went to Galt's Gulch to set themselves free of government intervention. Going to India is more realistic. It has huge ready-made markets and cutting-edge high-tech industry.'

'And the connection to our corporation?'

'Twofold: lucrative opportunities will arise from the economic reforms, and I will be in the best position to spot them. Second, I suggest you consider moving your businesses, lock, stock and barrel, to India where there will be low taxes and no political interference. I am relocating now.'

'But I don't expect you to act immediately on the basis of my crystal-ball-prediction. I just ask you to watch the markets and the financial pages, and don't take too long. The sooner you come the bigger the opportunities.'

'We'll see' said the Chairman. His meaning was clear, but he carried on. 'One swallow doesn't make a summer. I know India. Like America, it has deeply entrenched parties with unassailable national structures and loyalties, apart from an inconsequential small floating vote. I'll eat my hat – really, I mean it, we'll have a hat-eating party – if this character, whatever his name, ever amounts to more than an obscure loner in Parliament for more than one opportunistic term.'

Parliament, December 2013

As the eye-recognition software registered Sudesh's identity the security door slid silently open, allowing him into the parliamentary complex.

He was early. He wanted to savour this moment, of which he had dreamt since he was seven years old.

As he headed towards the main entrance he gazed up at the twice life-size bronze statue of Gandhi, seated cross-legged in contemplation. He felt as if the Mahatma was sharing his elation, along with the frangipanis covered in white and yellow blooms, and the great leafy trees that spread their shade around.

Sudesh turned from the statue and gardens to look at the large circular Parliamentary building, designed by Baker and Luytens and completed in 1927. Constructed of russet and gold sandstone and encircled by stately columns, Sudesh found it magnificent.

He entered the giant main door and made his way upstairs to the imposing, beautifully proportioned colonnade that encircled the upper floor, and provided the link between the Lok Sabha (Lower House) and the Rajya Sabha (Upper House). As he gazed across the verdant gardens towards New Delhi, he wondered at the splendid vision of the architects and the strenuous labour of the working men who hewed the giant blocks of sandstone, and transported them from Rajasthan. Together they had built this grand complex.

And he thought about the greedy, self-aggrandising men who clustered in its chambers now, making lofty speeches about the well being of the citizens whilst enriching themselves at their expense.

Sudesh's mood darkened. The government that is housed here, he thought, is like a cancer in India's gut. A cancer that spreads its cells through the country's blood stream, to settle and grow unchecked in states, cities, towns and villages, draining the nation's vitality.

He entered the semicircular chamber of the Lok Sabha and looked for his seat. He knew that the Speaker's seat was in the centre front, and the ruling alliance would be to the Speaker's right. In the front row would be the Prime Minister and his Cabinet members, in the back row the newcomers to Parliament, the backbenchers. To the Speaker's left the Opposition would be in a similar order of seating.

Despite being a newcomer, as the leader of his Party Sudesh would be seated in the front left row, with other Opposition leaders.

The chamber was nearly empty. A handful of other MPs in their seats, lowered their heads over papers and talked softly with each other.

Sudesh walked across the thick, springy bottle green carpet and took his numbered place in a blue upholstered chair with carved wooden arms.

As he gazed up at the domed ceiling, admiring its perforated stone work he set upon himself the task of treating the cancer of over-regulation and corruption. He wanted to bring back the Golden Bird.

The difficulty, he thought, is that the treatment for cancer sometimes nearly kills before it cures.

A Penthouse in Hyderabad, February 2014

Lanco Hills Towers was the world's highest residential tower and Vaneshri had chosen to stay right at the top. The asymmetrical building was set in a parkland with jogging tracks, outdoor and indoor pools and a cutting edge gymnasium. Not choosing to use any of these facilities; she simply preferred to enjoy the view.

Smog levels being low, her eyes saw for miles through her windows. As she admired the outside view, many thoughts about her new business, SecuriTech, sprung to mind. 'Technology to Aid Criminal Assassination' was what she wanted to keep as her company's slogan, but her father suggested it was too harsh. He advised her to go for something mild yet catchy like 'Bid Farewell to Crime through Technology'. The latter slogan had received a higher approval rating.

Vaneshri intended to market her products aggressively, catering to both the public and private sector. She was confident about finding clients through her father's reference and influence. She knew everyone needed high-end security measures to counter sophisticated crime syndicates. Vaneshri made the initial pitch to decision-makers, and her staff followed up. Her secretary set up appointments in all the major cities, focussing on potential targets of terrorism: major hotels, train stations and airports, embassies and legislatures. She also had National Intelligence and the army on her mind.

She kept her schedule tightly packed, flying from one city to another in very short intervals leaving herself no scope and time to miss Sudesh.

Flames, GK–II M-block market, Delhi, March 2014

'It happens every five years, naïve dreamers like Sudesh Kumar try to throw a spanner in the works' said Ashok to Hitesh over a drink at Flames, a favourite haunt of parliamentarians.

'You are right. We have a good system that has been working well for many years,' said Hitesh.

Ashok nodded and drank sparingly from a glass of cognac.

'What a wonderful thing education is!' added Hitesh, smiling. 'We can help these new boys to grow mature into the system. They will soon learn what they can and cannot do.' Hitesh shook his head cheerfully as he spoke.

Their conversation stopped as Sudesh walked into the bar with another young MP.

'Come and join us,' said Ashok. He was a tall imposing man with strong, noble features. 'We were talking about your ideas of welfare, Mr Kumar. Don't you think you are going too far?'

Silence spread across the bar. Ashok Mahajan was respected and feared.

'I don't think so,' said the younger man, 'I think my proposal will deliver better welfare at a very small cost.'

'So you think all our government welfare agencies should be closed down?'

'That's right,' said Sudesh. 'I am suggesting we replace them with community-based organisations which identify and allocate welfare money to people in need. That will entitle the poor to spend the money as they wish, using a smart-card.'

Hitesh snorted, and Ashok walked out as his phone buzzed.

'How did you reach me?' asked Ashok.

'Is this a secure line?' asked his caller.

'No. I'll call you back in ten minutes.' Ashok returned to the discussion.

'I am interested in knowing how you came to such a position?'

'There are many ways of doing that,' said Sudesh. 'Foremost, by getting rid of the bloated bureaucracy we could curtail the budget by eighty percent, and lower taxes accordingly. Alternatively, we could maintain the present budget and put the extra eighty percent into the hands of the poor, instead of lining the pockets of the wealthy and the corrupt.'

'Market fundamentalist, aren't we?'

'Certainly,' Sudesh said feeling a little anxious, 'How can I not be in this day and age?'

'Look, we all know that it's important to keep the markets happy, and maintain macro-economic fundamentals,' Sudesh nodded and Ashok glanced around, noting the confused expressions of the bystanders. He continued, 'But that doesn't mean we should take things to extremes. Why change a system that is working? Even if the system is not perfect? Surely moderation is the rule!'

'Not necessarily,' said Sudesh.

'In terms of what you are saying,' added Ashok Mahajan smoothly, 'there are obviously many ways in which the present system can be improved.' He continued, 'Yet it is a good system overall. Intelligent people understand that a level of corruption, though we cannot agree with it, sometimes makes things work that would otherwise not happen at all.'

❦

'Sorry' Ashok spoke on the phone as he climbed into his car, 'What did you want to tell me?'

'We have been told by the Department of Welfare that the ten billion rupee project has been approved.' 'Well, that is good news.'

'Your commission is in your off shore account, and there will be more. The contractor we've secured is masterful. It's great to see what can be achieved with low grade concrete,' the speaker chuckled. 'The dam will last for ten years before problems begin.'

'And how could we have possibly predicted that they would? There could be an earth movement or something.'

'That's right, Ashok.'

'Don't use my name.'

'Sorry. I'll try to remember.'

'What else have you got in the pipeline?'

'We want to extend the orphan children programme. That's going well. The cost of running the programme absorbs about fifty percent of that revenue, our commission comes in at about twenty-five percent, and the remaining twenty-five percent that goes to the orphans still generates positive publicity.'

'Good, good. We mustn't get greedy.' said Mahajan.

'Thanks, my friend. Sorry to keep you waiting but I had to speak to one of the new young MPs who could be dangerous to the cause. I need to befriend him, and neutralise him, if you know what I mean.'

The caller suddenly spoke in an animated tone, 'We can neutralise him anytime you like, Ashok. Sorry for using your name! Like that last guy we did.'

Ashok closed his eyes, 'How many times have I told you never to mention that. Ever.'

New Delhi, March 2014

Sudesh entered the government building breathing like a horse that had just finished galloping twenty miles.

'I must admit the way you took on Ashok was impressive, Sudesh,' said his companion, rushing to keep up with him. 'He's one of the grand old men of the Lok Sabha. And he plays hardball, perhaps you should be careful!'

Sudesh was still breathing fast.

'Look. I believe in tolerance and giving everyone his space.' His voice was higher and louder than usual. 'But when you encounter absolute evil, you have to stamp it out.'

'Absolute evil, Sudesh, what kind of a Hindu are you? It's another part of the elephant, you know the story.'

Sudesh didn't look at his companion; he spoke instead to the rapidly passing wall. 'There are parts of elephants and then there are centres of pure vested interest that condemn people to decades of poverty. And that I won't stand.'

'You can't beat the system, Sudesh.'

'Then I'll die in the attempt,' said Sudesh disappearing down the corridor.

SecuriTech Showroom, Delhi, March 2014

Madhumati walked into Vaneshri's showroom. It looked like the inside of a space-ship, courtesy of Bollywood. 'Vaneshri, it is so good to see you again. You look great!'

'Hi Madhu, how can I help you?'

'I'm interested in everything, show me around.'

Vaneshri's showroom was full of high tech gadgets and Madhumati was like a child in a toyshop. 'Look at these night vision goggles with an in-built camera,' said Vaneshri explaining, 'they allow you to see and take photographs in darkness. They use an image intensifier to convert weak light to visible light. Like most night vision goggles they display a green image, because the peak sensitivity of human colour vision is around 530 nm.'

The CBI agent nodded.

'How about these fake prints. They can fool expensive biometric security systems. Researchers in Japan tricked a high security system by using fake fingerprints lifted from a gelatine mould.'

'Really? That could be useful.' 'Would you use those in the special branch?' asked Vaneshri curiously.

'Sure, we spies make use of all kinds of tricks,' Madhu smiled.

'Okay, well how about this wrist mounted dart gun? You see it's so tiny it is easily hidden beneath a shirt sleeve.'

'Reminds me of James Bond.'

'Yes. Our experts derive some ideas from Bond movies. For example, these ground-based robot surveillance cameras,' Vaneshri pointed to the other side of the room, 'or the low frequency bleeper that attracts sharks to targets in the water.'

'How does that work?'

'In nature, sharks are attracted to the low frequencies given off by dying creatures. This simulates the frequencies.'

'I'll take a couple of those, as well as the fake print kit.'

Vaneshri looked at Madhu who spoke furtively, 'Ask me no questions and I shall tell you no lies.'

'Okay,' assured Vaneshri, 'Cool. And lastly, more defensive and definitely not pocket size, this 2m high, super-powered electron magnet. No bullets will get past this without being attracted to the magnet.'

'Very useful if you expect a location to get attacked.'

'I see.'

Sivananda Kutir, Uttarkashi, March 2014

By the time Janardan arrived at the Ashram, he had made up his mind.

'Today is a special day' he said, 'And I would like to take you out for dinner.'

Chanda smiled, 'It is always special for me when you visit. Is there anything more special today?'

'Yes,' said the soldier. 'I will be telling you soon.'

They walked through the village, mesmerised by each other's company and the cool breeze.

They went into a small restaurant and ordered vegetarian delicacies and caught up on some news on television that was kept at a corner. There was a companionable silence, then, as Chanda finished eating she looked up and asked 'So, what is your special news?'

He looked at her with serious intention, 'I have been thinking about this for a long time, Chanda, and now I have finally decided. Over the years of my visits I have grown fond of you to the extent of loving you.' As he spoke, he took her hand and she looked down, blushing.

'Earlier, I did not ask you to marry me because I was stationed at the front, and thought it would be too dangerous for you to stay with me there. My job would spare me with very little time for you.' She looked up as he continued 'I also knew that you were happy at Sivananda Kutir. But now,' he paused a little, 'I know that you also love me, and I wondered, if I bought a small house in this village, would you become my wife?' She tried speaking, but he rushed on, 'I know we would still not see more of each other than we do now, but you could live in the house and still work at the Ashram, and when I can get away from the front we could be together.'

Chanda's heart overflowed with emotion. 'I would love to be your wife. How soon do you think we can get married?'

The Palande residence, Hyderabad, April 2014

Shalini and Sabyasachi Palande welcomed the Singhs into their palatial reception room.

'Nanek, it is good to see you again. Madhumati you look beautiful as ever. I always wonder how you keep in such good shape.'

Madhumati smiled as she kissed Shalini on her cheeks.

'She works out,' said Nanek. 'She has spent hours working out rigorously ever since she joined the police force. She can run twice as fast and twice as far as I can.' The Chief Superintendent patted his stomach.

'I think we all have a bit of that,' said Palande, checking his flat stomach smugly. 'How are my daughter's products working for you?'

'Excellent,' said Nanek, 'Many of her innovative gadgets are well suited to Madhu's line of work.'

'I always said we could change the world with good people and technology.'

Nanek smiled, 'And the next person to help in that capacity will be Sudesh Kumar.'

Palande sat up straight.

'You've heard of him, no doubt?' said Nanek, noticing Palande's reaction. Now, however, the IT chief was relaxing back.

'I have,' he said cautiously, 'but perhaps not in quite the same context.'

At this juncture the servant discreetly drew their attention to the drinks table, and the small party placed their orders.

'Well, as you probably know,' continued Nanek, 'Kumar is one of us.'

'An aristocrat?'

'No, Saby,' the other man said patiently. 'An incorruptible, honest man.'

'Even rarer,' said Sabyasachi dryly.

'I have known him since he was a teenager. We used his ideas for that Crime Stop system we ran using your software. He also won an award for providing crucial inputs leading to arrests and captures.'

'Did he? That's redeeming.'

'Redeeming?'

'Never mind, please continue.'

'Well,' said Nanek. 'He was elected to the Lok Sabha last year, as the leader of his own political party, and he has been causing a stir. He is a gifted public speaker and is shaking up Parliament with incisive questions and innovative ideas. The poor trust him because he is promoting a first-rate plan to improve welfare and he comes from a poor village, and the rich people like him because he speaks the language of free market economics and property rights.'

'Really?'

'Yes, I am advising everyone to support Sudesh Kumar in every way they can. India hasn't seen anything like this since Gandhi.'

'Well, all I can say for now is that ... I should keep myself more updated about the country's politics.'

'What?' Nanek looked confused.

'I think I may have misjudged the man.'

Washington DC, April 2014

Katy Chan was meeting with Goldman Sachs' lobbyist, David Kaplan, at Willard Hotel in Pennsylvania Avenue.

'We are perhaps in for a crisis.'

'What's the problem?'

'Congressman Henderson is supporting a new law forbidding the use of petrol powered cars on interstate highways. We've been told that punters are already betting on the Upton Exchange that the law will not be passed. The UE has a powerful effect on public opinion, so now there is less chance for the Bill to pass.

'Congressman Henderson wants to know what can be done to influence the Exchange. It's my job as his aide to provide answers, but I don't understand how the exchange works. Can you explain it to me?'

'Sure,' said David, 'in essence the UE is a gigantic, international betting agency. Punters bet on whether or not a law will succeed in its purpose, whether it will cost more than anticipated and whether it will deliver its promised outcomes.'

'But surely it is difficult to measure the consequences of a policy?' said Katy.

'True. But where the government has published a regulatory impact assessment or cost benefit analysis, then it's simple. All Upton's analysts need to do is see whether the outcomes are as predicted. Alternatively, a cost benefit analysis is undertaken by a top accounting company, working according to published rules and procedure.'

'And a figure is produced estimating how much the legislation has benefited or cost the country?'

'Exactly.'

'Okay,' said Katy, 'I get the picture, but how does Upton make money, regardless of whether or not the policy succeeds?'

'He takes a betting fee just like any other gambling or betting service.'

'From what you are saying, David, I assume there is nothing we can do to influence the exchange with respect to our policy?'

'Nothing at all.'

Parliament, New Delhi, May 2014

Sudesh Kumar rose to address the house. He made an effort to overcome the feeling of anxiety that sprung in his veins before making his maiden speech.

'Honourable Speaker and members, Indian technology competes with the best in the world.

'We have developed a rope from carbon atoms so thin it can hardly be seen, yet strong enough to suspend a person. We have invented paint that repels dirt and graffiti. One day it will be possible to assemble anything from its component molecules or even from its atoms.

'You may think this might sound good in science fiction,' his eyes scanned the faces of those on his left and right, for once attentive and quiet, 'but it is not merely restricted to fiction. Such technology is available in India, right now.'

There was a murmur of interest.

'Yes, fellow brothers, we have the technology to transform a particular product into different products. We can do such transformation in unlimited quantities. Millions of tonnes can be changed.

'Unfortunately, we have many laws that make this harder to accomplish, that drastically reduce the number of goods that can be changed and transformed.'

The journalists in the press box made rigorous notes. His warm, deep voice, persuasive manner of speech and confident body language made people listen.

'I am now going to reveal the secret of how this technology works. Every year India sends out thousands of freighters with millions of surplus products. And every year the same cargo ships return with millions of different products our country needs and wants.

'Every year millions of items are transformed from the goods of which India has a surplus stock to products we lack in. This extraordinary process is called "trade".'

'How strange it is then that we put up tariff barriers, impose quotas and introduce customs and excise restrictions to stop this profitable transformation.

'When we attempt to protect our industries we have the opposite effect. We force our citizens to buy items made locally, instead of cheaper better quality imports; and we prevent foreigners from buying the local products they seek and this way we prevent them from supplying us with foreign exchange.

'Members of the House, all Indians suffer losses from trade barriers, but those who suffer the most are the poor, it is they who are most affected by the inflation.

'I propose that all taxes and tariffs on trade are eliminated now, and that all quotas on trade are abolished forthwith.'

Sudesh sat down.

The media reporter turned to a fellow besides him, 'Well that woke them up, something new for a change.'

'Yes,' replied his colleague, 'refreshing.'

Of all the new MPs this was the one they would remember.

Twenty

A private function room, Sheraton Hotel, Delhi, March 2016

The room buzzed with noise. Waiters struggled to find space to move between the huge gathering of Delhi's political and social elite and media.

'The problem with Kumar's policies is that they are dressed up for the poor, but would only benefit the rich,' said Punita Banerjee.

'What benefit,' she continued loudly, 'do his policies have for the slum-dweller whose shack has been demolished to make way for property developers?'

'I want him to have tradable title to his house,' said Sudesh, but his voice was not heard.

'What benefit,' added Punita 'does a man who transports saris from place to place in Delhi gain from toll roads?'

'Faster transit, and hence better sales,' said Sudesh, but no one cared to lend an ear.

Eventually, she finished holding forth and Sudesh addressed her directly, 'If my memory serves me right you are Punita Banerjee, columnist, *India Finance?*'

'Yes, that's me.'

'I remember you from my campaign days. You have a poor opinion of my policies.'

Punita Banerjee was born into a family of teachers. When she asked "why" of things, the answer was never 'because I said so.' Detailed explanations followed every question. And that was the way she liked it.

Punita's father taught maths and her mother English literature. They both favoured socialism and throughout her growing years the inequalities of Indian society were constantly drawn to Punita's attention.

She reached the end of her degree in journalism with a fierce desire to fight poverty, inequality and injustice. Like Sudesh she wanted to solve problems of the world. But unlike him she believed government was not the problem, but the solution.

A small airstrip, West of Delhi, May 2016

Vasu approached the unused airfield at top speed. As his car screeched to a halt four lethargic guards stumbled to attention.

They knew Vasu and so opened the gate immediately. He slipped in through the side gate and ran to his Lear jet, jumping into the cockpit clutching only a small case and a copy of *Nuclear Terrorism* by Graham Allison.

He was glad that he had learned to fly. He hadn't put in the necessary hours to stay in practice, but he knew what he was doing. The plane was airborne in seconds; its undercarriage remained fixed as it soared northward.

❧

Members of the police force who had been chasing him pulled up and watched the aeroplane growing smaller in the distance.

'Too bad, we've lost him. What was he wanted for, do you know?' one of the younger cops was curious.

'As far as I know he's a major crime boss. The Superintendent has finally got something on him, but he has managed to dodge us. I believe there was something related to terrorism too, but I'm not really in the picture.' Constable Ramesh Chintak chewed his moustache. That the criminal had escaped despite the high speed chase irritated him. It shouldn't have happened, he thought.

'He seems to have eluded us, Sir,' one of the senior officers spoke into his radio mouthpiece.

'Eluded you? How does a man in one car escape from twenty squad cars?'

'When he takes off in a plane, Sir.'

❧

The pilot and his companion scoured air and ground for their quarry. Radar wasn't picking up Vasu's plane. He flew close to the ground, which meant they too had to fly uncomfortably low as they passed between the mountains, checking to see if he had landed in the trees.

'What is that?'

The co-pilot examined the snowy Himalayan landscape below.

'Looks like a crashed plane,' he said.

'It does. Should we try to get closer?' 'We'd better check it out.'

The two military pilots circled down to three thousand feet above the wreck, as close as they could safely get.

'No question, it's a badly mangled plane.' 'Good, the bastard couldn't have survived that.'

Golden Crown Movie Theatre, Mumbai, August 2016

As the killer turned on the small grey electronic device a unique combination of ultra high and low frequency sound waves invaded the auditorium.

Signs of discomfort spread quickly through the audience. Feeling nausea people rushed from their seats towards bins and rest rooms. Others grew semi-conscious succumbing to headaches, dizziness and sweating.

Commotion created the necessary distraction.

The hero and heroine of the Bollywood extravaganza stopped mid-step and the lights came on, revealing pandemonium in the exclusive movie theatre. Some of the audience in their luxury reclining chairs writhed and groaned with discomfort, others silently clutched their heads.

'I think it's a gas attack', the movie theatre manager called up the twenty-four-hour security company and yapped 'Come quickly!'

Within a few minutes a team of security personnel arrived, wearing and carrying gas masks. They spread out and moved quickly down the aisles: 'Gas attack, put on this mask. Gas attack, take a mask.'

The killer, dressed identically and indistinguishable from the security team, joined them and moved directly to the last row from the front right.

Manak Lal Patra was unaware that he and his two companions received different masks from the others. These were coated with a lethal combination of nerve agents. Tasteless and odourless the chemicals were rapidly absorbed through their skins, respiratory tracts and eyes.

Moving through the melee towards the exit door the killer turned off the sound waves. As the commotion subsided another of Mumbai's crime lords and his top two men slumped dead in their reclining chairs.

Parliamentary Offices, New Delhi, October 2016

It was late but Sudesh was still at work.

He closed his eyes and turning his head to one side took a break.

Shakti was also at her desk, working through a pile of administrative tasks. 'I have some headache tablets, would that help you?' she offered.

'No, I'll be fine thanks, Shakti,' Sudesh's face softened as he looked at her. Often she worked late into the night alongside him and her presence was a source of comfort.

He lifted the next document from the pile and started reading it. His aide helped him, summarising past and proposed legislation. But in order to grasp current developments at international, national and State levels Sudesh had to read a great deal himself.

He read investor documents, position papers and local and international journals. When he became too tired to work, he read obscure science and economic texts for fun.

Sometimes, as he sat at his desk, his thoughts would drift and he would consider new ways to overcome the monsters of nepotism, corruption and government interference.

Monsters have been defeated and rejected before, he thought, and that gave him courage. Hitler's monster of National Socialism had been vanquished. Twentieth-century communism had been banished from the world. Dragons could be slain, and Sudesh was sharpening his sword.

A Delhi slum, October 2016

Punita Banerjee walked down the dusty, unpaved street, both sides heaped with litter. Children in rags looked up from their play and waved as she passed. Mangy dogs, goats, cows and feeble old men searched mounds of filth for morsels to eat.

As she approached the recently opened clinic, a small congested room with many patients waiting outside, she noticed a familiar tall figure emerging from within.

'Hello there, it is you, Punita Banerjee, is it not?'

Sudesh recognised her heart-shaped face and petite frame from a distance. Although Punita did not believe in paying attention to her appearance, she had a naturally elfin prettiness that was at odds with her aggressive disposition.

'And hello to you, Mr Kumar. What are you doing here? Isn't this rather far from your stamping ground?'

'Researching policy. I just thought I'd come out and have a look at the health facilities and consider alternatives. I understand that you are involved with the NGO that sets up and runs these clinics?'

'Yes, we help many people here.'

'This is great work, Punita, way to go!'

He was rather attractive, she thought, despite his disgusting right wing views. Not in an obvious Abhishek Bachchan kind of way, but he was clearly intelligent and she was forced to admit, his eyes were kind and he seemed honest.

'So how are things going in Parliament?' she asked.

'Oh, plenty of long-winded speeches and proposals for new interventions. But next month I have my first chance to make an impact. I think even you might like my Private Members Bill.'

'I very much doubt it! What are you proposing? Less child support? Longer working hours?'

Although he knew where he stood with Banerjee, Sudesh had to do his best with every journalist. And, somehow, with Punita, he found himself even more driven to convince her of his good faith, even if he was unlikely to succeed.

'I am proposing a new way to fund welfare using smart cards.'

'What's that about?'

'Every welfare beneficiary gets a card with a small memory chip. Instead of the government supplying welfare services to the poor, the funds go directly to the beneficiaries, in the form of cash credits on their smart card, so that they can buy what they need from any supplier, not just from the government.'

'You mean the government gives people cash, instead of caring for them?'

'Yes.'

'No more government education or health? No feeding schemes or housing?' She faced him square on.

'These "Care Cards" are flexible' Sudesh explained, 'They can be used for anything the government chooses to subsidise. It would be a matter of identifying the needs of a given family. If, for example, a family is allocated funds for education – the money will be accessed from the card by schools, freely chosen by parents, whether government or private. It's the ultimate people's empowerment.' He smiled at her, hoping that the term "empowerment" would appeal to her.

'Are we going to stand here forever, or shall we sit?' Punita said abruptly, gesturing towards the bench placed outside the small administrative office.

Punita continued their debate, 'I hear what you're saying. Like most of what you say, it's superficially appealing until one finds the catch. Okay, so government schools would have to compete with community and other private schools for funding? Ah, I see the catch!' She leaned back and folded her arms, satisfied. 'You want the money to go to for-profit schools. You want commercial schools to be in on the scheme. And the same for hospitals, housing companies and so on?'

'Correct.'

'It's another of your concoctions to promote greed and profit.' Punita glared up at Sudesh. 'Educators will be more interested in profit than people. They'll leach rather than teach and hospitals will steal rather than heal!'

The two of them indulged into an animated debate for longer than either of them realised, oblivious to clinic staff moving past them into and out of the building, collecting and depositing files, discussing treatments due to patients.

'You realise, of course', Punita said, 'that you're up against a mighty vested interest, thousands of officials in welfare, education and housing?'

Sudesh looked at her. Almost – but not quite – she sounded as though she was coming around to his way of thinking. He continued his explanation: 'My plan utilises networks of local people on the ground to identify and sign-on beneficiaries. Once Care Cards are activated the beneficiaries will download monthly payments from ATMs. There would be advice offices in every community, but not much more in the way of bureaucracy.

'Initially, we could re-deploy many of the officials to offices in their own communities, but once the plan was up and running they would be helped to find other work.'

Punita looked at her watch. 'It is time. I have other things to do and I expect you do too.' She patted his arm and left him wondering what he had achieved, if anything.

SecuriTech Showroom, October 2016

Madhumati was back in Vaneshri's showroom on another procurement trip.

'Have you seen this?' asked Vaneshri. 'It can stop people following you or secure a site in an unexpected way.'

Madhumati took the small tube from Vaneshri.

'Squirt a little of this into any lock and no one will be able to open it again. It's a chemical preparation that fuses the lock.

'And here is the latest reconnaissance tool. It magnifies sound by up to forty decibels simply by using a powerful omni-directional microphone and amplifier with headphones. So from your position, far from where a conversation is taking place, you can hear everything being said.'

'Excellent. This is really useful stuff. Vaneshri.'

Ray Upton's permanent suite at the Imperial Hotel, Delhi, November 2016

Ray looked across the room that was teeming with Delhi's movers and shakers who had come to brighten the evening for him. Punita Banerjee had buttonholed Sudesh. As Ray headed forward to rescue Sudesh, he overheard Punita's words, 'So you managed to swing your Care Card pilot scheme after all. That was a surprise!' She sounded almost friendly, for a change.

'Yes. I managed to drum up my first supportive editorials during the week before I proposed the Bill and I got fellow MPs to agree to a radical compromise: there will be a pilot project in East Delhi.'

'What made them agree to it?' Punita was curious.

'They feared a drubbing for protecting vested interests if they opposed me, so they agreed to the pilot.'

Upton joined the conversation. 'Yes, Ms Banerjee,' he said, 'all the background work has been done. I have great hopes that the idea will eventually be imitated world-wide.' Ray smiled and nodded at Punita. The mentor gently prompted Sudesh to move ahead and join other dignitaries in conversation.

Shakti and Vaneshri stayed watching all this from a corner of the room.

'Ray is masterly,' said Vaneshri. 'Yes, replied Shakti, 'and thank goodness he has taken Sudesh away from that woman, I'm sure she is attracted to him.'

'Funny way of showing it, she attacks him in her column every week.'

'Yes, but she seems fascinated by him.'

Vaneshri smiled, 'Well, you would recognise it wouldn't you, sweetie? Are you still in love with Sudesh?'

Shakti blushed and looked away, searching for a distraction. 'Look, there's my brother. Inder, come over here, I haven't seen you for so long!'

Inder came striding over and enveloped his sister in a big hug, 'Hi there, little sis, and Vaneshri, great to see you again, gorgeous as ever. I see your new business is going stratospheric.'

Vaneshri looked up at him from beneath her thick lashes. Talk about gorgeous; she had forgotten how attractive this man was.

'I'm glad India's golden boy, India's number one all rounder cricketer, still has time to say hello to his sister and an old friend', spoke Vaneshri casting flirtatious glances at him.

'Have not only come to say hello but have come to invite you people for watching our one-day match against West Indies at Wankhede Stadium in Mumbai next Saturday. I can organise you a seat in the InfoSwish box.'

She laughed, 'Only if you take me out for dinner after the match. If you win you pay, but if you lose the night's on me.'

'Done,' said Inder.

A corner shop, East Delhi, July 2017

The small woman in a ragged salwar kameez approached the ATM cautiously.

She gazed into the device indicated by a stylised pair of eyes, and a voice that said in Hindi, 'Welcome, Mrs Basu, your welfare payments are available, please proceed.' The face recognition device was standard, and the machine was programmed to provide up to date information in simple language.

The woman put her Care Card into the device as she had been taught, and her credits were downloaded. She would use the credit limit to buy food for her family and support education of her two children.

'Thank you,' said the voice, 'have a nice day.'

'My word, can you believe it?' said Anju, shaking her head as she crossed the small shop to the counter.

'The social worker told me I can buy food with this card,' she said to the shopkeeper, 'do you know what I must do?'

'Sure, Mrs Basu. Just choose the items you want and bring them to me.'

After the shopkeeper had rung up the total, he produced a small card reading device and asked Anju to swipe her card. She placed her thumb on the fingerprint recognition pad.

'Done,' the man smiled at Anju. And here is a printout showing you the items you bought, what they cost, and how much you have left with for the rest of the month.'

Delhi, October 2017

Punita and Sudesh were on their way to inspect the progress of the Care Card pilot project in East Delhi. Punita was sceptical of its success.

Their car paused in heavy traffic near an intersection, and Sudesh leant out of the window to buy a pile of magazines from a small boy. He paid him more than the price of the magazines.

'Why do you buy these magazines?' asked Punita.

'To help the kids.'

'You're not so naïve as to think they don't work for some get-rich-quick distributor exploiting children, are you? Those kids should be at school!' She was quick to react, in an adversarial mode.

As their car crawled along between motorbikes carrying families of up to five people, and rickshaws pushing through every available space, Sudesh placed the magazines on the seat beside the driver.

'How does buying their magazines harm them?' he asked rhetorically. 'How would it help if I don't buy from them?'

'Rather than buying magazines which enrich their cruel employers, you should persuade your rich friend, Ray Upton, to round up those children and place them in shelters.' responded Punita in an annoying tone.

She flared up more thinking about the extra effort that she had made that morning to dress up in her favourite salwar-kameez. She did not understand her growing desire to make herself look captivating to this man whose political ideas were so abhorrent. She felt sick with herself.

'Isn't that unrealistic? There are millions of children working in India, as you know, Ray can't rescue them all personally. Besides, child labour is common world-wide.'

'That's rubbish, Sudesh. Child labour is banned in all first world countries and anyone found employing children is jailed.'

Sudesh leaned over and retrieved the pile of magazines from the front seat. He flipped through them and handed Punita the international children's fashion magazine, *Dashing*. 'Page through this and tell me what you see.'

'Clothes for children of course, but I'm sure this has not involved child labour in the first world.'

'Okay, now flip through *British Theatre Guide* and tell me what you see.'

'I have no idea why these western magazines sell on Delhi streets, but I see nothing relevant.'

'Well, look at that billboard.' Sudesh pointed to a Coca-Cola advert showing a happy family on a tropical beach.

'Get to the point.' demanded Punita.

'You've just made my point. When you see first world child labour you don't see it. You just ignore it. Euphemistically, they call it child "employment". Every western country has so-called "child employment" schemes. Kids work as models for advertisements, take to the ramp at a very tender age, are offered the bait of fame and money and are impelled to take up acting in movies and theatre. At many places children begin to supplement in family businesses, deliver newspapers and so on. You flipped past the advert for *The Sound of Music* currently on at the London Palladium and you never noticed its casting consists mainly of children. They work long hard hours in rehearsals, perform rigorously in daily productions. And they are compelled to spend long hours in compulsory schooling for which, incidentally, they don't get paid, so it's conveniently not called "work".

'Much of the work they do is gruelling. It involves exhausting travel schedules and working under harsh lighting, but you don't call it "labour". I call it hypocrisy.'

'I know you lost your sister because of child labour laws, so you're bitter, but you're talking nonsense.' Her voice was warm again. She castigated herself for her mood swings when she was around this man. 'Those kids are carefully screened and protected by social workers.'

'What matters is not whether they work, but under what conditions. I want what works for the poor in the real world. I support every child's right to choose better alternatives. I want a world where children can escape destitution by getting on-the-job training, food, shelter, health care, education and life skills.

And I want NGOs helping kids, but I want to persuade them to support policies that protect all children, and not just the few they can get hold of.

'I also want government to draft policies that can make every Indian capable of leading a decent life.'

'I'm sorry Sudesh, but, stripped of your pseudo-intellectual obfuscation, you're simply an apologist for the shameful fact that our country has forty million child workers.'

Sudesh gave up and Punita leafed slowly through *Splash*. 'I must spend less time with this man', she told herself. 'Somehow, when I'm around him, I feel confused'.

L&PP office, November 2017

'We need to run candidates for at least half of the Lok Sabha seats, which means fighting in 270 constituencies. We also need candidates for fifteen of the State Assemblies.' Habib Rahman, the L&PP's campaign manager briefed Sudesh. 'A good performance in the States will translate into seats in the Rajya Sabha.'

'It is a huge challenge. Do we have enough candidates and field workers to pull this off?' asked Sudesh.

'We have been trying to make sure of that.' Habib remarked, 'Jaival's IT team has increased their data base to twenty million, mainly from website queries. The names and contact details are organised according to territory, State and language. Our poll results indicate that the younger crowd and poor people are increasingly turning in your favour.

'We communicate instantly and frequently with your supporters, mainly through SMSs.

'Small donations come in every day, and small donations from millions of people amount to billions of rupees.

'Your team is ready, Sudesh. They are geared up. All you have to do in the run-up to the election is get out there and enchant the crowd. And don't forget to eat your breakfast and get at least seven hours of sleep.'

Twenty-one

Parliament office, New Delhi, March 2018

Sudesh picked up his phone, 'Kumar speaking.'
'Good morning Mr Kumar, you may remember me from the Crime Stop project back in the late nineteen-nineties. My name is Nanek Singh.'

'Chief Inspector Singh! How could I forget? It's good to hear from you,' said Sudesh.

'I have been following your progress,' said Singh. 'We really need someone like you to bring about a huge change in this country.

'I have called you to offer my support to your campaign. I will get in touch with your team, of course, and be available to help in any way I can. I want to help by bringing in my contacts, old-timers like me, over to the L&PP.'

Chandni Chowk, July 2018

Two men approached Sudesh as the hubbub of his campaign moved through the crowded, narrow streets of Old Delhi.

'What are you going to do for us?' shouted one of the men in Hindi.

'What work do you do?' asked Sudesh, stopping.

'I'm a street vendor and he's a rickshaw-wallah. The police keep raiding us and demand bribes. But we can't get licenses. Most of the money we make goes to our unions to fight the city council.'

'I'm not surprised. Did you know that in this city there are eight lakh rickshaw drivers and only two lakh licenses?'

Sudesh had their attention.

'And there are over two lakh street vendors with no formal legal status.'

'So, what are you going to do about it?' asked the rickshaw driver.

'I will abolish licenses for rickshaw drivers.'

'And street traders?'

'The same. Anyone will trade without a license, everyone from the smallest trader to the biggest entrepreneur. As long as they don't commit fraud and honour their contracts, and don't commit crimes, everyone will be free to trade anywhere. I will introduce complaint offices run by independent people whom you will approach if you are harassed by the police or public officials.'

'I'll vote for you,' said one.

'Yes, me too,' said the other.

Institute of Management, New Delhi, July 2018

Sudesh was nervous. He was at Delhi's renowned B-School to address a group of opinion-makers and financial journalists on his economic policy. That was not what worried him, it was the academics. He was not a trained economist and could not help feeling jittery about the opinion the academics would form of him. He was a bit low on confidence as he projected his views through his speech.

'The government can do more for the poor by doing less,' he concluded.

Punita couldn't let this pass.

'Punita Banerjee,' she jumped to her feet.

'Go ahead, Ms Banerjee,' said the chairman.

'If your ideas were introduced every upliftment programme in the country would lose its funding.'

'That's right,' replied Sudesh.

Punita's blood began to boil as she envisaged the faces of the destitute people she encountered daily. 'That is outrageous. These people need all the help they can get.' She stood her ground, staring him resolutely in the eye.

'I agree. But apart from basic welfare delivered through direct payments, as is currently being implemented in East Delhi through my Care Card project, the State shouldn't be helping the poor. Every one lakh rupee paid by the business community in taxes is another job destroyed.'

'But you can't only be on the side of business.'

'Ms Banerjee, governments have to impose tax in order to spend. Most of the money raised in taxes is wasted on these long chains of bureaucracies. Our government is the most bureaucratic in the world with the lowest percentage of revenue reaching the poor. Upliftment programmes should be financed and run by NGOs and charities. They do a much better job than the government.'

Whatever made her drawn towards this man, she wondered at her own feelings. He was so wrong about everything. 'I have seen hundreds,' she raised her voice, 'hundreds of people helped through State-aid programmes. People who would otherwise be in the gutter and you want to stop all that!'

'I do. I don't doubt that you have seen many people's lives improved through government spending, but you haven't seen millions of lives ruined as a result of money siphoned from the private sector? Well, you've seen those ruined lives, you care about them and work hard to help, but you haven't recognised over-taxation and over-regulation as the cause.'

Sudesh and Punita debated openly flouting an appropriate way of speaker-journalist interaction. Over time, their exchanges had become an informative and entertaining feature of Delhi journalism, and Banerjee's spiteful columns had become a vital reading dose for the politically informed.

'Progressive income tax and profits tax on corporations provide most government revenue in India, and that is as it should be,' she maintained.

'Maybe, but that's not how it works.' Sudesh knew he was on shaky grounds. Most economists accepted her proposition unquestioningly. Could he carry this off without making a fool of himself in their eyes. He spoke again to unleash another of his heresies.

'In truth, Punita, there's no such thing as company tax. Eyes in the auditorium widened in spontaneous disbelief. 'All tax is personal tax.'

'Companies,' Sudesh explained, 'are a concept, what lawyers call a "legal fiction", "juristic person" or "legal persona". They aren't even as real as flocks of sheep or bunches of grapes; they're an illusion, no more than a collective noun for people cooperating.

'No one has the slightest idea who really pays company tax: shareholders, managers, labourers, consumers, financiers? Put the other way round, if you abolish company tax, will wages or profits go up, will prices go down … it varies from company to company, and time to time. Imposing company tax is like firing a shotgun into a dark room full of people. You have no idea who you hit.'

As the chairman allowed the next question to follow, Punita left the auditorium. As she walked out she mumbled, 'This man is impossible. He undermines my value system, my entire life's hard work, and then talks unimaginable rubbish! Or, did he make sense?'

She locked herself in her office and fought back angry tears.

Flame's Bar, July 2018

'That young upstart is getting too much attention,' said Ashok to Hitesh.

'We should have neutralised him early on, old buddy.'

Ashok frowned, 'The problem is he comes across as so damn sincere that we cannot blame the public for liking him. Even our colleagues in the house are growing fond of the fellow.'

'If he gains influence through these elections, the power with the government will be reduced,' said Hitesh with a grin, 'then who will think of luring us with more money?'

'Watch your words,' replied Ashok, frowning deeper, 'people can lip read.'

'Your old fear again, they're all far too busy strategising.'

'To get back to the subject, we made a big mistake by agreeing to the trial scheme for that welfare project of Kumar. It has worked far too well. Every trader in East Delhi has a smile on his face.

'The newspaper and financial editorials are eulogising it for improving delivery and slashing costs. Even international journals like *The Economist* and *IT Delivers* have picked up on the scheme. If it's extended countrywide it will have a very adverse effect on our business interests.'

'Ashok, you'll have to do something about Kumar or we will be requiring his bloody Care Cards for our sustenance,' replied Hitesh.

India Finance, July 2018

'The Tyranny of Twaddle' the title of Punita's column for the July edition of *India Finance*, was the most scathing denunciation of Sudesh so far. After a short period of positive media attention that had accompanied the launching phase of the L&PP, journalists had painted Sudesh in a negative light. But seeing that nothing could curtail his popular appeal, Punita resolved to put an end to his growing popularity through her column.

'The Tyranny of Twaddle'

We have always been a democratic country and regarded diversity as one of our country's virtues. We elect communists and libertarians, conservatives and liberals, religious fundamentalists and atheists, bunny huggers and industrialists. In short, we elect sensible candidates to the left or the right of Centre.

The Sudesh Kumar phenomenon is shaking everyone's faith in democracy. That he should garner more than a few lunatic fringe votes, that he now heads a party, growing in national importance, is democracy's Achilles heel. Are we to conclude that democracy is no protection against extremes, no guarantee of balance, no perennial assurance of the tendency towards political compromise and the golden mean?

His fatuous arguments, superficial rhetoric and dangerous ideas have often been exposed through the column, but in his lecture at the Delhi Institute of Management earlier this week, he set new standards in making twaddle sound plausible. He denied that we are harmed by cheap imports, and insisted that government, our primary protector and provider, is a cosmic evil.

Blaming government for the world's financial crisis which is universally acknowledged as market failure, defending child labour, proposing to privatise the nation's wealth into the hands of the super-rich, and calling for an end to government welfare, is not enough for Kumar.

He now wants us to believe that companies don't exist. That's right, these global corporations, giant multinational conglomerates, more powerful than most governments, responsible for the financial crisis, resource depletion, climate change and third-world poverty, are, he told his audience of incredulous intellectuals, mere imagination, a "legal fiction", an "illusion". He would have us believe that when governments tax companies, as all governments do, they are really not taxing them at all, but, as if by sleight of hand, they are taxing the rest of us. They are such a fantasy, according to Kumar, that by some mathematical magic, taxing them less means we'd get more.

When governments regulate companies, as all governments do, it is as pointless as regulating a shadow. There's nothing there to regulate. We pass straight through them and end up regulating hapless folk beyond the mirage, especially consumers and workers.

If companies are illusory, for whom are workers working? What if anything, are stock exchanges trading? From whom do we buy groceries?

Where to next? His imagination knows no bounds. Next he will conjure out of existence all abstract nouns – all collective and abstract concepts – from flocks of geese to human rights, and from love to terrorism. With him anything is possible. Except reality.

Sudesh read the column over and over again. Placing his elbows on his knees, he buried his head in his hands and sat motionless for thirty minutes. Character assassinations were part of political life, but this column got his head spinning. The column revealed a profound misunderstanding or misrepresentation of what he thought he'd said. Maybe it was because he'd failed so completely to communicate in the right sense and therefore lacked the most essential skill of politics. Perhaps, Punita was right and he was a naïve dreamer, or was it that he had started really paying heed to what she wrote after they had seemed to be getting on well with each other. He was wrong to feel that she was growing in agreement with his ideas!

The Radisson Hotel, Cape Town, South Africa, September 2018

Inder and Vaneshri were seated on a comfortable basketwork chaise longue. A few metres away the Atlantic Ocean lapped the terrace of Cape Town's Radisson Hotel. Vaneshri curled her legs up and leaned against Inder. A rug was tucked around their knees protecting them from the cool ocean breeze.

'I'm so glad I joined you on this trip,' said Vaneshri, sipping her Moët. 'Even though South Africa won the series, you were spectacular, and all the women are green with jealousy because you are mine,' she smiled at him. 'And now that the test is over we get to spend time alone together in this beautiful city away from the Indian paparazzi.'

Inder tightened his arm around her, 'I am happier than I have ever been. You are the most beautiful and brilliant woman in the world and I'm crazy about you. I wanted you from the moment I saw you in New York all those years ago. Despite Shakti's low opinion of my morals,' he grinned, 'I resisted trying to steal you from Sudesh. I still can't believe he let go of you.'

'He didn't let go of me, I let him go. My father made me an offer I couldn't refuse. But put me in the same position with you instead of Sudesh, and the business deal might not have won out.'

'Do you think Sudesh minds that we are together?'

'No. He's in love with India. Nothing and no one else has ever mattered to him.'

'Well, at this stage I don't care about Sudesh.' Inder reached for Vaneshri's slim hand, and slipping a beautiful diamond ring onto her ring finger he continued, 'You are the only woman I have ever loved. Vaneshri, please say you will marry me.'

India, October 2018

Elections are the price paid for democracy.

Sudesh focused on the moment at hand, it was the only way to survive.

Another city, another airport, another rally, another round of media attention.

The same stump speech, over and over again.

Raising flags, shaking hands, raising spirits, kissing babies.

Walking hand-in-hand with local politicians, posing for mutual benefit.

Being careful to say the right thing and never to say the wrong thing.

Listening to the people, following the polls.

Showing statesmanship. Proving leadership.

Twenty-hours a day. Tiring days and sleepless nights.

Another campaign.

And then it was time to count.

L&PP Office, December 2018

In 2018, India's electorate comprised over eight hundred million people. The elections were more than twice the size of those for the European Parliament, which was the next largest.

Even with improvements in voting technology, and with electronic voting machines used throughout the country, it was an elaborate process.

When polls closed on the day of the national elections, the voting machines were stored in a strong room under heavy security. It would take two more days to complete the different phases of the regional elections, and only then would the votes be counted.

During the wait the L&PP, like the other parties and the national media, occupied themselves obsessively with exit polls, trying to predict the outcomes.

On the day of the count Sudesh sat with his innermost circle comprising Kaamini, Jaival, Anil, Habib and Shakti, surrounded by television screens tuned to a range of local, national and international TV channels, all discussing the likely outcomes as they awaited the results.

After thirty minutes, in fifty results announced for the Lok Sabha, the L&PP had won only one seat. They were making inroads into some of the State assemblies. At this stage it looked as if they might win no more than ten seats in the lower house. That would make a modest difference.

Despite their progress, they were devastated. All that hard work, all that money, all that enthusiasm from the public, seemed to have lost its meaning with so few votes in hand. Did this mean the L&PP would never amount to much, that it would never be in a position to affect profound change. These doubts clouded Sudesh's mind.

Two hours later, Sudesh could scarcely contain himself: despite no strong regional presence the L&PP had won ninety-five seats in their second election. It was unheard of.

'He's different,' said voters interviewed on TV, 'He'll fight against corruption,'; 'He seems to be honest.'

The newly registered young voters and the poor had turned out in record numbers, as predicted by the L&PP pollsters. It was a ringing endorsement for Sudesh.

And here was another camera.

'You must be very pleased with the election results, Mr Kumar. You are a force to be reckoned with now.'

'Yes, we are very pleased. We can now do more for the people of India.'

'And with whom do you expect to form an alliance?'

'It is too early to answer this question, but we will enter into negotiations with all the major parties and perhaps some of the minor ones too.'

{❦}

As the election results were analysed it became apparent that the unexpected success of Sudesh's L&PP and other fringe parties was more significant than analysts had predicted based on opinion surveys and early results.

Since 1992, no single party had achieved a majority in the Parliament. They had had to depend on coalition building with other parties to form a bloc with sufficient votes. A simple majority was required to form the government.

In most democracies a handful of leading parties contest the middle ground, but Indian politics had seen growing number of voters vacating the Centre and congregating on the fringes. This increased the fluidity of coalition politics.

Speculation was rife as secret meetings, phone calls and negotiations between aspirant coalition partners proceeded apace.

BJP leaders approached the L&PP and smaller 'conservative' parties. The two most obvious scenarios to rule India were a conservative BJP coalition or a leftist Congress coalition.

Senior BJP representatives approached the L&PP. Negotiations were promising, but Sudesh was not available to agree on the critical details. At the most crucial moment in his political life he had disappeared.

Communist Party Headquarters, December 2018

The walls were plastered with paper and posters saying:

'Vote Naipal.'

'Discussion in the upcoming meeting: The working class and globalisation.'

'Conference: Resisting the erosion of workers' rights.'

'Solidarity: stand together or fall apart.'

A small man entered the room, bearing an open letter in his hand.

'You will never guess what I have here!'

'Someone has offered you a job? No wait, that would never happen. A marriage proposal? Nope, even less likely. Your utilities have been cut off? That must be it.'

'Very funny,' said the slight figure. 'Kumar wants to meet you.'

The other man raised his eyebrows, 'the same Kumar?'

'Yep,' said the other man, 'Mr Sudesh Thatcherite Kumar, the opponent of workers' rights, the one who wants to privatise everything.'

'And why would he want to talk to the supporter of the poor and oppressed?'

'Guess he wants to make a deal. We don't have to believe the same things to do that, do we? Ideology doesn't preclude alliances. This is India not the European Union.'

'True. Can't think of anything we have in common, but let's meet him. We have nothing to lose, but he must pay for lunch. We can't be seen to be subsidising capitalism.'

The other man laughed. 'That's right, it's only fair. Let's redistribute his wealth.'

❦

Some of the twelve communist parties of Inida had formed an election pact not to contest for the same seats.

All of their leaders were invited to the Communist Party of India's campaign headquarters to meet Sudesh. His ninety-five seats made the L&PP too large to be ignored.

'Welcome Mr Kumar,' said the leader of the CP of India, Rohit Jayaraman, 'We are surprised by your request to meet with us, but we are willing to listen. What do you wish to say?'

'I'm here to propose forming a ruling coalition with you.'

'Are you crazy? We're political opponents,' said the Marxist Party leader.

'Maybe not,' said Sudesh, 'Hear me out.'

'We're listening,' said Jayaraman.

'Let's start with what matters most to you. You would get most of the ministries, government appointments and the Prime Minister's portfolio. We are willing to settle for a few functions and some policies you would need to implement in your ministries. Beyond that we would each have full control over our respective ministries. This means you will have by far the most power.

'Everyone knows we disagree on many issues, so we would retain full freedom to disagree and debate in public. No need for a "party line" and no common party whip.'

'Where's the catch?' asked the leader of the Revolutionary Socialist Party.

'There is none. Shall I get to specifics?'

'Go ahead,' said Jayaraman, fascinated.

'Between you, you choose the Prime Minister and I will be his deputy. Of the forty-eight ministries our party wants only three, Law and Justice, Commerce and Industry, and Social Justice and Empowerment.'

'Ah, there's the catch, you want welfare so you can sabotage what matters most to us,' exclaimed a young man who wore a Democratic Youth Federation T-shirt.

'No, we guarantee that welfare spending will not be cut. Indeed, we propose to increase welfare spending on every recipient by one percent more than the economic growth rate. Further, we agree to remove any law or regulation that prevents needy people from improving their own welfare or that prevents others, including government, from helping them.'

'And what do you want from us?'

'Only one thing, a law of equivalence,' Sudesh tossed this out as if everyone knew what he meant. 'A law saying government can't exempt itself from the laws it imposes on others, equality.'

'But that would mean government can't tax and convict criminals unless people also get the right to do the same?', ventured the youth leader.

'No, no,' responded Sudesh, 'equivalence isn't about the government's ability to make or enforce laws. It simply requires that everyone is subject to those laws, including officials and politicians.'

Disgusted by years of 'establishment' and 'bourgeois' abuse of power, they needed no further convincing.

'What policy trade-offs are you asking for?' asked Jayaraman, leaning forward.

'I believe there is one issue to which you might have objections,' replied Sudesh. 'Commerce and Industry gives us control over foreign trade. We know you favour protectionism for workers and employers whereas we advocate free trade. But you gain control over what matters more to you, labour.

'The only concession we want with respect to economic policies including labour and taxation would be our ability to grant exemption from them in free zones. We will limit free zones to States whose governments agree to have them, and to a no greater area than that used in China.'

Rohit Jayaraman cleared his throat and sat up straight.

'One thing. Between us we have only 215 seats. We need another 60 to achieve a majority in the house.'

'Don't worry,' said Sudesh, 'I have approached a few of the other regional parties and discussed the proposal. Between them they have 70 seats, and provided we cater to some of their regional concerns they will join our alliance.'

'So, in summary, what you're proposing is we get all except three ministries. We also choose the Prime Minister and you give us guarantees on welfare spending. We have full control over our departments, we don't have to present a common front, and you'll ensure equality?'

'That's it, in a nutshell,' said Sudesh.

Sivananda Kutir, Uttarkashi, December 2018

Chanda smiled at her husband. Janardan had a two-week break and they were back in their favourite restaurant, where he had proposed to her.

Their two-year-old son, Sudesh, was with a neighbour, and they were enjoying uninterrupted time together.

As they conversed softly, the flickering television screen caught Chanda's attention.

'Oh my goodness,' spoke Chanda unable to contain her emotion.

'What?' asked Janardan.

'It's Sudesh!'

Janardan looked around for their son, nonplussed. Then he followed her eyes to the screen.

'Oh, you mean Sudesh Kumar, I didn't know you two were on first name terms.' Janardan laughed.

'He is my brother,' she answered slowly.

Janardan smiled, 'You are joking, right?'

'I couldn't be more serious. That is my brother Sudesh!'

'Oh! My god, your brother? So, we have named our son after him. Are you aware that he is the rising star in politics? His party won ninety-five seats in the Lok Sabha.'

Chanda gazed at the TV screen, but Sudesh's face had disappeared. 'He looks so sophisticated,' she said, 'so different from the skinny, barefoot boy I remember.' She paused, her eyes full of tears, of joy and pain. 'He always said he wanted to put things right in India. He seemed to have followed his dream.'

'From what I've heard, he might even accomplish it,' said Janardan, 'There are great hopes resting on the shoulders of Sudesh Kumar.'

He looked at his wife, 'Now you know that your brother is alive and doing well in life, isn't it time to go back and see him again, my darling?'

'How can I even think of doing that? If I get back in his life, it will damage his political career. I have brought shame on my family and village. No, he has a successful life. It has been twenty-three years since I disappeared. I am sure he has put me out of his thoughts.'

Janardan looked at her, 'I think he would welcome you back with open arms.'

The Communist Party Headquarters, December 2018

Sudesh paced the corridor for thirty minutes whilst the communists discussed his proposals.

'It seems Kumar is willing to sacrifice his principles in exchange for a little power,' said one.

'Typical capitalist,' said another, 'concerned only with his own, selfish interests.'

'We could call it the Peoples' Empowerment Alliance,' said the CEO of the Indian Federation of Trade Unions.

'Comrades, I lean towards accepting this proposal,' intervened Jayaraman. 'As leader of the biggest party in our group I assume you would all support me for the position of Prime Minister?'

'Let's vote on that,' said the Democratic Youth Federation leader.

They were so overwhelmed by this extraordinary turn of events that no one anticipated the implications of their seemingly minor concessions.

L&PP Office, December 2018

Sudesh strolled into the party office.

'Where were you?' exclaimed Anil, 'The BJP leaders are waiting for our answer, the press is yapping at our heels. How could you disappear at such a crucial time?'

Sudesh raised his hand and the room subsided into silence disturbed only by the hum of the air-conditioner and a phone ringing unanswered in the distance.

'We have a deal,' he said, 'I have formed an alliance that gives us three ministries. I will be deputy Prime Minister, and some of our core policies will be implemented. Crack open the champagne!'

The office burst again into noise. Cries of joy and congratulations filled the air.

'Give us the details,' said Habib, once order was restored.

For a moment Sudesh looked insecure. 'I expect this to surprise you,' he said, 'I'm not sure how to break the news.' He rubbed his nose, then continued in a rush, 'Our primary coalition partners are the communists.'

Laughter broke out. 'Jokes apart,' said Habib, 'what is the deal?'

'I mean it,' Sudesh replied, 'I have negotiated a deal with the communists.' He raised his voice, cutting through the response, 'I first approached the small regional parties with whom we have a lot in common and talked with them,' he closed the door to ensure no journalist could eavesdrop and sat on the edge of the nearest desk.

'Between ourselves, the communists and these regional parties we have over fifty percent of the seats.'

'But why do we want the communists in power?' asked Anil.

'We don't.' replied Sudesh.

Sudesh's team looked bewildered and fearful wondering if they had come that far only to be betrayed.

'Please, hear me out. Don't interrupt until I have finished, then I will answer your questions.

'This is the deal, we get three departments, Law and Justice, Commerce and Industry, and Social Justice and Empowerment, and the communists get the rest,' he explained.

'But,' started Anil, still bemused. Sudesh gestured for silence.

'Consider this, the communists will appear to have the important powers, but how much will they really be able to change? The principle of equivalence, to which they have readily agreed, will prevent any far-reaching moves. Think about it. They can no longer introduce new employment schemes that pay less than the minimum wage without allowing private employers to do the same. No government undertaking can enjoy special protections, unless the private suppliers are allowed the same terms.

'Our commitment to increase welfare at one percent above the growth rate per welfare recipient – notice that is for each recipient, not in total – will mean a shrinking budget for welfare. First, rapidly growing free zones and fewer regulations will reduce the number of people on welfare. Second, the widespread introduction of Care Cards will drastically reduce the cost of the welfare bureaucracy.

'We also have their explicit agreement to remove trade barriers, which means the financially backward classes in India will have access to the world's cheapest products.

'With few departments and powers we can still make important changes. The communists might increase taxes and pass more labour laws, but the public will see their policies and ours, side-by-side. Moreover, we will be free to point out their defects.

'I could go on, but I think you get the point. Are we agreed to proceed with the deal?'

L&PP Headquarters, February 2019

The Peoples' Empowerment Alliance (PEA) had proved its majority in the Lok Sabha in the vote of confidence. The alliance had been invited by the President to form the new government.

Back in the L&PP offices champagne corks popped. The party's new MPs, senior staff and party workers were crammed into the largest boardroom.

'To Sudesh, Deputy Prime Minister and Minister of Commerce and Industry!' they raised the toast.

Sudesh gave a short speech thanking everyone, and the crowds dispersed, breaking into small groups, spreading through the reception area and main offices, and filling the building with the noise discussing and arguing about the future.

Sudesh moved across to join Nanek Singh, now Commissioner of Police for Delhi.

'Nanek, good to see you. Congratulations on your promotion and thanks for your support during the campaign.'

Singh responded warmly and Sudesh continued, 'That Crime Stop system you ran in 1997, am I right in thinking it was successful?'

'Yes, extremely so.'

'Why did you end it so soon?'

'I'm not proud of this, but I received several calls threatening my daughter, Devika. The fear that she might be killed forced me to put an end to it.'

'I understand,' Sudesh nodded. 'Now that you are a Commissioner, and your daughter has grown up and become independent would you consider implementing a similar, upgraded programme throughout Delhi? The advances in technology should make it more effective than before. The Mafia Murderers seem to have decapitated organised crime,' he smiled at the unintended pun, 'but we still have a flourishing stolen goods market.'

'I'll start working on it without delay,' replied Singh.

Twenty-two

Centre for Policy Research, Delhi, January 2019

There was polite applause as Ray Upton approached the lectern and cast his eyes across his audience of students, academics and journalists. It would be an easy audience, he thought. They sympathised with his views and wanted to hear his analysis of the causes of the current international financial crisis which had become known as the Second Great Depression.

Ray was known for his ability to explain complex concepts in simple language. There was polite applause as he approached the lectern.

'You all remember the sub-prime crisis of 2008 and subsequent series of "bail outs" and "stimulus" packages introduced by governments?

'Such terms are misleading. Stripped of seductive rhetoric, they're nothing more than taking money from successful companies and transferring it to failed ones, that is from people who create wealth to ones who destroy it.'

Ray explained so lucidly what money is, how it is created, and how economies function that his audience, even professors of economics, felt for the first time that they had a clear understanding of monetary and financial economics.

Yet, he saw heads shaking disapprovingly. With what are they disagreeing he wondered.

He explained without complex formulae and obfuscatory jargon why government spending, however convoluted and disguised, amounts to taking wealth from people who create it and transferring it to people who consume it.

'Financial markets,' he said returning to the global financial crisis, 'are the most heavily regulated sector of every economy. It should therefore have been obvious that government failure, not market failure was the cause. Instead of liberalising markets so that they could correct the government-induced subprime crisis spontaneously, the massive diversion of resources from wealth-producers to wealth-consumers through bail-outs and stimulus packages was accompanied by even more controls. The world faced a repetition of the 'New Deal' which is mistakenly believed to have ended the 1930s' Great Depression. The facts and figures tell a different story, namely that it actually deepened the depression continued for a decade instead of a few months or years.

'By 2010, it looked as if the massive subversion of capital and stifling controls in these economies were working. Unemployment fell, investment resumed, and there was modest growth. Unfortunately, it was a malinvestment illusion. The Greek government could not pay its debt and others followed.'

Ray was surprised to see heads shaking more vigorously. Their body language gave no clue with what precisely they disagreed. He got the impression it was with his every word. Could they have forgotten the brief hiatus when politicians said the worst was over and congratulated themselves on their perspicacity?

'By 2014, economic indicators began to fall again. The Dollar, Euro, Pound and Yen were losing value. By the end of 2015, all of these economies were back to where they were in 2009.

'As you know, the 2015 recession became the current global depression, and the consequences have spread far beyond the economies where the problems began.'

The shaking of heads intensified. Ray had never solicited such a negative response. He assumed they did not get a word of what he said.

He soldiered on.

'Why were the positive results of the 2009 measures so short-lived? And why are the problems facing these economies so much more severe now?

'Billions of dollars squandered in these economies led to higher taxes, increased government debt, and double-digit inflation. Investors fled major markets in search of stability and freedom. Misguided governments reintroduced exchange controls.

'The result was more capital flight, and a brain drain of talented people taking their skills to investor-friendly countries and tax havens. As taxable income in the depressed economies fell, things went from bad to worse.

'The severity of this depression and the fact that people are finally attributing blame correctly to excessive government intervention, heralded the signs of unrest we have been seeing this year.'

Ray now faced a sea of furiously shaking heads. He saw no point in giving his full presentation and decided to cut it short.

'The Upton Index played a part. It was created in 2009 for people to place bets on whether the trillion dollar "bail outs" would work. These initial policy bets proved so popular that my internet service was soon running bets on most policies in what used to be the first world countries.

'It soon became obvious that the way people were betting was an accurate predictor of policy outcomes. The average of many people betting on how many beans are in a bottle, the weight of an ox and so on, is more accurate than the estimates of experts. It turned out that as a rule when governments do something, you should bet on expenses exceeding budgets and fewer benefits being delivered than promised, and counter-productive effects on balance.

'My betting system means governments can no longer get away with failed policies at the taxpayers' expense and that citizens are not as easily misled.'

Shaking heads now had smiling faces. Was the audience now laughing at him? Ray felt humiliated. He wiped sweat from his brow and continued as rapidly and positively as he could.

'To your credit, Indians avoided the mistakes of the first-world countries.

'Unfunded spending, nationalisation and bailouts for failed managers made the Second Great Depression inevitable. Discontent among citizens increased. Until those governments realise the only road to recovery is that proposed by the L&PP for India, their economies will stagnate.

'India now is the number-one haven for wealth and skills.'

With that, Ray nodded and left the lectern and heading towards Sudesh sat down behind him. As he sat, head lowered, he said, 'Sorry, I just didn't seem to reach them. That was the worst experience of my life.'

'Look!' said Sudesh, gesturing to the audience, and Ray looked up to see them standing as one, and clapping. It was a standing ovation. He was incredulous.

When he described his ordeal in New York, his attempts to demonstrate the distinctive way in which Indians shake their heads to indicate approval entertained his friends more than the story itself.

A Parisian Café, February 2019

Jacques Clemenceau liked catching up world's updates on CNN over his morning coffee in Café Blanc, one block from his apartment in Montmartre.

This is work, he told himself, politicians need to keep up with the latest news. His double espresso was now sans pastry due to his high cholesterol levels, but it still kick-started his day.

He frowned at the presenter's next statement, 'This morning the Upton Exchange listed twenty-four new wagers focussed on recently implemented French economic policies. Across the world self-styled political pundits are already placing bets for or against the question of whether these Acts will do any good to the French people. The current odds are thirteen to one against.'

As the presenter spoke, a ticker ran along the bottom of the television screen, showing the prevailing odds on pending laws internationally.

Clemenceau had been active in the Assembly debate on the Upton Exchange. Nobody liked it, but the legislators had realised there was nothing they could do to close it down.

'We have Ray Upton, here in the studio in New York,' continued the news anchor, 'Ray, it seems that millions of people are becoming addicted to your betting exchange.'

'Yes, there is a huge, international response that the exchange is gathering. Apparently, many people have a view on the efficacy of new laws, and they are willing to put money on their opinions.'

'But you are offering twenty-four predictions on the French economy, why so many?'

'France has an exhaustive legislative programme, and a habit of passing contentious laws.'

Jacques almost choked on his coffee. 'How dare he!'

The mogul continued: 'When millions of people bet on the outcome of legislation they hold up a mirror to the potential consequences of government actions. We think this is important for French citizens, and for the world.'

'And of course, as the middle-man you can't lose,' responded the interviewer.

'You get it,' agreed Ray.

'Well Ray, your exchange has thrown a cat among the government pigeons,' said the anchor, turning to smile into the camera.

The Palande Residence, Hyderabad, February 2019

The Palande household was in a state of merry din. Vaneshri's decision to get married to Inder Bhati thrilled everyone to the core. 26 October was the date chosen by the astrologer.

Vaneshri's relationship with Inder had become the talk of the town. Several gossip columns in page 3 newspapers and magazines tagged the twosome posing together in social gatherings. However, Vaneshri had refrained from discussing much about the seriousness of the relationship with her parents. She was still punishing Sabyasachi for his interference with her relationship with Sudesh.

When she finally brought Inder to meet them, and announced her engagement, Sabyasachi and Shalini were pleasantly surprised.

Sabyasachi raised no objections as Inder carried the tag of 'India's top cricketer'. Moreover, he earned, between his salary and endorsement deals, an annual income of more than fifty million US dollars. This was enough to make Vaneshri's parents glad their princess was getting married to a man worthy of her hand.

It was February and there were only eight months to go. Elaborate preparations for the wedding kept Shalini busy from morning to night. They had decided to invite more than two thousand guests, which included numerous relatives, business contacts and important people from the world of cricket.

Vaneshri was not very keen on involving herself in such complicated preparations and told her mother that she would be happy to marry Inder in the nearest registry office. She mischievously mentioned to her parents that if they wanted a big, traditional wedding they must take care of the planning on their own. Shalini was more than delighted to take the entire responsibility on her shoulders.

Deputy Prime Minister's Office, Delhi, March 2019

Two parliamentary researchers entered the office and glanced at Sudesh's schedule, which lay open on the desk.

'Can I help you?' asked Shakti who had now taken over as Sudesh's PA.

'We would like to have an appointment with Mr Kumar.'

'Let me know what you want to discuss with him, and I will do what I can. He will see you but it may take a while. He sees hundreds of people every month.'

'Why does he drive himself so hard? It's not a race. Poverty and crime will still be with us next year, and the year after that also,' said the taller man.

'For Mr Kumar, it is a race,' said Shakti.

'A race?'

'The best way to describe it is this. When you see government statistics regarding, for example, malarial deaths or people without sanitation or health care or clean water you see only a statistic. Sudesh sees the wheels turning, and those numbers moving. Every time he acts or makes a decision he considers the effect on those statistics. Always he is trying to bring the numbers down, to reduce the suffering.

'You analyse those statistics with your brains,' she concluded, 'Sudesh feels them in his heart.'

Paris, April 2019

As Vaneshri and Inder crossed the Champs Élysées on an April evening a blue Renault erupted in flames less than twenty feet away. They shielded their eyes and Inder instinctively moved between his fiancée and the blast.

A group of men ran off towards their next target. Some of them were young, others seemed older, and most of them were White.

'Is this safe, darling? I didn't expect an uprising on our holiday.'

'I'm beginning to wonder,' Inder looked up and down the now quiet street, 'What can be the cause?'

'This is the problem,' said a passer-by, pointing to a poster attached to a lamp-post.

'What does it say?' asked Inder. 'Your government has lied to you,' replied Vaneshri.

They walked along the wide avenue towards the Arc de Triomphe, disturbed but not frightened.

'There's another,' Inder pointed.

'They know how to help you. They choose not to,' translated Vaneshri. 'And look at that one, it says, "Your corrupt government is stealing from you".'

'I knew Europeans and Americans were angry about the depression, I didn't realise it was translating into violence.'

'In the early years, when the financial problems had begun, people thought their governments could help them. Now they are convinced their governments could have done something but chose not to.'

'I wouldn't like to be in government now.'

'Neither would I.'

'Inder, look!'

The young man turned to face an angry horde running towards them.

Imperial Hotel, New Delhi, April 2019

Sudesh met Ray at his favourite bar in the Imperial Hotel. He enjoyed the cool dimness and intimacy of the wood panelled room at this time of the day.

Ray wanted to hear Sudesh's plans for the future of India's Special Economic Zones or 'SEZs', which fell under his ministry.

'India's attempt to copy the Chinese model has achieved some success,' said Ray, 'but in this game you can't clone what has succeeded elsewhere and expect the same results. Given the choice, investors choose the area with the longest track record. To entice them to India you will have to offer something extra.'

Sudesh had done his homework. 'I worked through my department's files and you're right, crude replication is pointless. Most of the three thousand special zones around the world have failed They are expensive to set up and have attracted no investors.'

'So, what's your plan, Sudesh? India has a history of resistance to special economic zones, from both political parties, and from rural people whose land has been appropriated. Investors don't go where they're not welcome. Can you do better?'

'The former opponents of special zones are our alliance partners; they have agreed to give us autonomy regarding SEZs. With respect to the land, any new zones will only be put in place with the agreement of the State governments, and we will focus on barren land that is currently of no use to anyone.

'You taught me, Ray, that the best way to test the validity of an idea is to take it to its logical conclusion. That is our plan for the special zones. Normally, they have less government intervention and tax than elsewhere, but we will have none.'

'Many zones offer zero taxes.'

'No. They offer a five to ten year tax holiday, or very low business taxes, but there are many hidden taxes and charges. We're talking absolutely no taxes and no intervention.'

'Then what's in it for India?' Ray knew, but wanted to hear what Sudesh had to say on this.

'The answer is geographic. From a legal point of view the zones are not part of India, but geographically they are. They will employ Indians who will spend their income locally. They will sell products to our citizens who will benefit from the lower prices. And we hope and expect that the investors will settle here and bring their wealth.

'As you know this has already occurred to a considerable extent as a consequence of the depression.'

'Yes. We want to take it to a new level. Everything in these zones will be subject to free competition, driving efficiency up and prices down. I mean everything, infrastructure, courts, schools, hospitals, police, everything.'

'Who will pay for all these services?' Ray asked.

'People and businesses will pay user fees. Everything will be self-funded, mostly using electronic technology. In our free zones there will be opportunities for every business, including engineering companies who build basic infrastructure.'

'What do you plan to do with the government infrastructure already in place in existing zones?'

'We will sell it to the private sector. The existing businesses will probably be the first buyers. They will welcome the opportunity to take over infrastructure in exchange for no taxes or interventions.'

'In the business world,' commented Ray, 'we've learned that when things are too good to be true it is because they are not true. How will you create confidence if investors fear that the next government will scrap the deal?'

'We'll enter into binding contracts with investors which would allow them to sue us if we renege.'

'Why should investors trust those contracts?'

'We have approached Lloyds for a new political risk insurance. They will indemnify investors against breach of contract by India's government. For example, if a future government starts taxing SEZs, it will have to exempt existing investors. If it doesn't they can sue for damages. If the government doesn't pay, the businesses can recover from Lloyds. Part of the reason Lloyds is willing to provide the insurance is that, governments seldom break their contracts, because the consequences of doing so are too severe.'

Paris, April 2019

What a way to die, thought Vaneshri, crushed underfoot by a gang of thugs on the historic streets of Paris.

The two stood rooted to the spot, Inder mustered courage for action.

But as they braced themselves the group of men moved around and past them. There was panic on their faces. Soon Vaneshri and Inder could see the reason. Close behind the gang was a troop of gendarmes armed with truncheons.

'Just what I was looking forward to – a romantic, relaxing break in Paris,' exclaimed Vaneshri, 'Let's get out of the city centre.'

They hired a cab, picked up their luggage, and headed for Versailles.

Burnt out cars and lorries blocked most of the main roads, forcing their driver to divert through the back streets.

'We should have expected this,' said Vaneshri. 'There has been a growing unrest in France since the beginning of the depression.'

The placards around the city said it all. "Nous savons que vous nous mentez," (We know you are lying to us).

&

Settled in their suite in the Chateau d'Esclimon, Vaneshri and Inder glued their eyes to the news on CNN. The Parisian riots received extensive coverage interspersed with reports from Italy and Greece where demonstrators could be seen becoming increasingly unruly.

Outside the Houses of Parliament in London, and Congress in Washington DC, protestors marched with placards.

'It's surreal,' said Inder, gazing at the scenes on the five foot wide flat screen.

'And it's different from anything we have seen before,' said Vaneshri. 'Largely thanks to Ray's Upton Exchange the public is no longer willing to listen to excuses.'

Department of Law and Justice, New Delhi, May 2019

'What part of "objective" you don't understand? What's so complicated about "equality"?' asked Ashina Mehta, the Minister of Law and Justice from L&PP.

She directed herself at the group of lawyers around the U-shaped table in the Legislative Department's committee room. The meeting was taking place in the 'A' Wing of Shastri Bhawan, where national laws are drafted and screened for constitutionality and compliance with principles of good law.

Ashina had positioned herself beside the department head, Secretary Advaita Rizal.

'No need for formalities,' she said when Rizal started introducing her and explaining why she'd requested the meeting, 'let's get on with clarifying how laws must be drafted in future.

'You all know that the L&PP requires all laws to comply with the Act of Equivalence, which was adopted last month?'

The lawyers nodded.

'Well, we have a problem here. Let me take you through this Bill you have drawn up for the Department of Labour, the Public Works Bill.

'In Clause 6(2) it allows the government to employ people on public works and projects at below the minimum wage.' She looked up.

'The Bill is aimed at addressing unemployment,' said one of the younger lawyers.

'I am aware of that,' replied Mehta. 'However, the Act of Equivalence requires that laws apply equally to the private and public sector. So if this Bill is adopted, private companies would also be entitled to pay employees less than the minimum wage.'

'But what about the minimum wage law?' blurted the young man.

'Precisely,' said Ashina Mehta, looking at him, 'we have a contradiction there.'

'Does this apply to laws already on the statute books?'

'Yes.'

'So every law, old and new, except those regarding taxation, must apply equally to government and private business?'

'Yes, that is correct.'

The lawyers looked at her aghast. The implications were mind boggling.

Delhi, June 2019

'The wedding is going to be huge,' said Shakti to her mother. 'Shalini has booked the Umaid Bhavan Palace for the occasion. Its Rathore Durbar Hall is the only large and glamorous space available to accommodate the huge gathering that will be there. The guests are flying in from America and UK and from all over India, and the wedding planner has organised a "wedding shop" for the westerners that will stock saris, bindis, turbans and kurtas.

'We even have to learn a Bollywood dance to entertain the guests!'

The two were on their way to the design studio of Mukherjee, who had been chosen as designer for the entire bridal party.

'Do we have any choice as to what we are to wear?', asked Aruna Bhati.

'You do but I don't. The bridesmaids' outfits are already planned. Vaneshri is wearing traditional red and gold, and we will be in shades from nectarine to bright orange. You will choose from a range of gorgeous colours and exotic designs that tone with our *lehengas*. I must say Mukherjee is a fabulous designer.'

'Are you envious, my love?', asked Aruna.

'A bit. Not so much of the trappings, the wedding is much too big for me. Vaneshri and Inder are immensely happy. I am envious of that.'

'Sudesh is going to be the centre of attraction. Is he bringing a partner?'

'I don't think so, Amma. I sometimes think he likes that journalist Punita. But when I consider that she gives him so much trouble then I see no reason why he should like her.'

'I remember the time when you all were kids and loitered around together barefoot in the village. Look at you now: Sudesh is Deputy Prime Minister with you running his office, and Inder is a world famous cricketer.'

'I just wish Chanda was here too, then it would be perfect.'

Government Office, West Delhi, August 2019

Sudesh had habits that made people uncomfortable.

He often walked into remote government offices and enquired about the status of the work. He didn't stand on ceremony, and treated everyone, from the highest to the lowest official, with the same disarming charm.

Nothing would remain the same after his visit. One visit from the Deputy Prime Minister was enough to raise an alarm. The hot dusty rooms with their slowly rotating fans never dared to experience the same sluggish air.

Today, twenty astonished faces looked up at him.

'I want to see that report by the end of the day, that is midnight. Is that understood?', Sudesh instructed the staff.

Nobody replied, but everyone nodded. Cancelling their respective plans for the evening, the staff members geared up to finish the work by day end.

Los Angeles, USA, September 2019

Dr Jason Etheridge controlled a tiny robotic device that scraped the plaque from the interior of arteries. It was a technique he had invented and the process had become automatic.

His mind was engaged with other matters.

'So the government is changing the rules again,' said his surgical assistant, reading his thoughts.

'So it seems, Todd. Congress wants us to spend a third of our time working with patients who can't afford the normal fee.'

'Which might have been acceptable if Congress had not caused high fees in the first place.'

'Exactly. Since the new administration in 2016, national regulations have increased the cost of health care by fifty percent.'

Etheridge pressed a control switch for his tiny robot and it closed the patient's incision with a line of perfect stitches.

'And that's not counting the cost of allowing people to sue for punitive damages out of all proportion to any harm done by negligent or unlucky doctors.'

The two doctors left the surgery heading back to their hospital consulting rooms.

'Let's not fool around,' said Todd, 'The cost of our legal insurance is passed onto the patients in their medical bills.'

Etheridge turned into his office. 'You know, Todd, this new directive is the last straw. I've had enough.'

As he disappeared into his room, his receptionist buzzed through.

'Ray Upton is here to see you.'

'Show him in.'

Sudesh's apartment, Delhi, September 2019

Sudesh was tired and depressed before he went to bed that night. The L&PP's approval ratings were down. People didn't understand what he was trying to do.

They didn't realise that the policies he was introducing now would lift them out of poverty permanently in ten years' time.

The positive results of the Act of Equivalence were not yet evident, and though it had considerable support in business circles, the Communist Party was trying its best to make it appear purely obstructive.

Although the sale of Special Zone infrastructure had brought money into the treasury, the other parties, and the media had heavily criticised the loss of tax income. Hundreds of thousands of enquiries were being registered on the website, but so far only a trickle of new investors had actually signed on.

He didn't mind waiting. In time the public would experience the positive effects of his policies and understand his actions.

Or was he being unrealistic. Wasn't this just the way politics worked. People had short memories. Any progress he achieved before the next election would be claimed by the Communists, and as the major party in the alliance, who would deny them.

Maybe he should leave politics, join an NGO and help people at the grass-root level.

Umaid Bhavan Palace, October 2019

Shakti gazed up at the brilliant showers of coloured light filling the night sky above acres of manicured lawns surrounding the Umaid Bhavan Palace. The fireworks heralded the end of a perfect day.

Donning a cream and gold kurta with tinselled turban, mounted on a white horse followed by four elephants in full regalia, her brother had looked like a Maharajah as he arrived in the *baraat*.

Sabyasachi beamed with pride as he handed Vaneshri to her groom. For him there had never been a more beautiful bride. Her jewellery and wedding attire did not overshadow the radiance on her face. As she and Inder circled the sacred fire they could hardly take their eyes off each other.

Shakti felt shy in a gathering of affluent people and so chose to stay in the background, helping her mother. Sudesh had not brought a partner, and she could see no sadness in his eyes when they strayed to the wedding couple.

When the dancing began he sought her out, 'My dear Shakti,' he said, 'how lovely you look in your finery! I forget how beautiful my little friend is, when she works so hard in the office,' and as he whisked her off in his arms she felt as if her heart would burst.

Twenty-three

The Himalayas, July 2020

The simple house stood alone on the side of a mountain flanked by massive, snow-capped peaks. A man sat in front of it and waited for the four figures, who were heading out of the valley, to approach him. When the four Jaish-e-Mohammed operatives arrived, they were offered black coffee by their host who had spent two hours following their progress since he had spotted them with his binoculars. The four men with black turbans sat comfortably inside their host's cottage.

'We greet you in the name of Allah.'

'So, are the explosives and detonators ready?'

'Yes, I have made double the amount you requested,' he informed them, 'There is nothing better that I can do out here.'

'Double?' The Taliban leader sounded impressed.

'Double,' confirmed the man.

Standing up, he went into the smaller room of the cottage and brought out four packages, distributing one to each of the men.

Mumbai, July 2020

The lady was plump and stout. She guardedly watched Nirav enter the restaurant and waited for him to settle at a table. After the waiter handed him a menu, she waddled off towards his hotel suite.

As she approached the door, she wore a smile. There was a peep hole. Glancing around to check for observers she drew a five centimetre long cylinder from her pocket. Not everyone knew that peepholes could be reversed. She placed the device over the hole and looking into it she traced a complete view of the interior of the suite. As she expected there was nobody there. She had no problem in opening the door, she had bribed the front desk assistant and obtained a duplicate key.

The lady closed the door behind her and moved swiftly to the desk. Her gloved hands touched nothing unnecessarily.

'Ah, that could be it.' she said to herself as she grabbed an envelope.

She sprayed liquid onto the sealed A4 envelope, which became translucent, enough for her to read its contents. 'Interesting!' she told herself. She replaced the envelope and watched as the substance evaporated leaving no trace.

Grabbing the information she wanted, she left the room, heading for his car. With surprising dexterity for one so large she attached a magnetic box, less than half the size of a cigarette box, to the underside of the car. The GPS would allow her to keep track of his movements.

A good day's work.

'Mafia Murderers Strike Again', *Delhi Times*, 16 November 2020

Kolkata's crime boss, Nirav Choudhary, became the twenty-third victim of the mysterious 'Mafia Murderers' yesterday.

Responding to an anonymous tip-off the police discovered Choudhary's body late last night. Forensic investigations indicated that he died after ingesting an unknown poison that caused the blood to congeal in his veins and arteries.

Leaders of organised crime have been murdered in all of India's major cities, and for the past ten years a special unit comprising senior detectives from Delhi, Mumbai, Kolkata, Bengaluru, Chennai, and Ahmedabad has been working on the murders. The high-powered team is pooling resources to track down the killers and the organisation behind them.

All these murders have certain common aspects. They have breached sophisticated security. Each murder has been done by a different person, and all the murderers are highly skilled killers. That there are so many professional killers is especially baffling.

There are some who regard the 'Mafia Murderers' as heroic. With most of the top leadership dead, organised crime is in disarray. Law-abiding Indians sleep soundly in their beds.

It seems that whichever group is responsible for these deaths, its members are clever and prudent and seem to be hell bent on eliminating the entire tribe of criminals.

Police Headquarters, Delhi, May 2021

Nanek Singh looked at the docket that had come to him for routine review.

'Jay, this death of Vasu in a plane crash.'

'Yes Sir, five years ago. He went down in the Himalayas.'

'Are we sure?'

'The men pursuing him saw the wreckage from the air.'

'But if Vasu is dead, who is behind the killing of crime lords? The only person I can think of who could get a network together of killers and who could pull off this series of murders is Vasu. He could be acting on a fantasy of taking over organised crime throughout the country.'

'So you think when his plane crashed he survived?' 'Anything is possible. I think we should check it out.'

The Himalayas, May 2021

Two Sherpas and four police officers trekked through the snow towards the plane wreck.

They knew they were in for a long hike. They had been dropped off with their equipment approximately five days from their target. Given the depth of the valley in which the wreck lay, and the height of the surrounding mountains, it was not possible to land a helicopter any closer.

The six men clipped on their cross-country skis, shouldered their packs of supplies, and took on the most inhospitable mountain range in the world.

The Bhati Penthouse, Delhi, May 2021

'Are you ready darling?' asked Inder, checking his knotted bow-tie in the mirror. 'We don't want to be late.'

'Okay. I just need to Google my earrings,' said Vaneshri.

Inder wasn't sure if he had heard correctly. 'What did you just say?'

Vaneshri smiled, 'This is my new toy. I've done it for you too. Look at this.' Vaneshri picked up her PDA and touched the screen. 'Chaumet emerald earrings,' she said into the tiny speakers. She handed the multi-purpose organiser to Inder so that he could see the screen where he read "Google Personal Items."

'What on earth?' he thought, looking closer. Beneath the writing was a 3-D plan of their bathroom; a red dot flashed on the marble surface left of the hand basins.

'That's where I left them!' Vaneshri crossed the bedroom in the direction of the bathroom.

As she returned to the room, attaching the emerald stones to her ears, Inder folded his arms, 'How does that work?'

'All our valuable items are marked with encoded spray. Anything we can't find we Google. If the item is in the house it will appear on the little 3-D plan, just as my earrings did. If it is somewhere else, the GPS function kicks in and a satellite picture appears with a dot indicating its position and giving the address. Clever?'

'Yes, my darling, just like you,' replied Inder, kissing her on the cheek.

The Himalayas, May 2021

The wind drove the fine, dry snow into their safety glasses, limiting their visibility.

'We're getting close now.'

'The GPS shows us within a hundred metres.'

'Look over there.'

'That's it!'

The men made their way to the wreckage, hidden by snow.

'Well fellows, we have reached our target. Let's set up camp and search for the pilot's body in the morning,' said the leader.

'Wait a minute,' it was Atul Sethi, second in command, 'I don't think this is the plane we're looking for.'

'What do you mean?'

'Well, this fuselage is steel, not aluminium.' He walked around examining the twisted metal closely. 'Vasu was flying a jet. This is not a jet, look at this piece of propeller. This is a World War II bomber.'

The Chief joined him, looking carefully. 'You're right, Atul. This is not the plane Vasu took off in.'

'You know what I think we've found?' said Atul.

'What's that?'

'This could be the plane of the freedom fighter, Netaji Subhas Chandra Bose. He supposedly died in a plane-crash in Taiwan in 1945, but his body was never found and the Taiwanese have denied any such crash; their evidence was supported by the American state department.'

'It's certainly worth investigating,' replied the Chief. 'The plane dates from the 1940s, and if Netaji's body is found in this plane a long-standing mystery will be solved. Meanwhile, I wonder what has happened to Vasu?'

CNN Studio, New York City, September 2021

'Damian Knight, welcome to AC 360.'

'Glad to speak to you, Anderson.'

'Last time we spoke,' said Anderson Cooper, 'your campaign for Free Citizens had just been launched. Through your advertising and website you were reaching millions of people in depressed economies across the world.'

'That's correct. Our goal was to educate citizens and voters about the reasons behind the Second Great Depression, and to encourage them to pressurise their governments to change their tactics.'

'But look at what is happening around the world today; protests, riots, vandalism. Isn't your campaign responsible for this, hasn't it backfired?'

'First of all, Anderson, let me say unequivocally that at no time has the campaign for Free Citizens advocated rioting or destruction of property, including government property.'

'You don't officially endorse it, but isn't it the result of your campaign?'

'No. All we did was provide information proving that governments caused the Depression, and that unless they changed their policies, things won't change.

'When people understood what was happening they applied pressure on their governments in peaceful ways. They e-mailed their representatives, created citizens' lobby, and did their best to influence the process. But their governments ignored them.'

'You're talking about the USA, Europe and Japan?', confirmed Anderson.

'Correct. The governments that ran into trouble during the financial crisis of 2008 and 2009 and who attempted to fix their economies through massive spending programmes. These governments have ignored the people who elected them. Now the people are desperate. They have lost their homes and sources of income. They are surviving on private charity and community service.

'Desperation has led to anger, anger to rage, and that has finally spilled over into violence.'

'Yes Damian. But you gave them the information in the first place, and now you can't take it back. Without your campaign these riots might not have occurred.'

'The people would still be starving, Anderson. They would still have lost their savings, their homes and their jobs. The only difference is that they would be ignorant of the reasons.'

'Now that you have opened a Pandora's Box, do you have any solution to set things right?'

'You know, Anderson, there is no quick fix. Even if governments were to accept reality, stop spending, and repeal laws that prevent people from making money, it will take a few years to rebuild what has been destroyed.

'But there are many parts of the world, previously known as the third world, that have not made the same mistake, because they didn't have sufficient resources for profligate spending. Those countries and India in particular, are growing rapidly and offering huge opportunities.'

'Why India?'

'The Minister for Commerce and Industry, Sudesh Kumar, has created special zones with total economic freedom.'

'The same as in China?' queried Anderson.

'Similar, but with no government involvement at all. These free zones are beginning to take off. They are attracting investments from people who still have wealth but have given up on the Great Depression countries. There are businesses drawing on India's immense pool of labour, and there are plenty of opportunities for people in every walk of life.'

'You mean not only business men?'

'Doctors, lawyers, engineers, architects, IT professionals. I mean anyone who has had enough of government.

'America was built by pioneers escaping the old world, maybe the time has come to emigrate again, to the Third Millennium New World in India.'

Abbottabad, Pakistan, April 2022

Seven hundred boys between the age of six and fifteen sat shoulder-to-shoulder in the mosque school in Dakhan.

This is better than learning the *Koran* by heart, they thought, though none would dare mention it.

'You have all heard about nuclear bombs. You know that Pakistan owns such weapons and you must wonder why a government of the faithfuls does not use them to destroy the infidels?'

Some of the boys nodded.

'The reason is that the infidels also own nuclear bombs, and they would retaliate. They would destroy Pakistan.'

More boys nodded.

'When we have to act against the infidels, we should make sure that they never track us down. Think of 9/11, the Americans couldn't find us, could they? With all their technology and money! Allah be praised.'

The Madrasa was filled with laughter; this was a cause for happiness.

'Now, consider the benefits of incendiary weapons such as napalm B,' said the new mullah. 'When a napalm bomb is dropped it burns and destroys anything, or anyone in its path. One suicide bomber can create maximum damage.

'The modern form of napalm is composed of benzene and polystyrene, which are easily available. It is mixed with gasoline and burns at very high temperatures, immolating its targets. It creates carbon monoxide that deoxygenates the available air, causing suffocation.

'It is not a nuclear bomb; it uses ordinary materials, but it causes more fear than any other method, and fear is our greatest weapon. Provided we create sufficient fear Sharia will prevail throughout the world.'

Everyone agreed. People spoke freely here, unlike in the cities. Seldom did any westerner visit these deserted mountainsides.

'We may need to call on you for the difficult and dangerous work of building and deploying these bombs.' The boys looked at one another, elated by the prospect of adventure.

There would be no lack of volunteers.

Bhati Penthouse, New Delhi, May 2022

'We're doing some fascinating work in the Visakhapatnam Free Zone,' said Vaneshri, pouring a glass of lemon water for Inder and a Spritzer for herself.

'Yes?' said Inder relaxing back in his chair.

'We're using the resources of two million people to find a cure for tuberculosis and to investigate the link between genes and various illnesses.'

'What? You are getting everyone to do research?'

'No, no, just using their resources.'

'How are you doing that?'

'Well, you know about the new cities springing up in all of Sudesh's Free Zones?'

'The "anarchy cities"?'

'Yes. That's what the leftist press calls them, because there are no government regulations or taxes. In fact they are incredibly orderly and first world.'

'But how do they deal with criminals?' asked Inder.

'They have private police and law courts which are as efficient as their businesses. But listen, we put down large quantities of fibre optics which gives us huge bandwidth everywhere in the Visakhapatnam Free Zone city.'

Inder stifled a yawn.

'Everyone in the city is requested to leave their computers and playstations turned on when they're not using them, then we use them to process complex problems.'

'How does that happen?'

'The whole city becomes one huge, mega-computer. The idea was first used in the US at the turn of the century, but this is the first time it has been put into practice in an entire city, and we expect the other free cities to join the network soon. Without the usual bureaucratic red-tape to worry about, we can introduce it very quickly.'

'What did you say you're doing with it?' His interest had been regained.

'Scientists are using the network for complicated biological calculations related to finding a cure for tuberculosis.'

'And you mentioned something else?'

'We are going to correlate genetic profiles with medical histories, exercise and eating habits to search for the effects of genes on health.'

'Interesting.'

'We do this for the whole city, except for a few people who have opted out. We replace names with numbers, so the trials include many more people than normal, and are anonymous.'

'So, one day you might be able to look at an individual's genetic profile and say which diseases he is most likely to suffer from, and how he might prevent them?'

'Precisely!' said Vaneshri.

The Lok Sabha, New Delhi, July 2022

'This is capitalism gone berserk,' exclaimed Prime Minister Jayaraman during a parliamentary debate.

'I don't understand your objection,' countered Sudesh. 'The new schools and clinics are being run by religious groups, cultural and civic organisations. Small traders and peasant farmers are running many of the new businesses. This is people's revolution in the real sense.'

In three years since the Act of Equivalence had been passed, there had been an explosion of innovative alternatives to virtually everything done by the government.

Countless community, religious, corporate and informal schools and hospitals had been granted full equality with government institutions. This included equal funding, zero tax and more.

The Act required that security services receive the same funding and facilities as police, and that arbitration services compete on equal terms with courts. The same applied to the provision of electricity and telecommunications, as well as the financial and legal branches of the State.

It soon became apparent that it was not possible to extend all the subsidies and tax exemptions government enjoys to the private sector. There simply was not enough money in the budget. Instead, the government had to outsource most functions and compete with private business on equal terms.

There were two consequences. Now that government no longer enjoyed an unfair advantage the private sector came up with a wide range of creative alternatives, and the outsourced government departments, forced to compete, became increasingly efficient.

Office of the Deputy Prime Minister, November 2022

'I'm sorry to disturb you Sir, but I think this is important.'

'Come in! It's good to see you,' Superintendent Patel.'

The two men sat at the round table, and Sudesh looked at the policeman enquiringly.

'Regarding the Mafia Murders.'

'Yes, Superintendent?'

'We have traced a pattern.'

'Okay, go on.'

'It has been found that during each murder Special Agent Madhumati Singh was out of contact. That is to say, Sir, we cannot account for her movements at the time of these murders. We felt this observation might be significant.'

'Does Commissioner Singh know about this?'

'No, Sir.' The Superintendent spoke. 'Due to the nature of this information, Sir, we thought it best to bypass him.'

'Okay, Superintendent, I understand. Leave the report with me and I will give it my attention. However, difficult though it may be, you will have to inform the Commissioner as well.'

Frankfurt, November 2022

The German entrepreneur, Gerhard Vehr, was working on a strategy to market his Internet banking plan.

This would be a bank with no branches, no head office, one-hundredth of the employees and one-tenth of the charges. But he was finding it difficult to concentrate. The noise from the picket line was distracting.

'Can't we do anything about them?' Vehr asked his personal assistant as he entered the room.

'No, they are legally entitled to be there.'

'They are entitled to be unproductive and disruptive and still get paid!'

'For the first ninety days. That's correct.'

'And if we fire them?'

'You must pay them two years' salary.'

'Wonderful!'

'And remember, that includes medical benefits, pension, compulsory sick pay, children's school allowance, and of course, tax.'

'Why don't the politicians and union leaders realise that extra benefits mean we have to pay lower wages?'

'Most people who make laws don't understand economics, Sir.'

'These unions destroyed Britain in the 1960s and 1970s. Now they are destroying us. I've had enough!'

'Indeed. Mr Vehr, there is someone here to see you.'

'Who?'

'An American, his name is Upton.'

'The very man I want to see, send him through.'

Deputy Prime Minister's office, November 2022

Sudesh looked at the file, still lying on his meeting table. He pondered over the coincidence of Madhumati's absence at the time of every assassination.

Could she be involved in the murders, he dreaded the thought. Thinking about her extent of involvement with the CBI, Sudesh knew she could.

On the other hand, all of the evidence indicated that the murders were committed by a number of different individuals. He could not envisage Madhumati liaising with a network of killers.

He thought about Nanek and Devika. How would they feel, what would happen to their lives if their beloved Madhu turned out to be behind the Mafia Murders.

Sudesh picked up the file and put it in the bottom left drawer of his desk. He would think about it later.

Twenty-four

BBC Radio Commentary, 20 May 2023

'Seems like a perfect day for the World Cup final One Day International match between India and Pakistan. Kolkata's Eden Gardens, the world's biggest stadium, is filled to capacity with a hundred thousand cricket fans.

'Eden Gardens is India's oldest stadium, established in 1864.

'In 1917 these hallowed grounds hosted India's original first class game. Since the first international test in 1934, Eden Gardens has hosted more tests than any other stadium, including the 1987 World Cup final.

'In its illustrious history, this stadium has witnessed many records set by Indian cricketers. It saw India's first test hat-trick in 2000 and its best bowling attempt by Anil Kumble who took six wickets for twelve runs ...'

Kolkata's Eden Gardens Stadium, 20 May 2023

With two wickets in hand India needed 209 runs in 23 overs. Inder Bhati, regarded as the world's greatest batsman, was left at the crease with only two of India's tail-enders to follow. Pakistan's victory seemed inevitable.

Dejected Indian fans started moving towards the exit gates.

Inder spoke to his partner, 'Leave it to me, Sanjeev,' he said, 'Just hang in there, don't go for runs that'll give you the bowling, and don't think of losing for one second. Just stay in, whatever you do, stay in. Keep the ball off your wickets, keep it down, keep it safe.'

The game continued according to Inder's plan. Inder was now on a scoring spree. Pakistan's captain tossed a ball to Yawaar Khan, the fastest bowler of his team. Bhati–Khan clashes were legendary, and the crowd held on to its seats.

Yawaar's first delivery was fast and straight. It should have been a regulation dot ball, but an aggressive front-foot charge by Inder lifted it over his head and down the ground into the sightscreen stand for a six. As Khan turned, shaking his head in frustration, he heard Inder say belligerently, 'Sweat man sweat, there's more to come.'

A Farm near Kolkata, 20 May 2023

The Jaish-e-Mohammed terrorists performed their tasks, eager to replace 9/11 in the annals of history. To achieve this goal they needed only fourteen 45-gallon plastic drums filled with napalm B, an Air Tractor crop-sprayer and enough fuel to fly twenty-five kilometres.

The pilot was the 'chosen one'. He knew the small green and yellow plane well; he'd been a crop-sprayer for three years. Everything not essential for the short flight had been removed, and the fuel tanks kept nearly empty. The drums of napalm were heavy, so the plane must be kept as light as possible.

❧

Inder reached his 150 and Sanjeev notched up 22, breaking his previous record. The partnership had miraculously narrowed the deficit to 106 runs when Sanjeev was clean-bowled by a ball he appeared not to have seen.

Inder walked calmly to the centre of the pitch to give the same briefing to his new partner, Aditya, who was known better for his crafty leg spin. Inder knew he was in top form and kept repeating his favourite motto to himself and his partner, 'It's not over till it's over.'

The gap narrowed to ninety, then eighty, and then seventy. When it was down to forty the crowd were on the edge of their seats.

India was still twenty-seven short of victory at the beginning of the fiftieth over, with Aditya facing the first ball. He got a lucky inside edge and the ball rocketed between the bat and his legs narrowly missing leg stump, and racing away. They could have picked up two runs, but Inder knew he had to take on the bowling.

Now, India needed twenty-six off the last five balls. Having got this close the crowd believed anything was possible and Inder knew he had to throw caution to the winds. He stood upright holding his bat high in the ultimate Bhati–Khan stand-off position.

❦

Ahmad felt elated as he pushed the lever to full throttle. He would be airborne by the end of the short airstrip. He ascended very slowly and flew at low altitude below the range of radar and surveillance devices. He knew where to gather speed to rise briefly above power lines and areas of thermal turbulence. He had been trained and was prepared.

Residents looked up as Ahmad flew overhead, his thoughts focused on the stadium packed with Indian infidels, international visitors, and local and foreign dignitaries.

There would be many Pakistanis supporting their national team, but most were seated at the High Court end of the stadium, the only area which would not be bombed directly. Even if some of his countrymen died, it would still be a small price to pay in the Holy War.

❦

The first ball was a 150 kilometre per hour out-swinger. Inder swung with all his might and sent the ball over the third man boundary for a six. Now he needed twenty runs off four balls.

The next ball was a straight bouncer. He spun into his famous pull-shot to hit it over the mid-wicket boundary, but it landed short. A fielder who flung himself at the bouncing ball slowed and deflected it, somehow keeping it in the field of play. Though they could have run three, they settled for two so that Inder could retain the strike.

The last three balls would all have to go for six. The fielders who'd encircled the batsmen inside the ring spread out to the boundary ropes looking for the match-winning catch.

Inder's swing at the next ball missed and he was clean-bowled. There was a collective groan of despair intermingled with howls of delight from the end stand filled with Pakistanis. In the din no one heard the umpire call a 'no-ball.'

❦

Ahmad was in no hurry as he flew low over Kolkata's north eastern suburbs towards the elbow in the river Hooghly where he would find Eden Gardens on the far bank. He saw children playing cricket in streets, fields and parks. They paused to stare up and wave at him.

His flight had been timed so that the end of game climax would be Allah's. The plan was made in Paradise, he thought. Nothing would go wrong.

❦

When the crowd realised that Inder had a free hit and was heading back to the crease they settled down, once again riveted to the game.

India still needed three sixes off three balls. Inder made no error with the next two deliveries, one lifted over long-on's head into the tenth row of spectators; the next swept over the square leg boundary into the scoreboard.

This last would be the most important ball in the lives of two legendary cricketers. At 156 kilometres per hour it was the fastest ball of the match, intended as a toe-crunching yorker, but a few inches longer than Khan had planned, just long enough for Inder to bound forward, turning it into a low full-toss. The tip of his bat lifted the ball and sent it soaring towards the South East end of the stadium. As two hundred thousand eyes in the stadium and millions more on TV followed the disappearing red dot skyward they saw it morph into a roaring flame.

Moments before he entered the air space above the stadium, Ahmad had tugged the red cord on his left to release the steel latches holding the first seven drums. As they fell, steel wires secured to the aircraft tightened and pulled the pins from their sockets in the grenades.

The detonations were small, but when the phosphor fused with the air it flared to a searing heat and melted holes in the drums causing them to fracture against the air pressure of their high-speed fall. The napalm ignited and spread through the air leaving trails of flames descending into the crowd.

Ahmad's timing was perfect. The roaring of the engine initially conflated with the din of ecstasy over India's victory. Inder, exhausted yet elated, saw nothing as he walked towards his team-mate. He raised his bat in acknowledgment as the crowd cheered and applauded.

The plane rose slightly and disappeared leaving the northern side of the stadium on fire. From all around the conflagration people ran, fighting to breathe and struggling to escape the inferno.

Many spectators froze in horror and some ran to help the injured ones, the aircraft reappeared as unexpectedly as before.

Ahmad had circled and returned to launch his remaining drums of destruction into the southern stands.

Inder stared into the cockpit as the plane came nearer and saw the pilot look back over his shoulder towards the Club House stand – holding the commentators' box, and the suites packed with dignitaries. Vaneshri was in one of the suites.

In that instant Inder knew, for reasons he could not later explain, that the plane would reappear to crash into its final target, the gathering of foreigners and dignitaries.

'It's coming back! Clear the stand!' Inder shouted to the other players on the field as he ran towards the tiered seating. 'Clear the stand!'

Following his lead the cricketers leapt onto the fence separating the crowd from the field. It collapsed beneath their combined weight and they ran forward shouting and gesticulating wildly for the spectators to leave.

As before, it took Ahmed seven and a half minutes to circle back, just long enough for the crowd to take safer refuge.

The plane swooped down across the centre of the stadium over the length of the famed pitch heading for its third target. By the time Ahmad realised the stands were empty he was too late to adjust his flight path. He entered his Eden from their Eden cursing as the plane smashed into the empty grandstand.

By now the fire-fighters and paramedics who had been stationed nearby were dousing flames and helping the victims. Inder and the other cricketers ran to assist. Unharmed people were dispersed as quickly as possible so the wounded could be treated initially on the field and then transferred to hospitals.

Then began the dreadful task of counting the dead.

'Cricket's Greatest Match becomes India's Darkest Memory', *The Telegraph*, Kolkata, 21 May 2023

What should have been a day of national rejoicing translated into a day of mourning as the estimated number of deaths resulting from yesterday's terror attack at Kolkata's Eden Gardens rose to 15,473. Over 28,854 casualties, many in critical condition, were rushed to hospitals and clinics.

Volunteer groups are helping people search for their missing relatives and friends. As they become known, names of the dead and wounded are being made available through the Indian Red Cross. The identities of many of those who died from immolation and asphyxiation will not be known until DNA testing has been completed.

Inder Bhati, hero of the match that ended in horror, will go down in history not only for his extraordinary innings, but also for the lives he saved.

It was because of Bhati's quick presence of mind that the Club House stand was cleared before the pilot crashed his plane into it. As his final act, the suicide bomber had intended to wreak havoc amongst local and international dignitaries. Bhati along with other players emptied the stands saving an estimated three thousand lives.

CBI and Anti-terrorism Squad suspect Jaish-e-Mohammed, a Pakistan-based terrorist organisation, to be behind this suicidal attack. Three members of the terrorist organisation who have been captured are currently being interrogated.

Analysts fear that the Eden Gardens' attack, of 20/5, could precipitate a nuclear war with Pakistan.

The Singh Apartment, Delhi, 22 May 2023

Nanek read the newspaper headlines when Madhu joined him with a bowl of fruits at the breakfast table.

'The CBI is doing a good job,' he said, looking up.

'Yes, we're pleased with our results.'

'How did you round them up so quickly?'

'We used Google Earth' satellite footage recorded for the time immediately prior to the attack. With the software I bought from Vaneshri we were able to rewind their satellite video service and see where the plane took off, from a small landing strip in the grounds of a farmhouse. The anti-terrorism squad surrounded the area within an hour of the attack.

'We caught the perpetrators red-handed. They were unaware that our new technology could lead us to them so quickly.'

'I see the Pakistan government is attempting to cooperate by swooping down on fifteen known Jaish-e-Mohammed centres. I presume your unit briefed them?'

'Yes, we found lots of information in the papers, computers and cell phones at the farm house, and the suspects provided more information under interrogation.' She grinned at him wickedly.

Continuing more soberly she said, 'One outcome from this tragedy is that it could herald a new era of either cooperation or an all-out war between India and Pakistan. We could finally rid the world of Jaish-e-Mohammed, the principal terrorist organisation in Jammu & Kashmir, or we would have the world's first nuclear war. I fear the worst. Our nation is baying for Pakistan's blood.'

The Kashmir Front, June 2023

Janardan helped the families load their household goods in a truck and assisted the older members to struggle up to perch on top of their possessions.

He climbed into the driver's seat and set off along the potholed road, away from the border, raising a cloud of dust. He drove slowly, allowing a group of boys to follow on their bikes to keep up.

During a brief hiatus in the shelling, Janardan helped people relocate from villages within the line of fire. He took them to an army-run relief centre situated in a school building, at a safe distance from the mortar bombs and rockets.

On their arrival he helped the families unpack their household belongings and piled them alongside heaps of other people's.

The new refugees were offered a share of the government ration, chapattis that were cooked on griddles and tea that was prepared in cavernous cauldrons. As they settled, Janardan walked through the makeshift camp, checking if people were reasonably comfortable, and started to listen to what they were saying.

An old lady squatted with a baby playing in the dirt at her side. 'When is the war going to begin,' she grumbled, 'it can't be worse than this, moving here, moving there.'

'Yes,' replied a young woman, bending to give the child a piece of *roti*, 'it's time to put an end to all of this, once and for all.'

'Our houses are under fire, our people and our cattle are dying,' added another, 'For us the war has already started, now they should get on and finish it.'

As Janardan, now a major in charge of 120 men, returned to the truck he reflected on their words. He wished that this interminable conflict ends, but the end must not be reached through nuclear missiles.

Wheeler Island, July 2023

Prime Minister Rohit Jayaraman stood in the control centre with Dr Natrajan, gazing at the Agni-VII. The gleaming canister was sixteen metres long. It ended in a black point, strangely reminiscent of a thick gold pencil with a sharpened end.

'It has a range of ten thousand kilometres. We have perfected the use of the ring laser gyroscope and accelerometer, first used in the Agni V and this one is extremely accurate.'

'Was the test last year successful?'

'Yes, Sir. We have had no more problems since 2006. All our missiles are on standby.'

Jayaraman looked at the nuclear warhead with awe. Within thirty minutes this missile could destroy Lahore or Islamabad. But with blast damage reaching a seventy kilometre radius neither of these cities could be chosen as revenge for the years of terrorism and to end the Pakistan problem. Both were too close to the Indian border. Rohit Jayaraman felt the weight of his responsibility.

The Kashmir Front, July 2023

As mortar shells flew overhead, the officer gulped down his rum and gorged on his lunch in a jiffy. He was deep in his bunker; one of many along the two-thousand-kilometre border stretching from the Siachen glacier in the north to the plains of Kathua in the south.

'When are we going to have a go at them, Chief?'

The soldier all braced up for the battle also carried a book.

'As soon as I get the instruction. We'll waste no time, I can't wait to punish the bastards for murdering our people at Eden Garden.'

'I thought the CBI caught all the Jaish-e-Mohammed people who were responsible, Sir?'

'You mustn't believe everything you read, Sergeant Major. What about the fifty-five thousand people who died in the Kashmir struggle before the stadium attack? If those gutless politicians don't retaliate they are begging for more atrocities.'

'If they do attack Kashmir do you think they'll make use of us, Sir? What about that Agni VII and other missiles they've been stock-piling?'

'If we get orders to evacuate we'll know they've chosen that route, and they will have my support.'

'Yes Sir,' responded the Sergeant Major half-heartedly.

Army Headquarters, July 2023

General Aram Jacob pushed his seat back and stood, glowering at the Prime Minister.

'Rohit Jayaraman, I think I've known you long enough to tell you that we can delay no longer.'

'Aram, I don't want to be the first democratic Prime Minister since the Second World War to drop a nuclear bomb.'

'You must at least allow us to destroy their army installations.'

'That might precipitate a nuclear attack from them, General.'

'Our intelligence believes Pakistan is on the verge of launching a nuclear missile. The destruction of Jaish-e-Mohammed may have received international support, but internally it has resulted in more political pressure from the militant Islamists.

'They can drop their nuclear warheads on Hyderabad with no danger to themselves. You must act immediately or they will beat you to it.'

'I don't doubt the seriousness of the situation, Aram, but you know this is not a decision I can take alone. I will have to meet Sudesh Kumar, my coalition partner.'

The frustrated General banged his fist on the table, 'You must act, Prime Minister. You must act! You know as well as I that all-out nuclear war is inevitable, which means we must strike first.'

On a boat in the disputed waters of Sir Creek, August 2023

Sudesh extended his hand to greet the Pakistani Minister of Commerce. 'Thank you for meeting me without formal diplomatic clearance, Dr Rabbani.'

'I am assured you have a proposal sufficiently important to justify this,' replied the Minister.

'I believe I do.'

Sir Creek runs through the Rann of Kutch marshlands where the Indo-Pakistan border meets the Arabian Sea. India claimed the border as midway between the troop-lined banks of the creek, and Pakistan said it was on the Pakistani side. Sudesh arranged the meeting on a Swiss boat in the disputed area so that each could regard the meeting as taking place on their territory.

'Please take a seat,' said Sudesh. 'Dr Rabbani, despite your country's cooperation after the Kolkata stadium attack, I believe you will agree that India and Pakistan are now on the verge of a full-scale war.

'We all know that a nuclear war would destroy both the countries. We also know that even if we find a way to avoid war now, the conflict over Jammu&Kashmir will not end.

'I have a proposal which may bring about a permanent resolution.'

'But you're not in power, you're a junior partner in a tenuous coalition with your ideological adversaries,' interjected Rabbani, 'and you and I control commerce, not foreign policy. I see no point in this meeting.'

Sudesh recalled the same reaction from the communists when he proposed the coalition. With an effort he brought his mind back to the moment and focussed all his strength of personality on the man opposite.

'Dr Rabbani, thanks to thirty years of high growth, India's economy is ten times bigger than that of Pakistan. The annual increase in our defence budget is three to four times greater than your total defence budget. What chance is there that you will ever drive us out of Indian occupied Kashmir?'

'Where is this going?'

'You are in charge of foreign trade, struggling to promote exports, earn foreign exchange, create employment and settle international debt. India, your neighbour, is one of the biggest, fastest growing economies in the world, but we have mutual sanctions: nothing crosses our three thousand three hundred kilometre border.'

He paused, his eyes still fixed on the Pakistani Minister. 'My proposal is that we remove all restrictions on your exports to India in return for you accepting the Line of Control as the permanent Kashmir border. That would be worth billions of dollars to you annually.'

'Is that all you have to say?'

'Yes.'

'Why do you think we'd be interested in free trade with you? My job is to protect our economy from foreign competition. You have wasted my time.' Rabbani placed his hands on the arms of his chair as if to stand.

'I am not talking about free trade. I am offering to remove restrictions unilaterally.'

The Minister settled back in his chair and stared at Sudesh, 'You mean we get unrestricted access to your economy and maintain full sanctions against you?'

'You got it right.'

'And our countries sign a treaty accepting the LoC as the permanent border?'

'Yes.'

'My government would never give up our claim to Kashmir.'

'Consider this; it's unlikely that you will ever recover Indian-occupied Kashmir. The dispute is a financial drain on both of our countries and may plunge us into a mutually destructive nuclear war.

'If you accept my offer it will massively boost Pakistan's economy and strengthen your personal credibility. The choice you face is between a dangerous expensive conflict with no end in sight, or immediate growth and opportunity. Please discuss it with your fellow ministers.'

The National Assembly Building, Islamabad, August 2023

Dr Rabbani presented Sudesh's proposal at an emergency meeting of Pakistan's National Security Council.

The Chief of the Army Staff was called in to brief the Security Council on the current military situation with respect to Jammu & Kashmir. In camera he confirmed what Sudesh had told the Minister of Commerce regarding the relative military strength of the two countries.

Economists and Business leaders from SAARC (South Asian Association for Regional Cooperation) presented estimates of the value of free access to India's economy. They urged the government to accept the offer. Labour representatives said they welcomed the opportunity for Pakistanis to repatriate income from India.

At the end of three long days and nights, hundreds of cups of coffee and very little sleep, the thirteen members of the National Security Council agreed to accept the proposal. The Cabinet rubber-stamped the NSC's recommendation and an envoy was sent to Sudesh.

'Do you have the agreement of your government?' asked the envoy when conveying Pakistan's acceptance to Sudesh.

'No,' replied Sudesh, 'this is a trade deal, I don't need it. I am ready to sign.'

'But confirmation of the new Kashmir border is a matter for Foreign Affairs, not Trade.'

'India already regards the Line of Control as the border. All that is needed is for Pakistan to accept it.'

The Cabinet Meeting Room, New Delhi, August 2023

'This is an outrage!' exclaimed the Minister of Defence when Sudesh presented the Cabinet with the fait accompli of his trade agreement with Pakistan.

'They bomb our stadium and we reward them. It's absurd. I repeat my view that we should occupy the rest of Kashmir and all strategic areas on Pakistan's side of the border. They are military minnows. We should teach them a lesson once and for all!'

'They will never back down without a nuclear war which neither of us wants,' said the Prime Minster, looking worried. 'This may be the best we'll get, but it seems very one-sided, it means terrorism has triumphed.'

'Don't forget,' said Sudesh, 'the Pakistani government cooperated fully in destroying all of the Jaish-e-Mohammed cadres. The few remaining terrorist groups are divided and disorganised.'

The other cabinet ministers welcomed the prospect of an end to the conflict with Pakistan, but they were concerned about the impact on Indian business and workers.

'We should never have given you control over foreign trade,' said the Minister of Mines, 'we will be flooded with cheap minerals, our marginal mines will shut and we'll lose crores of jobs.'

'Perhaps, but our industries will have cheaper raw materials, our economy will be more competitive and our consumers will benefit.'

'We need to improve our terms of trade, increase exports and earn forex' said the Minister of Agriculture. 'This will have the opposite effect. It's one-sided in their favour.'

'It is one-sided,' replied Sudesh, 'but you get the sides wrong. It's one-sided in our favour. We get their cheap goods, services and labour, they get our money.'

'Spending our forex on them and allowing them to take jobs from our workers and block our exports isn't in our favour,' argued the Minister of Finance.

'We don't want exports; we want imports. The whole purpose of exporting is to get imports: the cheaper, the better. If we export to Pakistan or anywhere else for that matter, it benefits them and harms us; it's import promotion we want, we want to export less and import more.'

'Surely you're not suggesting that established trade theory is wrong!' objected the Minister of Statistics.

'Yes I am,' confirmed Sudesh. 'It is wrong. Think about it, we get richer only if we get more for less. If we had only exports and no imports we'd be poor, only imports and no exports would enrich us. The established consensus is nonsense.

'In reality India has no trade surplus or deficit, only people do, individuals and firms. They trade because they value what they get more than what they give. Every transaction makes them and the country richer.

'This deal with Pakistan is to our benefit, we end all border disputes and we get their exports, or at least the people do who buy from Pakistan.

'I repeat, the only thing we can do with foreign exchange is import, we want more for less, and that's what we get with this deal.'

'But we lose foreign exchange, our forex goes to them', objected another minister who'd studied economics.

'No, no, no,' insisted Sudesh so confidently that his colleagues were speechless. 'Money never leaves a country. All that happens is that foreigners get to own it. All they can do with it is spend it locally. Importers will buy only if they have money – foreign exchange – and it is exporters who provide it. Increase in imports automatically leads to increase in exports to pay for it and everyone benefits.'

Sudesh had not expected to undo economic mythology of decades in a single Cabinet briefing and he was thankful he had not needed their consent to his trade deal. In the end some of his Cabinet colleagues were partially convinced by his arguments, and the most passionate opponents of free trade admitted that the 'peace price' might be worth the deal.

'Frankly, I think it's a waste of time, not just the deal, but also discussing it,' said the Prime Minister, 'Even if you're right, and most experts disagree with you, it isn't nearly enough to appease Indians. Our nation is seething with rage, they want blood and they want it now.'

They were not prepared for Sudesh's bombshell. 'Oh no, you misunderstand me. I'm not suggesting that getting Pakistan to agree to the LoC is enough.'

'What other concessions do you have?'

'None, not from Pakistan, not directly anyway, and not that they know of or have agreed to. But it is substantial and will humiliate them in the eyes of our people.'

'You're talking in riddles, get to the point.'

'As we speak a press release is going out to the effect that Pakistan has gained nothing from the deal. They will be the laughing stock of the world for having made such substantial and historic concessions.'

'How so?'

'My press statement announces that we are giving the same benefits to all countries, that immediately after Pakistan signed, we declared unilateral free trade for everyone. They would have got precisely the same had they never signed.'

There was a collective gasp. Ministers stared at each other, then all eyes turned to Sudesh.

'You mean every country can now dump anything on us without any reciprocity? Are you mad!' exclaimed the Minister of Finance, followed by a chorus of astonishment and discontent.

'If what I said about trade with Pakistan is true, then it is true for all countries,' insisted Sudesh.

Ministers decided to end the meeting and convene urgent party caucus meetings to decide whether to dissolve the coalition and call early elections. Their problem was that polls showed Sudesh and the L&PP gaining popularity which made it increasingly unlikely that anyone could govern without them. A new coalition, however, could negotiate terms that would clip his wings.

Communist Party Caucus Meeting, Delhi, August 2023

By the time they got to their caucus meeting at which a decision to dissolve the ruling coalition was presumed to be a foregone conclusion, delegates had seen the public and media reaction to Sudesh's announcement. Cartoonists and satirists in every newspaper had lampooned Pakistan for having fallen for Sudesh's ploy. Public outrage and demands for military action, including nuclear war, had been replaced as if by magic with a sense of victory. Pakistan was as humiliated by the treaty as it was bound by it.

'I was not duplicitous', said Sudesh when his integrity was queried by an ever-aggressive Punita at a press conference convened hastily in the Communist Party office originally intended to announce their withdrawal from the coalition.

'That I and my party have always been for unilateral free trade has never been a secret. You, Ms Banerjee, have denounced us for it in your columns. I never said or implied in negotiations with my Pakistani counterpart that they alone would enjoy the blessings of unconstrained access to our economy. After inviting Pakistan to sign the treaty, their entire Cabinet agreed to it unanimously. I had nothing to do with them, so was not privy to how or why they agreed to it.

The Communists agreed to retain the ruling coalition after securing the concession from Sudesh that he would negotiate a reasonable phasing-in timetable with organised business and labour. Everyone agreed that there could be no such compromise regarding Pakistan as there was an unbreakable deal with them. And everyone ignored economists who exposed the obviously flawed logic of treating Pakistan and the rest of the world differently – goods from any part of the world could move to India through Pakistan.

A Cocktail Party, New Delhi, September 2023

Punita stepped into the Bhati penthouse lobby and saw Sudesh interacting with a small group of guests. Not that man again, she thought, hoping illogically that he would see her and come over.

Over the years she and Sudesh had encountered one another many times in their roles as journalist and politician. Punita had repeatedly attacked his policies in the press but he seemed to be impervious to her assaults. An argumentative camaraderie had developed between them.

Punita still felt attracted to Sudesh, but she had decided not to budge from her principles.

Sudesh strolled towards her waving his hand, 'Miss Banerjee,' he said with a warm smile, 'it's good to see you. I didn't know you knew Vaneshri and Inder.'

'I've been interviewing Vaneshri about the technology in your free cities, she does respond very enthusiastically.'

'Yes, she's always been a creative thinker, and now that there's no red tape to trip her she's unstoppable.'

'And no red tape to prevent American millionaires from exploiting Indian workers?' Punita commented pointedly.

'Correct,' he replied, still smiling.

'Don't you think it is wrong for people to be paid so little?'

'Who is doing the wrong thing?'

'The businesses that employ the workers.'

'So, shouldn't they employ them?'

'No, they should pay them more.'

'You mean the government should tell them how much they must pay? There are problems with such laws. For example, if wages are fixed too high, machines are bought to replace people.

'The more important question is how to improve the workers' circumstances as quickly as possible.'

'And how do you plan to do that?'

'In the free zones the workers are not taxed, which means the employers can afford to pay more than when they have to deduct income tax.'

'What about the employers, they don't pay any tax either, do they?'

'The zones are tax free. And there are no regulations. The employers are not required by law to provide benefits such as medical aid, child care and pensions. Most of the businesses offer these services through choice because when workers feel their employers care about them they are loyal and work harder.

'Some give their workers the choice between a lower salary and benefits, or a higher salary without benefits.

'Because the businesses are saving money which is normally spent complying with regulations and trying to minimise a multitude of taxes, they grow very rapidly and employ and train more people. As people become trained and gain experience they are in a better position to negotiate higher wages.

'The zones are developing at a great pace, and are providing hundreds of thousands of fresh employment opportunities, soon we shall lose count. I hope to see such policies as followed in the Free Zones extended to all parts of the country.'

'You are a hopeless radical!' said Punita, smiling despite herself.

'Remember all those stimulus packages in the USA and Europe that worked for a while and then resulted in another collapse?'

Punita nodded.

'I am stimulating India's economy in a way that brings about natural growth in response to real needs. Instead of using tax-payers' money to reward people who undertake my pet projects, I am leaving entrepreneurs to discover for themselves what the market wants. If they succeed, they make money, increase employment and stimulate the economy naturally. If they fail, they go out of business, but not at tax-payers' expense.

'And, dear Punita, increased employment, in other words increased demand, is like increased demand for anything – labour is no special case – more demand means higher prices. Remember there's been high growth without inflation for three years, which means real living standards have risen exponentially.'

Dal Lake, Srinagar, September 2023

Ashok and Satya relaxed back on the velvet cushions of their shikara enjoying the views of the houseboats and mountains across the shining waters of Dal Lake.

Traders approached them, pulling alongside and offering the goods piled high in their boats. The couple rejected the flowers and jewellery, computers, cell phones and tinned food good-naturedly.

'Enjoy your shopping with Abdul, sweetheart, I have a business meeting,' Ashok told Satya as they approached a houseboat bigger and grander than most.

Vasu was waiting to greet his old friend who led him inside, away from prying eyes.

'So you are back from the dead?' said Ashok, patting Vasu on the back. Vasu nodded, indicating the couch and heading for the bar to prepare two glasses of whisky.

'Yes, they finally realised my plane didn't crash.' He grinned. 'But they still don't know about this hideaway, so I hope you weren't followed.'

'No chance of that. The CBI is far too busy worrying about the perpetrators of that napalm attack to worry about an old parliamentarian like me taking a holiday,' Ashok shuddered.

'And Sudesh managed to make capital out of it,' responded Vasu. 'Can you believe the Indians would let Pakistan off with a trade deal!'

'It's incredible.'

'The Deputy Prime Minister has been busy during the past four years. He has destroyed my bread and butter.'

'You mean the stolen goods market?'

Vasu frowned, 'Yes, city and State police throughout India have been imitating Commissioner Singh's Crime Stop programme. With modern technology the volunteer workers can use their cell phones to enter the numbers of vehicles visiting possible outlets directly into the central data base. It doesn't take long before the correlations emerge, and the cops come down on my guys.

'They also search the second-hand dealers and pawn shops, and any goods that can't be accounted for are confiscated. They are either traced back to their owners through the serial numbers, or given away to charity organisations for the poor.'

'Speaking of the poor,' said Ashok, 'all our sources in the welfare department have dried up since this Care Card thing has been put in place nationwide. With money going directly to the people, there is nothing left to skim off. And the officials are so busy trying to keep their jobs while competing with the private sector there are far fewer opportunities to do deals on government contracts.'

'I've been out of the loop for a while, what's this about competing?'

'Kumar controls the Justice Department, and he introduced something called the Act of Equivalence. It means any measures applied to private business must also be applied to government.'

Vasu nodded, taking in the implications. 'And I read in the financial papers that if he wins a majority in the elections he will privatise everything?'

'Correct. And then you and I might as well retire because all our opportunities to make money on the side will dry up.'

'Is there anything we can do to stop him from winning?'

'It won't be easy. The guy is India's hero. He's ended the seventy-five-year-old conflict with Pakistan. People are moving freely across the border and troops on both sides are dispersing.

'He has a vast following among the poor who can now easily feed their families, get medical care and send their kids to school. They are also getting jobs, especially in free zones that are mushrooming everywhere.

'Those free cities have had huge publicity. Everyone can see how well they are working, how fast they are growing with entrepreneurs and money pouring in from the West. They are becoming the world's leaders in innovation and technology.

'Now, when Kumar talks about extending the free zones to all of India the response is positive. The State legislatures are enthusiastic. He paints a picture of India as the most successful nation in the world. He takes them back to the time when India was called the Golden Bird, when it was the world's richest nation, and people have started believing that it will happen again. They even believe he can end poverty.'

'What if he was suspected of murder? Would that help?'

'What are you suggesting, you old dog? If the timing was right, if it happened just before the elections he might lose his momentum. You know how fickle voters are. Do you have something in mind?'

Vasu tapped his nose. 'You leave that to me. But if we can get reasonable people back into power don't forget your partner in crime. Now, that's enough about business. How is that beautiful wife of yours?'

L&PP Headquarters, Delhi, October 2023

Barack Obama had become a touchstone of exemplary campaigning since his first win during the 2008 US elections. Many candidates contesting elections in different countries had tried to imitate his panache but all failed in their attempt.

Obama's speeches had an extraordinary spark, his conviction and honesty enamoured his audience exponentially.

Sudesh Kumar was the world's only politician who shared Obama's charm. Sudesh had succeeded beyond expectations in his first two elections, and showed signs of a historic victory in his third election.

Unlike Obama, Sudesh was not everybody's favourite in the world. The first world countries were too busy worrying about their economic problems to take much interest in an upcoming Indian politician.

But in India Sudesh had become a national hero. He had gathered massive positive response as his various policies began to bear fruit. Care Cards had brought ample relief to the poor. With the introduction of Crime Stop programme, rate of property crimes had decreased in all cities. The free zones boomed as investors around the world realised there was still one democracy in the world with great opportunities and a sound financial system. The Act of Equivalence began to pay dividends in an efficient government.

And now, to cap it all, Sudesh had single-handedly ended the Kashmir conflict and averted a nuclear war. In a politically fractured country he stood as a unifying bond.

Sudesh's team had been building their databases and resources for ten years and with the 2023 general elections only three months away they worked ceaselessly.

Like Obama they had used Internet based social networks to reach out to people. With an e-mail list of ninety-two million, fifty million cell phone numbers and fifteen million volunteers they had raised eight trillion rupees over the past year, ninety percent through small on-line donations. This enabled them to field candidates in every Lok Sabha constituency, and to inundate regional and national television channels with advertisements illustrating the ways in which Sudesh had changed the lives of ordinary Indians, and his plans for the future.

With by far the world's biggest electorate of eight hundred and ten million voters an election campaign of this size would have previously been impossible. Now Pan-Indian wireless broadband internet access was available free to all Indians and Kumar's team's investment in its data base paid off very well.

Nearly five million volunteers had worked to register new voters and as the time for the election came closer the number of people knocking on doors asking to support and work for L&PP increased to over twelve million.

The L&PP had created a nation-wide web of community-based networking organisations. In houses, offices and halls across the land people met and exchanged ideas, strategies and progress reports as they rallied voters to Sudesh Kumar's cause.

Jaipur, 15 October 2023

The Rambagh Palace Hotel of Jaipur stood in all its glory. Water from the fountains gently splashed lending a magical charm to the evening. Peacocks posed gracefully and enamoured the surroundings displaying their brightly hued plumes. The Prime Minister Rohit Jayaraman, escorted by a phalanx of aides, climbed its sparkling white marble stairs leading to the city side of the hotel to join a meeting with his closest allies. The Communist Party deputy leader walked ahead and greeted Jayaraman with a smile.

His smile froze within seconds as he saw a crimson dot appear on Jayaraman's chest. It was followed by a sharp crack and Jayaraman's steps faltered. The laser beam moved swiftly to his temple. Another shot sang out and he collapsed to the ground.

The nation heard the shattering news: one shot in the heart and another in the head had caused immediate death.

Within seconds the security team cordoned off the area and sealed all exits from the premises.

Sophisticated forensic equipment calculated the trajectory of the bullets as having been fired from a room on the first floor. Details were radioed to the search team.

Entering the room, guns drawn, the guards found a high calibre rifle lying on a table by the window but the assassin had vanished into thin air. How he got into the room and disappeared puzzled experts for many years.

Shock waves rippled across every corner of the world.

India Finance, 20 October 2023

Punita Banerjee

The hope of the poor, the youth icon and the golden boy of the intelligentsia Sudesh Kumar enjoys unprecedented popularity in India. Indian public has received a big jolt after learning about the circumstantial evidence linking our Deputy Prime Minister to the death of Prime Minister Jayaraman.

Kumar was spotted at the Rambagh Palace when Rohit Jayaraman was shot. The security cameras revealed that Kumar had entered the men's washroom, and made an exit after some time.

With a national election only four weeks away, Kumar has now stepped into Jayaraman's shoes. The Communist Party is in disarray. This has improved L&PP's chances to win the elections by an outright majority. It has also been suspected that there is a common background to PM's assassination and Mafia Murders. CCTV camera footage and DNA samples show that each murder was perpetrated by a different person, almost all men, who were obviously hired killers. The assassins have managed to evade not only the police, but three top teams of private investigators.

Although Sudesh Kumar has gained popularity for his involvement in Crime Stop and the subsequent drop in crime, it should be remembered that his way of fighting crime is becoming a subject of condemnation.

Indians have a right to a full inquiry.

Central Police Command Centre, New Delhi, 23 October 2023

'I don't like to tell you this, Commissioner,' said the Director of the CBI.

'Tell me what?'

'Your friend, the Acting Prime Minister, cannot be eliminated from our investigations.'

'What do you mean?'

'He's the one who said India must be cleansed of organised crime. And see this; he is the one who directly benefits from Jayaraman's assassination.'

Singh raised his eyebrows. 'I'm aware of these facts, but I can't believe that Kumar is involved. He is a man of integrity.'

'You know it Commissioner, that anything is possible, and personal views have to be put on one side during an investigation.'

'That is true. All lines of investigation will be kept open. But I do not believe Sudesh Kumar is behind the killings.'

National Prime Time Television, 1 November 2023

'My name is Kanak and I have a story to tell. This a true story of my past. Once as a child I was alone in a playground.

'Sudesh Kumar does not know that I am running this campaign on his behalf. Now that he is the centre of unfounded rumours and allegations I feel it is my duty to do my bit.'

An Indian village scene appeared on the screen as this lean, middle-aged man addressed the nation.

'As a boy I lived in the same village as Sudesh. He may not remember me, but for me he is a very important person.'

A dramatised version of a past incident appeared showing a big strong lad pounding a small timid boy. 'I was the small boy who was attacked by the school bully. Sudesh stepped in and saved me from being beaten to a pulp. He didn't even know me.'

There was a third lad, not much bigger than the victim, stepping forward to intervene, then the camera returned to the speaker. 'Sudesh stood up to that boy whom everyone feared. He had the courage to tell the bully that his actions were wrong. When the bully turned on him, Sudesh used his wits to protect himself and defeat him, just like David vanquished Goliath.

'He fought for good and against evil as a boy, and he is doing the same today. Vote for Sudesh Kumar.'

L&PP Election Rally, Goa, 3 November 2023

A tall man rose from his seat to address the rally. He towered above the chairman as he replaced him behind the microphone.

'My name is Loknath and when I was a boy Sudesh Kumar saved my life.'

The crowd roared.

'By taking his hand off my windpipe.'

The roar of approval turned to laughter.

'You have all seen the campaign run by Kanak Jaising. I was the bully who attacked Kanak. At the age of twelve I was bashed up by Sudesh who broke my jaw and humiliated me in front of the entire school. But over time I have thought about that incident long and hard. I have listened to Sudesh during his rise to fame, and I have learned from him.'

The audience clapped.

'I have abandoned force and achieved success in life by working hard and providing what other people want and are willing to pay for. And that is what Sudesh's policies are all about. I don't know much about politics, this is the first time I have spoken at a political meeting, but I think I know Sudesh.

'Why did he attack me against the odds, as he now attacks poverty and corruption in India against the odds? Why?'

The crowd was quiet.

'Because Sudesh Kumar hates injustice. He hates injustice and he loves liberty. Because of these beliefs he has devoted his life to fighting for the Indian people, especially those unable to fight for themselves. Give Sudesh Kumar your vote, he deserves it.'

Twenty-five

New Delhi, 10 December 2023

Two and a half million people gathered at Rajpath to hear Sudesh Kumar's victory speech. The L&PP had won 378 of the 550 Lok Sabha seats, and majorities in nineteen of the twenty-eight States and territories.

As Sudesh gazed at the ocean of people on the two-mile-long Rajpath he was struck with awe, pride and humility. He took a deep breath and began to speak.

'India is poised to lead the world in peace and prosperity.

'To become the world's leading nation is not a matter of destiny; it is a matter of choice. Today, more than seven hundred million people went to the polls and joined hands to eliminate poverty and corruption and pave way for liberty, justice and prosperity.

'In the days and months ahead we will face challenges. Much of the world is gripped by economic depression and nations are controlled by governments who refuse to acknowledge that they are the cause of the problem, not the solution.

'India has escaped depression by avoiding excess. For this we give credit to previous governments who resisted the temptation to overspend. During the past five years my party has introduced measures that have attracted investors and innovators from across the globe. Many people who were not able to participate in their own failed economies have seen a new hope in India.

'You have granted me the mandate to continue along this road. To eradicate poverty, minimise corruption and liberate entrepreneurship and invention.

'We seek not to imitate western capitalism. Our vision is of a prosperous, principled and caring society. A society in which people look after one another instead of relying on government to do so, where personal compassion replaces welfare-by-plunder, and where the emphasis is on community and the common welfare rather than personal aggrandisement and selfish greed.

'Today we are entitled to celebrate. We are no longer the world's beggar-nation. Mothers in rich countries can no longer force their children to eat by citing the "starving children in India". We are in a position to help others, not with aid, but by demonstrating the means of success.

'We have put an end to our conflict with Pakistan and countrymen from both the lands can move without any fear across a peaceful border. We are beginning to rebuild trust, relationships and divided families.

'We have transformed Special Zones into centres of exponential economic growth. We are constructing free third millennium cities that are building on the discoveries and hard work of the past to fulfil the promise of the future.

'The Act of Equivalence has unleashed the power of private enterprise by levelling the playing field with government. We have replaced official discretion with judicial objectivity and due process and in doing so we have reduced corruption.

'The rate of poverty in our country is falling remarkably. Free enterprise has created so many jobs that the number of welfare recipients has fallen by one-third. Care Cards have given independence to those who still need assistance.

'I am deeply optimistic about India's future. We will extend the freedoms of the Special Zones throughout our country. We will close government departments and agencies so that crores of State employees can become high income wealth producers instead of low income wealth consumers. We will unleash India's wealth to create employment instead of allowing it to be sucked into the black hole of taxation.

'During the golden age of the Gupta Empire, fifteen hundred years ago, our forebears made significant achievements in religion, education, mathematics, art, literature and drama. Education included grammar, composition, logic, metaphysics, mathematics, medicine, and astronomy.

'The Indian numeral system and the decimal system, now universally used, were developed. Indian philosophers proposed that the earth was not flat but round, and that it rotated on an axis. They made discoveries about gravity and the planets of the solar system and originated the game of chess.

'Indian physicians excelled in pharmacopoeia, caesarean section, bone setting, and skin grafting. These ideas spread throughout the world through trade. Indian medical advances were adopted in the Arab and western worlds, and the great universities in central and eastern India received an influx of students from many parts of the globe.

'Today, we are on the brink of a Third Millennium Golden Age. The initial steps have been taken. I call upon my fellow Indians to rise to the challenge, take advantage of opportunities, fulfil your destiny, and show the world the way out of darkness and into light. The Golden Bird will soar again!'

Sudesh's Apartment, January 2024

Shakti burst into Sudesh's flat. Preparing his breakfast in his small kitchen, he turned to smile at her as she flew towards him holding a magazine high in the air.

'Look Sudesh, have you seen this yet? It's just come out!'

Sudesh gazed at his own face on the cover of *Time Magazine*. He was lost for words. 'Person of the Year,' read the type reversed out white on black across the centre of the Time banner.

'You're "Person of the Year",' said Shakti, smiling gleefully. 'You're not only famous in India, you're recognised all over the world!'

Sudesh frowned slightly, 'But that's not what it's all about.'

'No, of course not,' said Shakti, 'but look at what they say. During your first five years as Deputy Prime Minister, India has been the only country in the world that has experienced rapid economic growth. We used to have the most bureaucratic government in the world, but you have already reduced it by twenty-five percent. You are the first Indian politician ever to make a real difference to the lives of the poor. They call it a miraculous achievement.'

Sudesh started to speak but Shakti stopped him.

'I know, I know, the miracle is that most governments stop growth from occurring. But Sudesh, they say that now that you have won a mandate to deregulate the Indian economy you might set an example for depressed countries to follow. They can rebuild their economies using your ways. So you see, not only are you going to save India, but you might save the world!'

Sudesh couldn't help laughing, Shakti's joy was infectious. He stood up, caught her in his arms, hugged her tight and lifted her off her feet. As he put her down he said, 'I don't know about the world, but we are well on our way to transforming India, and that is enough for me.'

As Shakti crossed the room to fix a celebratory cappuccino Sudesh watched her affectionately. She was alight with happiness. She's loyal, clever, hardworking and pretty, he thought. She is a treasure. How is it that she is still single?

News Broadcast, Zee TV, February 2024

The Prime Minister announced today that all government assets in India are to be privatised. Indian and foreign buyers can place their bids through any of ten accountancy companies that include the biggest international companies and the four largest firms in India.

All government land and government buildings in India are for sale, with a few military exceptions. This includes school buildings, hospitals, police stations and recreation facilities.

In future no private goods or services will be funded by taxation at the national level or in any State or territory in which the L&PP is the elected majority. Public goods and services that require tax funding will not be supplied by government departments but by competing private agencies.

Private businesses will take over government departments and services and they will be required to employ current workers, or to pay them a severance package negotiated with the unions.

The Singh Household, Delhi, February 2024

Nanek Singh found his wife in her studio. She was sitting in the lotus posture, eyes closed, meditating.

'I think you might be involved,' he said.

She opened her eyes and smiled up at him, 'Involved in what?'

Nanek sat down on a padded bench, looking at her. 'For a long time now I have noticed that you are always missing when the Mafia Murders are committed. In recent months I have watched and listened carefully.

'I have a feeling that you are responsible for all of those killings. It still doesn't make sense, because the evidence shows that a number of different individuals were involved.' He lowered his face after speaking.

Madhu rose swiftly to her feet and sat at his side. She put her arms around him and rested her head on his shoulder. 'If it was so, my love, would you have me arrested?'

'Madhu, you know that these murders are against everything that I stand for as a police officer. They are outside the rule of law. If we get concrete evidence that you are involved in these murders, I will have to turn you in.'

Parliamentary Press Room, 2024

'In this press conference I will explain what we plan to do with government assets.'

Cameras flashed.

'We are going to give them away.'

Sudesh paused, expecting a reaction, but journalists stared as if nothing had been said. He repeated, 'We are giving the State's assets away. We are returning to the people what is theirs.'

Questioning hands shot up.

'Let me explain,' he glanced at the large contingent of ministers, officials and consultants standing by to answer technical questions.

'Every Indian will get a booklet of Restitution Vouchers representing a certain value, equal for all. Think of it as a cheque book for buying government assets. People might choose newly listed shares in government enterprises or departments, or a municipal bus to be owner-operated, or perhaps membership of a farming commune. Everyone will be shopping in a giant store called "The State".

'Unlike vouchers given to citizens in the Czech Republic, ours will be freely tradable; our people will be treated like emancipated adults who can decide for themselves what to do with their assets. They can, for instance, sell them to investors.'

There was a lot of commotion and agitation; journalists were raising hands and shouting questions and interjecting.

'I will answer your questions once I finish,' said Sudesh. 'We expect a lively market to emerge. We do not want our people to be hasty, we want them to wait and see what prices emerge, unless, of course, they need cash urgently. A temporary Restitution Service will offer training to the public.

'Regarding the fear that civil servants may lose their jobs we will provide transitional guarantees against retrenchment, seek other employment for redundant people, and help government employees take ownership of businesses in which they work.

'The differences between various options such as companies, cooperatives, employee trusts and investor clubs will be explained.

'Lists of available assets will be published shortly. They will include almost everything the State owns, public enterprises, transport services, hospitals, schools, roads, harbours, airports and buildings. Now I will take questions.'

Punita leapt to her feet, unable to contain herself, 'That is outdated free market privatisation; it's been tried and failed.' Some of her colleagues applauded her.

'Call it what you wish, Punita,' replied Sudesh. 'We call it "restitution", because that's what it is.' He nodded to another journalist, 'Mr Kamil,' he said, smiling.

'The Czech vouchers failed because ownership was too dispersed amongst millions of people and as a result there was no effective control over self-serving managers,' said the man.

'You're right, that happened because the government did not let the public trade their shares. In our case, people with no interest in being active shareholders will be free to sell to serious investors.'

'In other words,' said another journalist, 'you want the poor to get a massive handout that they can spend on alcohol and gambling?'

'We give pensioners cash every month and trust them to spend wisely, which, with rare exceptions, they do. In the village where I grew up, poor people spent the little they had with care. People who are entitled to vote in elections should be free to spend their own money.'

.'What happens to assets no one wants?'

'I keep them,' said Sudesh. 'No, that was a joke. Experts such as merchant banks will value the assets with a view of ensuring they're all taken up. The ruling value of vouchers will soon be general knowledge. The voucher price of unpopular assets will be lowered, as in year-end sales in shops, until someone wants them. Speculators will be free to hold out for bargains.'

'How will people pay for everything they now get free? When you dispose of social services like schools and hospitals, public buses and roads, no one will be able to afford them.'

'I said nothing about reducing subsidies,' said Sudesh. 'We will continue to assist the poor with Care Cards. They will choose between efficient, innovative and competitive suppliers. We will fund demand, not supply.'

'If the market is better at producing and supplying everything, what does the State do best?'

'Collect tax and consume wealth,' said Sudesh.

There was a reluctant chuckle, but this time he was not joking. 'The Restitution will allow government to tax less and supply more.'

Cabinet Meeting Room, February 2024

'Let me explain,' said Sudesh. 'The Guillotine is a technique for getting rid of obsolete and inappropriate laws and regulations. It works like this: all departments must re-motivate all their laws by a specified date. Any law not compellingly motivated by that date is automatically abolished. The result is that superfluous laws fall by the way side.'

'Has this been done before?' asked the Minister of Corporate Affairs.

'Yes, the first country was Sweden during the 1980s; subsequently the method was used throughout Eastern Europe, and elsewhere. It's a good system but I think we can improve on it. We want to do more than merely scrapping superfluous laws; we want to get rid of all counter-productive laws.'

'How?'

'Firstly, when laws are added to the register they must reveal, in numbers, what they are intended to achieve, by when. They must also disclose what they will cost government and the public in cash and kind, and they will survive only if they're shown, by independent audit, to have benefits exceeding costs.'

'A cost/benefit analysis,' said the Minister of Agriculture, 'Good idea, the smallest irrigation project is subjected to a cost/benefit analysis, but not laws that affect the whole country with costs running into crores.'

'There should be one date by which the regulations must be registered, and a subsequent date by which we must receive the cost-benefit analysis,' suggested the Minister of Communications and IT.

'All the information should be published on the Internet for public scrutiny,' she continued. 'If any interested party maintains that the cost of a regulation would exceed the benefits, they should be entitled to present their case in open court. Should they win their case the regulation would have to be referred back for reconsideration by the Lok Sabha.'

'They have such systems in a growing number of countries', Sudesh added, 'commonly known as regulatory impact assessments. We can build on their experience by adding a requirement that secondary effects and unintended consequences must also be assessed, and that the process has to be repeated at fixed periods. In the UK they have to show what other laws there are that may be causing problems which new laws are intended to redress, and should therefore also be guillotined.'

The Minister of Justice had kept silent until now. 'Do you have an example of a law that would be guillotined?' Bharat Jaitley loved laws and his department had spent a lot of time and money on getting them properly drafted and enforced.

'In the UK the effective cost of registering and monitoring all dangerous dogs was found to be so high compared to expected benefits that the proposal was scrapped despite popular sentiment calling for "control". The process protected politicians from public pressure to pass a bad law, and enabled them to apply scarce resources productively.'

'Will this guillotine measure save us from negative publicity generated by the Upton Exchange, asked Pravim Gordam, Minister of Finance.

'Yes, of course, it will mean we're ahead of it, pre-empting it. Thank you for your ideas, ladies and gentlemen,' said Sudesh. 'We appear to have sufficient consensus on this. I will refer the Guillotine to the Department of Justice for drafting.'

Flame's Bar, March 2024

Ashok sat for a drink with an old friend, a senior intelligence officer. The two mulled over their common state of decline. The primary source of their income had dried up. To add to their disgust, now there was no corruption for the government no longer controlled licenses or highly priced projects.

'The file linking Agent Singh to the Mafia Murders was given to the PM over a year ago, when he was still deputy.'

'Are you sure?'

'Absolutely. He said he would follow up, but never did. It seems that the woman is responsible, and the PM must know that. He has daily security briefings. But he has conveniently forgotten that file.'

'Very interesting,' Ashok nodded slowly, 'this could be exactly what we are looking for.'

Los Angeles, March 2024

The surgeon ran up the stairs to the ninth floor of the hospital, 'Where is Dr Etheridge?'

'He's gone.'

'Gone? Where?'

'Gone to India, don't you read the newspapers? All our top people are going there.'

'Why?'

'Because they're tired of being fettered with regulations. They are going where the latest technology and best conditions are available, and they will be free to put their training and talent to proper use. And will get opportunities to work with other gifted people.'

'But we can't replace Etheridge, he's the only specialist who understands the whole picture.'

'Do you think Congress cares about that?'

'Never mind Congress, I need Etheridge.'

'Perhaps you should mind Congress as it has made people like Etheridge run away from the country.'

'Maybe we should go to India ourselves. Maybe we should practise there.'

'Not a bad idea.'

CNN World News, April 2024

'This is Samantha Cook reporting for CNN World News.

'Today the British Government acknowledged the seriousness of what has come to be known as the "Leaders' Strike".

'Europe, North America and Japan are losing many of their top entrepreneurs, doctors, architects, engineers and scientists to India. Loosely led by maverick British industrialist, Damian Knight, more than ten thousand highly trained individuals are building businesses in the free cities of India, where there are no taxes and no regulations, but efficient privately run law and order services.

'India's new Prime Minister, Sudesh Kumar, is currently extending many of the rights enjoyed in the free cities and enterprise zones to the rest of India. Governments throughout the depressed world are increasingly concerned about the brain drain.

'At a recent press conference Kumar answered accusations that India is encouraging the "Leaders' Strike".'

Sudesh appeared on the screen, speaking into a microphone against a backdrop of royal blue curtains, 'All we have done in India is to provide conditions in which free thinkers can flourish. Countries concerned about the loss of their top people have a simple solution. They should deregulate their economies, reduce taxes and the brain drain will end.'

Twenty-six

New Delhi, August 2024

'You cannot dive into the middle of the demonstration,' said Sudesh's aide Anil desperately, 'You will be torn limb from limb. These people are angry, they feel insecure.'

In response to the news of a gathering of fuming fifty thousand government workers with their leaders threatening a national strike in the Delhi Stadium, Sudesh had headed out of his office. He walked rapidly in the direction of his car, Anil close behind.

'I want to speak to them. How can they understand what we are doing if I don't speak to them?' was the Prime Minister's reply.

❦

Sudesh pushed through the crowd. As he strode between angry masses, Sudesh heard their caustic remarks, 'He's the one who is responsible,' 'What's he doing here?' 'He has let us down.'

He continued steadily towards the front, oblivious to the danger surrounding him. As he approached the stage the organisers recognised him and made way for him to speak. They were all astounded to watch Sudesh walking to the microphone. He turned to address the crowd.

When the protestors realised who stood before them they shouted slogans in protest. Sudesh spoke, 'Colleagues, I too am a government employee, but that is not why I am here. I have come because I want you to hear me.

'My job, like yours, is threatened. You can fire me without notice in the forthcoming election. But unlike you, if I lose my job I will get no severance pay, no bonus, no retraining and no shares. You will get all of these.

'I know that I am more privileged than many of you, even without my job. But I understand how it feels to be unemployed, destitute, homeless and hungry.'

The crowd was sceptical. Their livelihood was being threatened by this man, they were in no mood for political sweet-talk. There were shouts and jeers. Media cameras jostled for better angles.

'If you allow me,' continued Sudesh, 'I will say just two things, then I will leave you to continue your deliberations.' The crowd settled a little.

'First, no government worker will be retrenched without guarantees. These include guaranteed employment until a new job on the same pay scale is found, as well as retraining for new work. We will do everything we can to anticipate problems and implement our policies in ways that benefit rather than harm you.

'As part of our Restitution Plan, popularly known as "the Big Giveaway," you will all be offered shares in your own departments, shares that will be freely tradeable.

'Some of you are employed in departments that will disappear, for example, those that control licensing, tariffs and other regulations that are being scrapped. We are considering union proposals on how to compensate these workers over and above the guarantees already mentioned.

'Now, as ordinary citizens, I ask you to think about this. In order to survive, private hospitals must save lives and provide patient care. Government hospitals continue regardless of how inadequate are their services. Parents will not pay for badly run private schools, so they go out of business. Government schools survive even if the children receive little education. Wherever we go we get better services from private businesses than from government-run enterprises.

'People think governments should provide important services, I don't think we can afford to have crucial services fail. If government is going to do anything at all let it be things that don't matter so much, like fashion, entertainment and sport.

'Let government make movies and run sports. Bad films and inefficient sporting events wouldn't threaten lives. Rather than telecommunications, let us nationalise cricket.' Groans and a chorus of "no" sounded through the stadium.

'Governments do not fail because there is anything wrong with their employees. On the contrary, we civil servants are decent people who want to be productive and get our work appreciated. We are victims of the system. I want to liberate everyone from the shackles of political agendas and bureaucracy to work productively and earn a decent wage.'

There was a hesitant cheer.

'Privatise yourself!' shouted one protester.

'He wants me to privatise the Prime Minister,' repeated Sudesh for all to hear, there was a ripple of laughter. 'I have good news for you. By the time we are finished there will be so little left for the Prime Minister to do. My job will, for all practical purposes, be privatised.'

Sudesh thanked the crowd and the organisers and prepared to leave the platform. As he re-joined the workers, the chief organiser announced that the rally would be adjourned until after negotiations with the government.

Sudesh made his way slowly through the stadium, pausing in between to shake hands and answer questions. Anil, no longer nervous, walked along with him. They neared their car when a man addressing Sudesh saw his eyes jerk wide with shock as he staggered forward about to collapse. A woman standing in front of him screamed with terror. Everyone stared in disbelief at the blood soaking the sleeve of the Prime Minister's shirt.

Anil swung around, looking for the gunman, but all he could see was a wall of bodies as the crowd clustered close.

A Houseboat on Dal Lake, August 2024

Madhumati stood at the side of the houseboat. She had chosen an overcast night for the task. The dark still waters were lit by the reflection of lights.

She saw the guard sitting on the covered front deck, silhouetted against the dim light of the curtained room behind, a submachine gun across his knees.

From the back of the shoe box shaped boat, where it sat low in the water, she climbed silently onto the roof and padded quietly as a cat to the front, above the seat of the guard. Turning her back to the water she gripped the edge of the roof and swung her body down, landing on the deck with a soft thump. As the guard turned his head she crossed to him in one stride and struck with the yawara stick just below his ear. He toppled to the ground and she tossed his gun into the water.

She moved to the left of the door and waited, black in her wet suit, for Vasu to appear. He was in his sleeping shorts. He held a gun and searched for the guard. Madhu's leg shot sideways, her flexed heel struck the side of Vasu's palm and his fingers flew open. The gun fell onto the floor and Madhu said, 'You master-minded Eden Gardens.'

As he bent, scrabbling for the gun, she raised the kongo and struck down with full strength, aiming for the killer spot on his temple.

A Private Hospital, Delhi, August 2024

The surgeon walked into the waiting room, in his scrubs with his mask pulled down. He smiled at Shakti and Kamla, 'The operation went fine and the Prime Minister is strong. He will be up and about in a few days.'

&

Sudesh opened his eyes. With a hazy vision he could see two women sitting in the corner of his room. He could recognise one of them as Shakti but he wondered who the other woman was. Her profile looked familiar, he thought she resembled his mother.

He looked at Shakti with questioning eyes. He gestured her softly to come near him. The other woman turned her head and smiled at Sudesh. Within no time after that Sudesh realised that it was Chanda.

His sister came swiftly to the bed and sat on the edge, reaching for his hands. Tears rolled down her cheeks and she spoke, 'Sudesh, forgive me for staying away for so long.'

Vijay's Lair, South Delhi, August 2024

Lata Malhotra was allowed entry into the building after an elaborate scanning process. The bullet-proof electronic door let her through and she waited for it to close behind her and the second door to open. She entered her husband's study, closing the door behind her. Vijay Malhotra sat reading in his armchair. He did not look up when she entered. She crossed the room and kissed him on the forehead and moved to the mahogany bar counter. She poured their the favourite Château Margeaux into two long stemmed glasses and passed one glass to Vijay who was reading *Stalinism and Nazism: Dictatorships in Comparison.* Lata picked up *Vogue* and gently flipped through its pages.

It took him fifteen minutes to look up at her and ask, 'How was your day?'

'Eventful.'

'What happened?'

'I finalised my plans to kill you,' her voice conversational.

He looked up sharply, 'What nonsense is this?'

She smiled, and for a moment looked like a stranger.

'Do you think I am your wife?'

He frowned, 'What are you on about, Lata? Is this meant to be a joke?'

'I'm not Lata, I'm Madhumati Singh, I've killed twenty-seven criminals over the past twenty years and you will be my last,' she sipped her wine. Her voice changed mid-sentence to an unfamiliar man's voice, and then a woman's.

He felt confused and passed his hand over his eyes again. He strained his eyes as if peering into a dark room. Apart from her strange voices, she was clearly his wife. He knew her better than anyone. But he had heard of Madhumati Singh.

'I had to imitate Lata to get to you and be alone with you,' she said in her own voice.

'What game are you playing, Lata? We both know that no stranger could get past the surveillance?'

'Replicating fingerprints is not a problem for me,' she said in a voice India's last great crime boss recognised as that of Bollywood star Shah Rukh Khan. He wondered if he was hallucinating. He reminded himself that his security was impenetrable.

When she divulged how much she knew about him, he was forced to accept that this was not his wife, but her double, a virtual identical twin.

This woman, the embodiment of his fears, made him feel strangely calm. He was as fascinated and curious as he was terrified; he had been puzzled for years about the identity of the Mafia Murderer. Could it really have been a woman? They had seen a multiplicity of men in surveillance footage, he reminded himself.

'That's why no one suspected me, everyone was looking for men fitting my disguises.'

'And your appearance?'

'The first time I saw Lata I noticed the similarities such as our height and shoulders. I had rhinoplasty to shorten my nose. I had collagen injected into my lips, and Bollywood's best prosthetics and make-up artists took care of the rest. I've gone to a lot of trouble for you, Vijay. You were my greatest challenge.'

Vijay could not believe his eyes and ears. He tried hard to come to terms with what he saw and heard. 'How did you beat our systems?'

'Lata is slightly taller than me, so I had to learn not just her gait, but how to walk like her in her shoes with added platforms and padding to make me taller. I had to have her proportions for your body and face recognition security cameras, I had to lose some weight and add a little body modification, some real surgery and some prosthetics. I like my new hips.'

'How did you know our systems?'

'I befriended Lata three years ago. Since then we have spent much time together.

'Your irises...?'

The woman touched her fingers briefly in both eyes and removed her contact lenses. His wife's striking green eyes lay staring at the ceiling.

'But ... I don't understand. How could you get past the dogs?'

Madhu enjoyed sharing her trade secrets with Vijay. She had nothing to fear because she would soon be helping him leave this world. Besides she knew if she opened up, Vijay too would share his secrets, she wanted that for records.

'I made Lata sit in the sauna and swabbed perspiration off her to dab all over my body, for the dogs, you know.'

'The voice?' he asked. It occurred to him that if he could keep her talking long enough, his guards would check on him, or he would get to his alarm button. If he could get her off-guard, may be he could even overpower her.

'As for her accent,' she switched back into Lata's familiar sensual tones, 'we taped her calls, conducted voice-analysis and I practised. I'm good with voices and accents.' She switched from one recognisable male voice to another. 'I practised for hours until the voice-recognition software couldn't tell us apart. That was pretty good, even if I say so myself, beating SecuriTech's best software.'

'How did you pull off all of those hits? Did you have a team?'

'No, I trusted only myself. I used disguises, switched methods and left false DNA or no DNA to confuse the force. I am conversant with all scrutiny methods.' She smiled again.

But she had questions too. 'I presume you were responsible for Prime Minister Jayaraman's assassination?'

'Yes, Vasu commissioned me for that.'

'And the attack on Kumar at the Stadium?'

'Also ordered by Vasu, but my guy botched the job. He won't be working for me again.'

'No, he won't,' said Madhu. Her eyes gleamed and he felt a sudden moment of fear. He tried to lunge for his panic button, but felt a rush of dizziness that made him slump back.

Madhu looked at him, her head on one side. 'It won't take long now,' he heard her say as he drifted into unconsciousness.

Madhu took a small ballpoint pen from Lata's handbag. She crossed the room, held the point of the pen to Malhotra's neck and injected a tiny dose of curare. He would be dead in five minutes.

She picked up the bag and left the room, closing the door gently behind her. She nodded to the security guards on her way out saying, 'Mr Malhotra doesn't want to be disturbed.'

A Private Hospital, Delhi, August 2024

'I'm sorry,' said Sudesh.

'Sorry for what, Sudesh?' Shakti spoke holding his hand as he lay on the bed.

'I've been such a fool for so many years. I've blinded myself to my own feelings. It's taken a bullet through my shoulder to make me realise how much I love you.'

Sudesh opened his eyes and smiled at her, 'My darling Shakti, will you marry me? I would like you to be beside me for the rest of my life, in my heart and in my home.'

'I would like that too,' she said, with an expression of exuberance on her face. She would have shrieked and danced with joy had she not been forced by being in a hospital to constrain herself.

৯

Nanek Singh had been waiting beside Sudesh's bed before he woke.

'We've followed up on the attempted assassination,' said the Commissioner after enquiring about Sudesh's arm, 'but there is not much to report. The gun must have been equipped with a silencer. We suspect that the culprit was following you and took a chance, trying to take advantage of the opportunity to disappear in the crowd.'

'I suppose I should take security seriously in future.'

'Certainly.'

Sudesh saw that Singh looked strained. 'Is there something else wrong, Nanek?'

Singh looked away then back again, 'I think she's dead.'

'Madhu?'

'I haven't seen or heard from her for two days, she always keeps in touch.'

'She's probably on a mission.'

'I hope so. I hope nothing has happened to her.'

'I hope so too.'

A village near Delhi, August 2024

Village folks eagerly awaited Sudesh. They expected to see their Prime Minister arrive in a blue-light convoy of big cars accompanied by guards and dignitaries.

What they didn't know was that his visits were preceded by elaborate security measures with sniffer dogs checking for explosives along carefully planned routes. They didn't know platforms were normally built for speeches and stands were constructed to seat national and local luminaries. And they didn't know that there would be dozens of journalists, photographers and TV cameras.

They assembled in the old quarry of the long-abandoned brickworks where many had worked when Sudesh was a boy. It was the only place in the village where they could all gather, and where there was a natural elevation from which they could be addressed.

They waited patiently on the hot day, buying nuts, sweetmeats and cold drinks from vendors and swapping stories of the Prime Minister's childhood. Suddenly a sound was heard above the murmur of voices. A sound as unexpected as it was familiar; it came from the motorised rickshaw approaching the village. It turned the corner down the dusty ramp where children played after school. Faces turned, in surprise. It was difficult for rickshaws to approach the quarry.

The bemused rickshaw driver thought his passenger looked like the Prime Minister; so did the crowd. A well-dressed man, tall and handsome, familiar yet unfamiliar, walked with purposeful gait from the rickshaw towards the elevated area backing against the hills. He showed no sign of recent injury. He was alone for the first time in public since being in office. Those who had wandered off ran back. An excited buzz rose from the group.

The man spoke clearly, his voice amplified by the quarry walls. They could hear every word.

'I came alone today, in a rickshaw, because that is how I left. That time there were no entourages, no cameras, no dignitaries and no police to escort me. My dear friends, I look amongst you and see familiar faces. Faces of my mother's and father's friends and family, faces of my school-fellows, faces of people who shared their food with me. The very dear faces that I can never forget.

'Many of you must have wondered why, while contesting elections, I did not seek your support, did not campaign in this district, and did not return to celebrate my victories with you.

'You may have wondered why I did not wield my power and influence to help you, and why I did not bring special development projects to my birthplace.

'When I was a boy in this village I dedicated my life to ending corruption and the abuse of power. Ever since I have gained power I have fought for justice and equal opportunity for all.

'I could not visit all of India's villages, so I did not visit you. I could not build new schools, hospitals and houses in all villages, so I did not build them for you. I was fighting against special favours granted by politicians to friends and relatives, so I could not single you out for special attention.

'But I have given you all I could give with integrity, and these things I have given to all.'

In rapt attention no one heard the rumble of an approaching SUV until it sped around the corner and squealed to a halt with a cloud of dust. Then there was another. And one more.

Sudesh's voice was drowned by the hubbub of the villagers who turned in bewilderment to see policemen jumping from the vehicles.

Uniformed men marched into the crowd, pushing people aside to clear a pathway, heading towards the Prime Minister. The clamour grew louder as the crowds jostled, pushed, and shouted trying to discover what was happening.

A tall broad-shouldered high rank officer accompanied by two others, marched up to Sudesh.

'Sir.'

'What can I do for you, gentlemen?' Sudesh sounded puzzled but soon adjusted into a helpful frame of mind.

The senior man stood to attention.

'We have received an urgent message from Police Headquarters, Delhi.'

'Yes.'

'Mr Prime Minister, Sudesh Kumar, you are under arrest for abetment to the crime of murder through non-disclosure of information. I am Deputy Superintendent Lalit and I have here a memo of arrest to be signed by one witness. You have the right to inform a friend or family member of your arrest.'

'What?' said Sudesh as his head began to whirl, 'What is the charge?'

The policeman studied his papers.

'Abetment to the crime of murder through non-disclosure of information.'

'Murder?'

The officer looked further down the page and read.

'The alleged murder by Madhumati Singh of twenty-eight leaders of organised crime syndicates.'

Sudesh gazed at the man, speechless.

One of the deputies approached with handcuffs.

'That won't be necessary. I will come,' said Sudesh.

Holding his head high, the Prime Minister of India began to walk with the policemen through the staring crowd of villagers towards the police vehicle.

Police Station, Parliament Street, New Delhi, August 2024

Commissioner Singh entered the cell where Sudesh was detained as his bail hearing was pending.

He walked to Sudesh, clasped his shoulder briefly, and then sat on the chair besides him.

'A lot has happened. Let me fill you in.

'The police have discovered, with incontrovertible proof, that Madhu, and Madhu alone, is the Mafia Murderer. Two days ago she managed to gain entry into Vijay Malhotra's house disguised as his wife. She poisoned him and left.

'She then returned to the isolated storage facility where she had locked his wife, Lata Malhotra, and released her.

'Lata returned home and found Vijay dead in his study. In theory she would have had no easy way to prove that Madhu committed the crime since the security staff were not able to watch the room when the couple were alone together.

'But Vijay had high-tech cameras and audio equipment in all rooms recording everything said and done. This information was radioed to an off-site centre where it was stored in a computer database.

'Lata knew about the process but didn't know Vijay's password. She told the police, and we brought in one of Vaneshri's people to hack into the database and access the footage.

'During the time Madhu spent alone with Malhotra she gave him her name and told him she had killed twenty-seven criminals and he was to be the last. She described how she had fooled his security, and in a broad outline how she had committed the other crimes.'

'Has she been arrested?' asked Sudesh.

'No, she has disappeared,' replied Singh. 'She probably decided to lie low in case Lata Malhotra was able to identify her. I hope that is the explanation.

'But before I answer your questions let me tell you how you came to be involved. Your old enemy, that MP Ashok Mahajan, somehow discovered that you had been given a police file linking Madhu to the murders two years ago. When the news of Malhotra's murder and Madhu's complicity broke, he laid a charge against you for abetment.

'Our people searched your office and found the file. Since you had never acted on the information, Mahajan's lawyers had sufficient grounds to push through for your arrest.'

Twenty-seven

Prime Minister's Office, September 2024

Sudesh had been released on bail, and was termed as innocent until proven guilty. He still was the Prime Minister.

There was no talk of impeachment. He was immensely popular and the media was universally outraged and sympathetic. The general view prevailed that it was just a matter of time until he was cleared of suspicion.

After one press conference in which he confirmed that the law must take its course, he was keeping public appearances to a minimum, but working as hard as ever.

Just when he started reflecting on the problems arising from his Guillotine measures Shakti arrived to tell him that Nanek Singh had come to meet him.

Sudesh stood up to greet his friend. 'How are you, Nanek? Any news about Madhu?'

'A massive police hunt has been launched, but there is no sign of her. My view is that if she doesn't want to be found, she won't be.' Sudesh nodded, noticing that the Commissioner looked less anxious than when they last met.

'What about you?' asked Singh, 'When is your trial date?'

'Next week, Tuesday,' replied Sudesh. 'It has been set for the earliest possible date to put an end to the uncertainty. The whole world is speculating on the outcome, investors' confidence has been badly shaken, and the stock exchange is falling.'

High Court, New Delhi, September 2024

The camera panned across the crowd gathered in front of the Courthouse. 'The trial of the Indian Prime Minister, Sudesh Kumar is about to commence,' said Anita Bal, news presenter for CNN–IBN. 'Inside the courtroom is Chief Justice Chakravorty, whose verdict may perhaps hold the Prime Minister "guilty". Outside the court are millions of self-proclaimed jurors who have already decided on a verdict of him being "not guilty".'

'No world leader has explained more clearly why no man should be above the law than India's Prime Minister, on trial here today. Sudesh Kumar has not only passionately espoused the Rule of Law, but consistently implemented it since he took control of the Ministry of Justice in 2018.' As the BBC World news anchor spoke, the television camera focused on *The Times of India* billboard, 'Rule of Law on Trial.'

Sudesh's trial was a huge media event. Never before had a Head of State in a peaceful democracy faced murder charges. Millions of viewers throughout India and across the globe were glued to television screens, awaiting the fate of this charismatic leader.

❧

It was the fifth day of the trial, and the courtroom was packed. At the front of the public gallery sat Shakti, Chanda and Kamla. Nearby were Vaneshri, Inder, Ray Upton and senior members of Sudesh's party.

The Press Gallery included representatives of every major network and publication, among them Punita Banerjee representing *India Finance*.

'Mr Kumar,' said counsel for the prosecution, 'would I be correct in saying that you have always insisted that no one should be above the law, and that you were responsible for repealing the Prime Minister's exemption from investigation and prosecution while in office?'

'Yes,' answered Sudesh.

'And have you repeated on many occasions that the Rule of Law means people's rights and duties must be determined by unambiguous laws equally applicable to all?'

'Yes.'

'Am I wrong when I say ...'

'Objection!' interjected Sudesh's counsel. 'These are leading questions.'

'Objection upheld.'

'I am willing to answer all the questions,' said Sudesh.

'Am I wrong when I say that you had reason to believe that Madhumati Singh might have committed murder and might do so again?'

'I knew only of inconclusive circumstantial evidence.'

'Evidence nonetheless, reasonable grounds for suspicion?'

'Perhaps.'

'Answer my question, "yes" or "no", Mr Kumar?'

'That is for this court to decide.'

'Are you aware that under Chapter Five of the Indian Penal Code omitting to prevent a crime constitutes abetment in the commission of the crime?'

'Yes.'

'I put it to you that you withheld information about past murders, which had you reported might have prevented future murders, and which, in law, makes you guilty of murder.'

'No.'

'Were you given a report regarding the Mafia Murders?'

'Yes.'

'Did you inform the police about the report you had received?'

'No.'

'Why did you not turn the report over to the police?'

'The report merely indicated that Special Agent Singh's movements could not be accounted for at the times of the murders. I told the CBI's Superintendent Patel to present the report to Commissioner Singh of the Delhi Police. I was not obliged by law to have a coincidence investigated.'

'Did you withhold information which, had you passed it on, might have prevented murder?'

'Possibly,' said Sudesh, 'given that Superintendent Patel did not give the report to the Commissioner.'

'You say the evidence handed to you dealt only with a coincidence, but why would it have been given to you unless it was significant?'

'I believe it was given to me because the CBI did not want to inform Commissioner Singh due to his relationship to Special Agent Singh. My view was, and still is, that Commissioner Singh is incorruptible, and I decided, and still believe, that he should have been informed. I was not aware that the CBI had decided not to inform him.

'At the time, and without the information we now have, I concluded that the evidence was coincidental and anyway could best be pursued by a task force.'

'Do you admit, Mr Kumar, that all of these assumptions might have resulted in more deaths?'

'It is possible,' answered Sudesh.

'I rest my case, my Lord, the accused is attempting to obfuscate the fact that his illegal omission was an abetment to murders of innocent people.' The judge raised his eyebrows and there were sniggers in the public gallery, inducing the prosecution counsel to abruptly add, 'That is, citizens presumed innocent in the absence of having been proven guilty.'

Chief Justice Chakravorty's Chamber, October 2024

'Come in,' a deep voice said. Ganesh Rawat entered the chamber. The Chief Justice was sitting in an old leather armchair in the corner nursing a glass. 'Sit there.'

'Ah, yes, Ganesh. And what do you think of our little predicament here?'

'Well, Sir,' Ganesh stammered. As a judge's clerk he hadn't expected to be asked his opinion. 'Prime Minister Kumar could be seen as being guilty of the crime of abetment under Chapter 5 of the Indian Penal Code,' he said pulling out his copy of the code. The Chief Justice reached across the space between them and jerked the book out of the clerk's hands.

Ganesh paused briefly, surprised, and then continued, 'But Prime Minister Kumar's crime was not intentional, it was a trivial technicality. And the information he withheld was just a suspicion of wrongdoing without clear evidence, and ...'

'And the law is an ass,' the old man interrupted. 'And he told his informant to tell the police chief. And the law is way too complicated for anyone to understand. There are a million little ways to ensnare good men for things that should not even be crimes. Such laws turn people into criminals for things they haven't done, and things they could never have known were crimes. The more complicated you make the law the more you turn innocent people into criminals.

'Do you see, my boy, such laws mean that if you want to get rid of someone you are not comfortable with, there's always something you can find to trip them up and ensnare them.

'Take this abetment law,' the Justice continued with his monologue. 'We make people tell tales on their fellow men, on their own family, and call it a crime when they don't. We force innocent citizens do our policing work for us; we throw them in jail if they don't. We turn them into scapegoats for our failed criminal justice system.

'Do you remember learning that people must have a guilty mind to be criminals?'

Ganesh nodded.

'This whole abetment chapter on crimes of omission should just go,' the Justice continued, thumbing to the beginning of Chapter 5 in Ganesh's copy of the Penal Code.

'And this endless litany of victimless crimes brought before my bench: consenting adults locked up for what they do within the confines of their bedroom, people fined for not taking care of themselves as well as the State would like them to–seatbelt laws and helmet laws. Not to mention the endless licensing laws that criminalise honest businesses. If it was up to me, we'd start from scratch.'

'From scratch, Sir?' Ganesh asked nervously.

When will the Chief Justice get to the judgment, Ganesh wondered. It has to be written, checked and edited.

'Yes, I would like a clean, empty law book – a small one, mind you. A few pages should do just fine, with a few simple rules everyone understands governing all human interaction. Don't cheat people. Don't take their stuff. Simple. A three-year-old could learn the law. Maybe a few others, but nothing that anyone who had spent more than a week on the playground at nursery school wouldn't understand and agree with.'

Ganesh reflected on his seven years at law school, and on the number of specialised branches of law that he dealt with in post-graduate studies.

'I have seen too many good men brought down and locked up for crimes where nobody could point to a victim. I fined many harmless people, and sent many to jail. And now, I must decide the fate of one of the greatest men of this country.'

Ganesh shifted uneasily in his chair. He had hoped that the Prime Minister would be found innocent, but now it seemed that the matter was not so simple.

The old man continued, 'Now, listen carefully. If our Prime Minister goes down for his mere omission there may be a huge outcry to get rid of the rubbish in the Penal Code and other silly laws.'

'Sir, you mean you might use our Prime Minister to teach India a lesson!' Ganesh almost yelled out.

'I plan to do no such thing. I will consider the law, as it is written, weigh up the evidence of the case and find for or against him as I would for any other accused.'

'Prime Minister Sudesh Kumar has not tried to pull strings or get special treatment. He submitted himself fully to the rule of law. For that I admire him greatly. He has allowed justice to take its course as it would have for any other person. I have seen far lesser men with influence worm their way around laws for which they are only too happy to see others prosecuted. Our Prime Minister has done no such thing. I have not had any of the usual visits from influential friends with suggestions on how I should rule.'

The room fell into silence for a few minutes as Chief Justice Chakravorty sipped his drink slowly. Then he looked up, repositioned his glasses on his nose and continued.

'Young man, get ready to transcribe my last judgment. Henceforth, I will leave the application of unjust laws written by over-zealous bureaucrats to younger, stronger men like you.' With that he slugged down the last of his scotch, and banged down the glass.

Ganesh sat upright, his pen and notepad ready.

☙

'Mr Sudesh Kumar,' concluded Justice Chakravorty when he handed down his judgment at 10 a.m. on Thursday, 17 October 2024, 'you are accused of abetment to murder because you did not pass on information. You admitted that this information might have saved lives. Lives of monstrous criminals perhaps, but nonetheless lives of people presumed by the laws you espouse to be innocent until proven guilty. In applying the law regarding illegal omission and abetment as this court understands it, I find you guilty of abetment to murder.'

Twenty-eight

India, October 2024

The shock waves of Sudesh's conviction for such a seemingly innocent transgression impelled men, women and children in homes, schools, factories, offices and shops to, down tools, switch off machines and take to the highways and byways. As if directed by an invisible presence they streamed towards the centre of every village, town and city.

In Delhi, where the verdict had been handed down, people rushed towards the Parliament, deserting their vehicles as traffic grid-locked, and continuing on foot, finally to emerge from the side roads to congregate at Rajpath, the great boulevard that runs from the President's residence, past the Secretariat Buildings next to Parliament, and through India Gate to Delhi's National Stadium.

Crowds filled the two-mile long avenue and lawns on either side. Mumbai, Kolkata, Bengaluru, Chennai, Hyderabad, Ahmedabad, Lucknow and every other Indian city and town witnessed similar outcry. 'Release Kumar,' roared the crowds, 'Su-desh, Su-desh, release Sudesh,' reverberated through the land.

The security establishments were prepared for a public protest, but not for the biggest demonstration the world had ever seen. Police and army had been called out in anticipation of trouble, but no one had expected tens of millions to take to the streets.

ॐ

Sudesh had no idea what awaited him when he was taken from his cell to an armoured vehicle and driven to the Parliament complex. There were no windows where he sat, so he could not see the determined and angry faces of the multitudes lining the roads through which his vehicle eased its way.

He had agreed to address the nation, but he had made no promises as to what he would say.

Thirty minutes later, he climbed the stairs to the East turret of the North Block of the Secretariat beside Rajpath.

He stood there, silhouetted against the sky, still light on the horizon but darkening to amethyst above, and observed the extraordinary spectacle below.

'Su-desh, Su-desh,' the chant rose to greet him. People were crowded at every available space. They packed the road and the flanking parks, and stood knee deep and shoulder-to-shoulder in the long line of rectangular ponds. People climbed *Jamun* and Java Plum trees to have a glimpse of Sudesh.

Gazing upon this supporting multitude Sudesh felt his eyes sting. People glued to television screens around the world watched Sudesh as he began to speak.

His words were captured and transported throughout India and across the globe by the bank of hastily assembled microphones and cameras before him.

Virtually every Indian owned a cell phone that had radio and television reception. No matter where they were, they could see Sudesh raise his arm or hear media reporters describe the scene before them.

Media and military helicopters hovered above, and specialists examined satellite images to estimate the size of the crowd. Around the world people listened and watched in awe as an estimated five million crammed together in and around Rajpath.

When Sudesh began to speak India fell silent.

'Do not demonstrate against my conviction, but celebrate India's new found liberty and prosperity. Do not protest injustice done to me, but demand justice for all. Do not condemn the court for convicting me, but fight the unjust laws that it enforces. Do not honour me, but embrace the values that inspired me.'

After ten minutes Sudesh concluded. 'I speak to you today not from humility but from pride. I know what I have accomplished, and why you have gathered to support me. I know what this great nation has achieved and the successes that lie ahead. Do not think of my conviction as the end, think of it as a beginning of the new epoch.

'As for me, do not fear, I will appeal my conviction and I will win!'

The crowd roared.

'When I succeed and I am free again,' he said, 'I will continue the work I have begun. Go now in peace.'

ॐ

By midnight most people were back in their homes. No violence had been reported.

But word had passed through the crowds and the following day, precisely at noon, people stopped whatever they were doing and for one minute they stood silent thinking their own thoughts. Pedestrians stopped in the middle of busy roads, vehicles paused at intersections and farmers stood silently in their fields. Then they continued as if nothing had happened.

And at nine that night the lights went out. They went out as planned, though no one knew by whom. 'An hour of darkness symbolised India's past,' said an All India Radio reporter.

When the lights reappeared they seemed to blaze brighter than before. People poured into the streets, holding burning candles high, creating across the land rivulets, then streams and finally great rivers of light, connecting all with each other, and celebrating India's new Golden Age.

Author's note

Ayn Rand's *Atlas Shrugged* (*AS*) leads amongst my favourite books. America crashes in *AS* when free markets are lost. *The Deal Maker*, which was conceived by me twenty five years ago, is of the rise of India as it moves from socialism to freedom.

In the meantime, India did move from the slavery of license raj, extortionate taxes, and tyranny of officialdom to a degree of freedom. Not enough but enough to whet our appetites.

I concluded that if I wanted to die a contented man, I had to finish this book. I had written enough award-winning articles in economics to realise that non fiction would never get an audience as big as fiction could.

Whenever someone told me that they wanted something, I would quip, 'what difference does wanting make? I want to be the Prime Minister of India, am I getting what I want? No. Then why should you?'

I wanted to be the PM not because of a desire to be someone but because I wanted to do something. Rarely do people have both capabilities: of coming to power, and then of knowing what to do after achieving it. Our politicians possess the first capability, and I only the second. In this book I live my dream through Sudesh.

I thought if I could not write the book alone (as I run businesses as well), then I would procure help. In 2000, twenty pages were written outlining what I wanted. I started my hunt for a partner. During a conclave in September of 2000 in Nepal, I talked about it with people who could be associated. Everyone readily agreed to assist, but nobody could promise partnership.

Finally it was Leon Louw and me. My co-author, Leon Louw, is one of South Africa's most highly regarded political analysts and is known for making extensive economic reforms in South Africa. He has received numerous international awards, and, with his wife, Frances Kendall, has been nominated three times for the Nobel Peace Prize. Presently he is the Executive Director of the Free Market Foundation (FMF) and of the Law Review Project.

Leon's passion for freedom matched mine and it was easy to get him excited about what I had in mind. Together we worked on the idea, together we developed it and together we came up with this book. Frances contributed some scenes and so did Nubby Patz and Jim Peron. Frances also edited the drafts and her incisive criticism added force in the literary journey. Douglas Shaw made substantial contributions to early drafts, and Libby Lamour made valuable editing suggestions.

In a meeting which I had in Santa Rosa, in California, USA, Leon came from South Africa, Manav, my son, wrote several pages of his comments, Shalini, my wife, gauged it from the feminist angle and gave her comments. Dr Douglas Lisle – a brilliant psychologist helped us with his valuable suggestions to make the narrative more gripping.

Nirmal Sharma's contribution came in form of the cover design. Kapish Mehra, Managing Director, Rupa & Co., chose the cover design from among several dozen options. I'm also grateful to Kapish for deciding on the title of the book from the 100 different title suggestions put forward by our team. There were people at Rupa particularly Sheerie who edited, and re-edited it a dozen times and brought the book into its present form.

Trust you have enjoyed the book and can visualise India as I visualise it. To carry dreams to reality, you have to dream first.

My dream was to write this book in the hope that it would become someone's dream to get India to freedom and prosperity – just as Sudesh does in the book.

15 August 2010
Rakesh Wadhwa